Main

Murder
of a Lady

Murder
of a Lady

A Scottish Mystery

Anthony Wynne

With an Introduction
by Martin Edwards

Poisoned Pen Press

Originally published in London in 1931 by Hutchinson
Copyright © 2016 Estate of Anthony Wynne
Introduction copyright © 2016 Martin Edwards
Published by Poisoned Pen Press in association with the
British Library

First Edition 2016
First US Trade Paperback Edition

10 9 8 7 6 5 4 3 2 1

Library of Congress Catalog Card Number: 2015946352

ISBN: 9781464205712   Trade Paperback

Poisoned Pen Press
6962 E. First Ave., Ste. 103
Scottsdale, AZ 85251
www.poisonedpenpress.com
info@poisonedpenpress.com

Printed in the United States of America

Contents

Introduction

Murder of a Lady, first published in 1931, is an excellent example of the "impossible crime" mystery, written by a long forgotten master of this ingenious form of detective puzzle. Set in the author's native Scotland, the story gets off to a cracking start, as the Procurator Fiscal calls on Colonel John MacCallien, and his guest Dr. Eustace Hailey, late one evening. He brings news that Mary Gregor has been stabbed to death in nearby Duchlan Castle: "I have never seen so terrible a wound." The dead woman was found crouching by her bed, but there is no trace of a murder weapon. The door of her room was locked, and so were all the windows.

Another murder follows, and suspicion shifts around a small cast of suspects. One tantalizing question is: why were herring scales found at the crime scenes? (The book had at one time an alternative title, *The Silver Scale Mystery*.) Luckily, Dr. Hailey happens to specialize in solving this kind of conundrum, although he opts to work independently of the police: "I'm an amateur, not a professional, and my studies of crime are undertaken only because they interest me...I follow a line of investigation often without knowing exactly why I'm following it—it would be intolerable to have to justify and explain every step...The detection of crime, I think, is an art more than a science, like the practice of medicine."

Later, he adds: "Detective work is like looking at a puzzle. The solution is there before one's eyes, only one can't see it… because some detail, more aggressive than the others, leads one's eyes away from the essential detail."

Hailey is, in other words, the archetypal "great detective" of the type so popular during the Golden Age of Murder between the wars. Anthony Wynne, his creator, contributed an essay about him to a book called *Meet the Detectives*, published four years after *Murder of a Lady*, in which Hailey expresses the view that: "The really interesting crimes are those committed by people who, in ordinary circumstances, would have lived all their lives without apparent fault." Hailey "never blames the criminal so whole-heartedly as to be unable to see and feel his tragedy". He maintains that the psychology of the criminal is key: "more often I come to the truth indirectly by an understanding of the special stresses to which he was subjected immediately before the crime took place."

Hailey and his creator were admired in their day, and Dorothy L. Sayers was among the critics who reviewed him favourably: "Mr. Anthony Wynne excels in the solution of apparently insoluble problems." Hailey first appeared in the 1920s, and his career lasted until 1950, but by then, readers' tastes were changing, and elaborately concocted whodunits were no longer fashionable—unless written by Agatha Christie. The late Robert Adey, author of the definitive study *Locked Room Murders*, lists no fewer than 33 books and stories written by Wynne which feature "impossible crime" elements. As he points out, Wynne "soon established himself as the champion of [a] form of impossible crime: death by invisible agent. Time after time he confronted his…detective with situations in which the victim was killed, quite on his own, in plain view of witnesses who were unable to explain how a close-quarters blow could have been struck."

There is, of course, a striking contrast between such elaborate game-playing plot material and the examination of criminal psychology, and Wynne's real focus was the former, rather than the latter. He did not lighten his books with as many macabre trappings or as much gleeful humour as did John Dickson Carr, the American novelist who is commonly regarded as the finest of all specialists in locked-room mysteries, and this may help to explain why his work has faded from view. But his best work remains attractive to readers who love a cunningly contrived puzzle.

Anthony Wynne was the pseudonym of Robert McNair Wilson (1882–1963), a Glasgow-born physician who developed a specialism in cardiology after working as assistant to Sir James Mackenzie, whose biography he wrote. McNair Wilson published on a range of scientific and medical subjects, as well as on historical topics, especially in connection with the French Revolution. He was also fascinated by politics (in the early 1920s, he twice stood unsuccessfully as a Parliamentary candidate for the Liberal Party) and by economics. His obituary in *The Times* noted that "he developed a deep interest in monetary problems; for a time they dominated his conversation, and he wrote several books challenging what he considered to be the unjustifiable power wielded by moneyed interests." These included *Promise to Pay: An Inquiry into the Principles and Practice of the Latter-day Magic Sometimes Called High Finance* (1934).

McNair Wilson was medical correspondent of *The Times* for almost thirty years, and was admired by Lord Northcliffe, whose biography he wrote; at one time he was also engaged to write chatty feature articles for another newspaper, the *Sunday Pictorial*. "His lively and inquiring mind could not be bound to any one subject for long, however great and however interesting," his obituarist said. "Writing and conversation were…his chief pleasures." He wrote little fiction in the last two decades of his life, but one likes to think that he would be gratified that a twenty-first-century revival of interest in Golden Age detective fiction has resulted in the re-emergence of Dr. Hailey after many years in the shadows, and the republication of this intricate mystery as a British Library Crime Classic.

Martin Edwards
www.martinedwardsbooks.com

Chapter I

Murder at Duchlan

Mr. Leod McLeod, Procurator Fiscal of Mid-Argyll, was known throughout that county as "the Monarch of the Glen". He deserved the title, if only because of the shape and set of his head and the distinction of his features. A Highlander, full length, in oils, dignified as a mountain, touchy as a squall, inscrutable, comic in the Greek sense. When at ten o'clock at night he came striding in, past the butler, to the smoking-room at Darroch Mor, even Dr. Eustace Hailey gasped, giving, by that, joy to his host, Colonel John MacCallien.

"I must apologize, gentlemen, for disturbing you at this unseasonable hour."

Mr. McLeod bowed as he spoke, like a sapling in a hurricane.

"Won't you sit down?"

"Thank you. Yes. Yes, I will. Dear me, is it ten o'clock?"

John MacCallien signed to his butler, who moved a table, furnished with decanters and siphons, closer to his visitor. He invited him to help himself.

"That's too kind of you. Well, well…"

Mr. McLeod poured what seemed to Dr. Hailey a substantial quantity of whisky into a tumbler. He drank the whisky, undiluted, at a gulp. A sigh broke from his lips.

"Believe me, gentlemen," he said in solemn tones, "it is not lightly that I have troubled you. I heard that Dr. Hailey was staying here. It seemed to me that the gravity of the case and our remoteness from help gave me title to lay his skill under contribution."

He moved uneasily as he spoke. Dr. Hailey observed that his brow was damp.

"There's been murder," he said in low tones, "at Duchlan Castle. Miss Mary Gregor has been murdered."

"What!"

"Yes, Colonel MacCallien, it's too true. Murdered, poor lady, while sleeping in her bed last night." The Procurator Fiscal's hand was raised in a gesture which expressed condemnation as well as horror.

"But, it's impossible. Mary Gregor hadn't an enemy in the world." John MacCallien turned to Dr. Hailey. "Even tramps and tinkers turned to bless her as she passed them, and with good reason, for she was constantly helping them."

"I know, Colonel MacCallien, I know," Mr. McLeod said. "Who is there in Argyll who does not know? But I state the fact, there she lies, murdered." The man's voice fell again. "I have never seen so terrible a wound."

Chapter II

A Fish's Scale

Mr. McLeod wiped his brow, for his habit was sudorific. His nostrils expanded.

"It was no ordinary knife which made that wound," he declared in hoarse tones. "The flesh has been torn." He turned and addressed himself to Dr. Hailey. "Miss Gregor was lying crouching beside her bed when they found her." He paused: the blood diminished in his face. "The door of that room was locked on the inside and the windows of that room were bolted."

"What, a locked room?" John MacCallien exclaimed.

"That's it, Colonel MacCallien. Nobody can have gone into that room and nobody can have come out from it. I have examined the windows myself, yes, and the door, too. You could not close these windows from the outside if you tried. And you could not unlock the door from the outside."

He shook his head, closing his eyes, meanwhile, as though he had entered into communion with higher powers. After a moment he turned to Dr. Hailey.

"The wound," he stated, "is in the left shoulder, near the neck. So far as I could judge it is three or four inches deep, a gash that looks as if it had been made with an axe. And yet, strange to say, there seems to have been little bleeding. Dr. McDonald of Ardmore, who examined the body, says that he thinks death was due to shock more than to the wound itself. Miss Gregor, it appears, has suffered for many years from a weak heart. There would not be much bleeding in that case, I suppose?"

"Possibly not."

"There's a little blood on the nightdress, but not much. Not much." Mr. McLeod gulped his whisky. "I telephoned to Police Headquarters in Glasgow," he stated, "but this being the Sabbath day I don't look to see Inspector Dundas, who is coming, until to-morrow morning. I said to myself, when I heard to-night that you were staying here: if Dr. Hailey will be so good as to examine the room and the body immediately, we shall have something to go upon in the morning." He rose as he spoke: "I have a car waiting at the door."

John MacCallien accompanied his guest to Duchlan.

They were greeted in the hall of the Castle by the dead woman's brother, Major Hamish Gregor, whom Mr. McLeod called "Duchlan". Duchlan looked like an old eagle. He shook Dr. Hailey's hand with sudden and surprising vigour but did not speak a word. Then he conducted John MacCallien to a room adjoining the hall, leaving Mr. McLeod to take the doctor upstairs.

"Who knows, this blow may be mortal," the Procurator Fiscal confided to his companion in a loud whisper as they ascended the oak staircase. "Duchlan and his sister were all things to each other."

The stair ended in a gallery; from this several passages radiated. They passed along one of these and came to a door from which the lock had been cut away. Mr. McLeod paused and turned to the doctor.

"This is the room; nothing but the lock of the door has been disturbed. I had a great shock myself when I entered and I would therefore prepare your mind."

Dr. Hailey inclined his head, responding to the Highlander's gravity with a reserve which gave nothing away. The door moved noiselessly open. He saw a woman in a white nightdress kneeling beside a bed. The room was lit by a paraffin lamp which stood on the dressing-table; the blinds were drawn. The kneeling figure at the bed had white hair which shone in the lamplight. She looked as if she was praying.

He glanced about him. There were framed samplers and pieces of fine needlework on the walls, and many pictures. The furniture was old and heavy; a huge four-poster bed in mahogany with a canopy, a wash-stand that looked as if it had been designed to accommodate a giant, a wardrobe, built like a feudal castle, and, scattered about among these great beasts, the small deer of tables and chairs, smothered, all of them, in faded and tarnished upholstery.

He walked across the room and stood looking down at the dead woman. Mr. McLeod had not exaggerated; the weapon had cut through her collar-bone. He bent and drew back the nightdress, exposing the whole extent of the wound. The look of pity on his face changed to surprise. He turned and signed to Mr. McLeod to approach. He pointed to a pale scar which ran down the breast from a point slightly above and to the inside of the end of the wound. The scar ended near the upper border of the heart.

"Look at that."

Mr. McLeod gazed for a moment and then shook his head.

"What does it mean?" he asked in a whisper.

"It's a healed scar. So far as I can see it means that she was wounded long ago nearly as severely as she was wounded last night."

"May it not have been an operation?"

"There are no marks of stitches. Stitch marks never disappear."

Mr. McLeod shook his head. "I never heard that Miss Gregor had been wounded," he declared.

He watched the doctor focus his eyeglass on the scar and move the glass up and down. Sweat broke anew on his brow. When an owl screeched past the window he started violently.

"This old wound," Dr. Hailey announced, "was inflicted with a sharp weapon. It has healed, as you see, with as little scarring as would have occurred had it been stitched. Look how narrow and clean that scar is. A blunt weapon would have torn the flesh and left a scar with ragged edges."

He pointed to the new wound. "There's an example of what I mean. This wound was inflicted with a blunt weapon. Offhand, I should say that, at some early period of her life, Miss Gregor was stabbed by somebody who meant to murder her. It's common experience that uninstructed people place the heart high up in the chest whereas, in fact, it's situated low down."

He had been bending; he now stood erect. His great head, which excellently matched his body, towered above that of his companion. Mr. McLeod looked up at him and was reminded of a picture of Goliath of Gath which had haunted his childhood.

"I never heard," he said, "that anybody ever tried to murder Miss Gregor."

"From what John MacCallien said I imagine that she was the last woman to attempt to take her own life."

"The last."

The doctor bent again over the scar.

"People who stab themselves," he said, "strike one direct blow and leave, as a rule, a short scar; whereas people who stab others, strike downwards and usually leave a longer scar.

This scar, as you see, is long. And it broadens as it descends, exactly what happens when a wound is inflicted with a knife."

He moved his eyeglass to a new focus over the recent wound. "The blow which killed, on the contrary, was struck with very great violence by somebody using, I think, a weapon with a long handle. A blunt weapon. The murderer faced his victim. She died of shock, because, had her heart continued to beat, the wound would have bled enormously."

The screech owl passed the window again and again Mr. McLeod started.

"Only a madman can have struck such a blow," he declared in fervent tones.

"It may be so."

Dr. Hailey took a probe from his pocket and explored the wound. Then he lighted an electric lamp and turned its beam on the woman's face. He heard Mr. McLeod gasp. The face was streaked in a way which showed that Miss Gregor had wetted her fingers in her own blood before she died. He knelt and took her right hand, which was clenched so that he had to exert force to open it. The fingers were heavily stained. He looked puzzled.

"She clutched at the weapon," he declared; "that means that she did not die the moment she was struck."

He glanced at the fingers of her left hand; they were unstained. He rose and turned to his companion.

"Her left hand was helpless. She grasped the weapon with her right hand and then pressed that hand to her brow. Since there was little bleeding, the weapon that inflicted the wound must have remained buried in it until after death. Perhaps, before she collapsed, she was trying to pluck the weapon out of the wound. The murderer was a witness of this agony for he has taken his weapon away with him."

Mr. McLeod was holding the rail at the foot of the bed; it rattled in his grasp.

"No doubt. No doubt," he said. "But how did the murderer escape from the room? Look at that door." He pointed to the sawn part of the heavy mahogany. "It's impassable; and so are the windows."

Dr. Hailey nodded. He walked to the window nearest the bed and drew back the curtain which covered it. Then he opened the window. The warm freshness of the August night entered the room astride a flood of moonlight. He relit his lamp and examined the sill. Then he closed the window again and looked at its fastenings.

"It was bolted, you say?"

"Yes, it was. The other window is bolted too." Mr. McLeod wiped his brow again. He added: "This room is directly above Duchlan's study."

Dr. Hailey moved the bolt backwards and forwards. The spring which retained it in position was not strong and seemed to be the worse of wear.

"Did Miss Gregor sleep with her windows open?" he asked.

"I think she did in this weather. I've ascertained that the windows were open last night."

The doctor turned the beam of his lamp on to the floor below the window and immediately bent down. There were drops of blood on the floor.

"Look at these."

"Was she wounded on this spot, do you think?" Mr. McLeod asked in hushed tones.

"Possibly. If not she must have come here after she was wounded. Notice how small the quantity of blood is. Only a drop or two. The weapon was in the wound." He bent again and remained for a moment looking at the stains. "The odds, I think, are that she was wounded here. When a blade remains in a wound it takes a second or two for the blood to well up and escape. No doubt she rushed back to her bed and collapsed just when she reached it."

"The murderer didn't escape by the window," Mr. McLeod declared in positive tones. "There's no footmark on the border below, and the earth is soft enough to take the prints of a sparrow. If you'll look to-morrow you'll see that no human being could climb up or down those walls. They're as smooth as the back of your hand. You would need a scaffolding to reach the windows."

He had evidently considered all the possibilities and rejected them all. He wiped his brow again. Dr. Hailey walked to the fireplace where a fire was laid and scrutinized it as he had scrutinized the window.

"At least we can be sure that nobody entered by the chimney."

"We can be quite sure of that. I thought of that. The chimney-pot would not admit a human body. I've looked at it myself."

It remained to examine the place where the body was kneeling. There was a quantity of blood on the floor there but much less than must have been found had the wound not been kept closed until after death.

Dr. Hailey moved the beam of his lamp up and down the little, crouching figure, holding it stationary for an instant, here and there. He had nearly completed his search when a gleam of silver, like the flash of a dewdrop on grass, fixed his attention on the left shoulder, at the place where the neck of the nightdress crossed the wound. He bent and saw a small round object which adhered closely to the skin. He touched it; it was immediately dislodged. He recognized a fish's scale.

Chapter III

Brother and Sister

Dr. Hailey asked Mr. McLeod to confirm his opinion of the scale. The Procurator Fiscal did so without hesitation.

"Yes, it's a fish's scale, a herring's. There's no other scale of any fish that looks like that, as any man or woman on Loch Fyne-side will tell you."

"If that is so we shall have to look for a weapon with a use in the herring fishery."

He spoke with an undertone of excitement in his voice. Mr. McLeod agreed.

"It looks like it. It looks like it. The fishermen use an axe sometimes, I believe, though I've never had much to do with them. It's a wonder there's no more of these scales. You'll get hundreds of them on your fingers if you so much as handle a herring."

"Still, the blade had probably been cleaned."

"It's very difficult to clean away these scales. You're apt to miss them because they lie close to whatever they touch."

Mr. McLeod's agitation was increasing. The discovery of the herring-scale seemed to have shaken him almost as much as the discovery of the murder itself, possibly because so many people in Argyllshire earn their living directly or indirectly from the Loch Fyne herring fishery. Dr. Hailey opened a penknife and very gently and carefully lifted the scale on its blade. He carried the scale to the dressing-table where the lamp was burning.

"There will be no objection, I take it," he asked, "to my retaining possession of this? Happily, you saw it in position and can confirm the fact of its presence."

He laid the knife down as he spoke and took his watch from his waistcoat pocket. He opened his watch. He was about to place the scale in the lid when Mr. McLeod objected that so important a piece of evidence ought to be shown to Inspector Dundas.

"I think, Doctor," he protested, "that it will be well if you leave the scale in the room here, for Dundas to see. He's a pernickety body that doesn't thank you for giving him advice, and if we remove any piece of the evidence the chances are that he'll make himself disagreeable."

"Very well."

Dr. Hailey put the scale in one of the small drawers of the dressing-table. He closed the drawer.

"I should like," he said, "to open the window again before we go downstairs. I saw a boat moored near the house."

"The motor-launch. It belongs to Duchlan's son, Eoghan."

When the curtain was drawn the moonlight made the lamp seem feeble and garish. Dr. Hailey threw up the window and looked out over the quiet waters of Loch Fyne, across which a silver streak that moved and shimmered below him led into the mouth of a burn. He could hear the gurgling of this stream as it ran round the side of the castle. He leaned out of the window. A wide flower-bed illuminated now by the light from the study window below, separated the carriage-way from the walls. The carriage-way ended at the front door, to the left of the window. Further still to the left, a steep bank fell to the burn.

The boat was anchored off the burn's mouth; its white hull gleamed dully in the moonlight and made sharp contrast with the black bulk of a jetty built just within the little estuary.

"Put the lamp out, will you?" he asked his companion.

He turned, when McLeod had obeyed him, from the loveliness without to the fear within. Miss Gregor's white hair shone in the moonlight with an added lustre that made her nightdress seem dull. In the dark setting of her chamber she looked remote, ghostly, pathetic. Mr. McLeod took the lamp, opened the door and went out into the corridor. He relighted the lamp.

When Dr. Hailey joined him he was holding the lamp in both hands. The glass funnel shook, making a small, rattling sound.

"I can't bear to look at yon poor woman," he confessed. "Did you notice the moonlight on her hair? I believe she was praying in her last moments."

He glanced about him. The doctor feared that the lamp would slip from his shaking hands.

"There's an awful eerie feeling about this house. I did hear once that it was haunted."

He seemed reluctant to leave the scene of the murder, as if the horror he was experiencing gave him some macabre kind of enjoyment. The association in his mind of religious ideas and gross superstition was, perhaps, the explanation. After all, Dr. Hailey reflected, it has taken mankind all the centuries of its history to effect a separation between the spiritual and the demonic.

"I'm afraid," he said, "that Miss Gregor had but little time after she suffered that blow."

"Oh, sir, sir. 'In the middle of life we are in death.'"

Mr. McLeod spoke the familiar words lovingly, nodding his head to give them emphasis. He belonged, apparently, to that considerable company of elderly men who find security and strength in accustomed phrases. But his fears were too lively to be dispersed for any length of time.

"It's an awful thought," he exclaimed, "that the hand of death may be here, within these walls, at this moment."

He began to gibber. He glanced about him like a dog watching shadows. His lively imagination made disturbing play with his features.

"Aye," he repeated, "Mary Gregor was on her knees during that last awful moment. Her strength was ever in prayer."

His voice fell. It had come to his mind apparently, that the dead woman's plea had not been granted, for he added in tones that carried a heavy burden of fear:

"The Lord gave and the Lord hath taken away."

His head was shaking in the manner of a man possessed of information which he is in no mind to disclose. The lamp began to rattle again. Dr. Hailey took it from him.

They went downstairs to Duchlan's smoking-room. Dr. Hailey had a quick impression of an antique dealer's show-room. The place seemed to be full of stuffed animals and antlers and old oak. The old man rose to receive them and presented them to arm-chairs with a ceremonious wave of his hand. Either he was dazed by the calamity which had befallen him or he was so schooled in courtly manners as to be incapable of forgetting them.

"Well, Doctor?" he asked, in a clear, rather shrill voice.

"I'm afraid I can offer no enlightenment so far."

Dr. Hailey shook his head. He was observing the room and its owner with an attention of which the vacant expression in his eyes gave no indication. Between the bedroom upstairs and this overcrowded apartment there was, he recognized, an affinity that deserved consideration. Both rooms revealed confusion of mind; in both the determination to cling to everything which the occupants had ever possessed was apparent. Duchlan kept the pelts and horns of the beasts and birds he had killed; his sister kept her samplers and good works. Both brother and sister seemed to set value on ugliness and discomfort. The chair in which he was sitting hurt the doctor's back; those he had seen in Miss Gregor's room were equally ungenerous as they were equally unlovely. But generations of Gregors had sat in them. Duchlan Castle, it seemed, contained the cast-off clothing of generations.

"My dear sister," Duchlan said, "was without an enemy in this world. It is not conceivable that anyone can have borne a grudge against her." He smoothed his kilt on his knees with a gesture that caressed that garment. "Believe me, her days were days of service."

He spoke with the assurance of an officiating priest. His face was set in an expressionless mask. But a trickle of blood had come to his cheeks.

"Her ways were ways of blessedness," he added. "And her paths were peace."

Silence received this tribute. Dr. Hailey felt uncomfortable. No doubt the old man meant what he said but his pride of family was so unashamed that he gave the impression that in praising his sister he was also praising himself.

"Will you tell the doctor all that you know, Duchlan?" Mr. McLeod said.

"It isn't much, I fear. Our lives were not eventful." Duchlan turned to his visitor and, at the same time, advanced his hands to grasp the ends of the carved arms of his chair. His hands were thin and white; and he raised and lowered his fingers in a way that recalled the movements of a spider's legs. "My dear sister and I," he stated, "dined together as usual last night. I thought she looked rather tired, for she had been very busy all day."

He paused to adjust the silver ornament which was attached to his waistbelt and which, Dr. Hailey saw, bore a coat of arms. This act, too, was caressing, as if a deep satisfaction resided in the possession of chieftainship. "My sister," he went on, "told me that she had a headache. I suggested, before we went into dinner, that we might, for once, dispense with the services of our piper during the meal. But she rejected the idea. 'My dear Hamish,' she said, 'surely you remember that our father had the pipes played at dinner even on the night of his death.' Our Highland customs were dear to her both for themselves and by reason of their associations. I knew that she was suffering greatly, but she welcomed Angus, my piper, with perfect grace, and, when his playing finished, rose and handed him the loving cup. I'm sure he knew and appreciated her courage. That, Dr. Hailey, was my dear sister on the last night of her life, thoughtful and careful of others; true to the traditions and customs of our family."

Tears gleamed in Duchlan's eyes. He wiped them away.

"We were alone at the meal, she and I, because my daughter-in-law was feeling unwell—and my son had not yet returned. Believe me, I felt my mind carried back to the days when my father, the late Duchlan, used to occupy my place and when he seemed to his children a being of supernatural goodness. Mary's thoughts had been moving in unison with mine, for she told me that she believed our father was the noblest man who ever trod this earth. 'His house,' she said, 'is full of his goodness.' Then she spoke about my little grandson. How earnestly she hoped that he would prove worthy of the traditions of which he is heir. 'If only it can be impressed on him,' she said, 'that there is no privilege except that of serving.' The coming of the little lad to stay with us a year ago, while his father was stationed in Malta, was a supreme joy to her, since it gave her an opportunity of influencing him.

"Believe me, she had made the very most of that opportunity. It was her sincere conviction that the basis of character must always be religion. 'The fear of the Lord,' she used to say again and again, 'is the beginning of wisdom.' She laboured to inculcate that fear in the child's heart. It was given to her, as to few others, to be able to penetrate the childish mind. I think the perfect simplicity of her own character was the explanation. She could suggest a whole world of ideas with a gesture. Her spirit delighted in love and beauty; but her thoughts were never suffered to escape from the control of conscience. If she believed in mercy, she never shut her eyes to justice. A child, she used to urge, must be able to count upon the divine attributes as upon the light and the air. He must learn to know all the loving-kindness of which the human heart is capable, but he must learn at the same time to recognize that even love is conditioned by righteousness. The texts which were most frequently on her lips were those in which testimony is borne to the holiness that limits and purifies even the most gracious of our human feelings."

Duchlan's face became grave. He raised his hand in a gesture which was part benediction, part protest.

"I will not disguise from you," he continued, "that these views of my dear sister were not welcome to all who had the duty of caring for the child laid upon them. In these modern times there is, everywhere, a relaxing of discipline. Sentimental ideas, corrupt in their essence, have too often replaced the old ideas of justice and responsibility. Children to-day hear too much about forgiveness, about mercy, about love, about kindness; they hear too little about the consequences which must issue from every breach of the moral law, however trivial. We are moving far away from the austere virtues of our fathers. It was Mary's task, her sacred mission, to do what lay in her power to correct that error."

The gravity of his tones was unrelieved by any inflection so that what he said sounded like a recitation carefully committed to memory. So strong was this impression that Dr. Hailey ventured to suggest that modern ideas were not necessarily wrong because they were based on the good rather than on the evil which is in human nature. He watched the old man as he spoke and saw him recoil sharply.

"My dear sister had a boundless faith in the goodness of human nature." Duchlan retorted. "But that faith was based on her deep religious conviction that man is born in sin. She hated evil too fervently to make terms with it, or to pretend that it was mere error. 'I have no patience,' she often told me, 'with the namby-pamby sentimentalism that excuses every fault in the name of love.' When she said that she always quoted the text: 'Whom the Lord loveth, he chasteneth'."

Duchlan's tones were passionate, as if the slight criticism he had encountered had awakened doubts in his own spirit that must, at all cost, be suppressed. He waved his skinny hand.

"Believe me," he added, "Mary's faith was a tower of strength. Again and again I found help and comfort there when my own faith wavered. Her character was built on the rock. She was steadfast, immovable. My own nature had never approached the degree of resistance to evil which was her outstanding merit. But she gave me strength."

The old man wiped his eyes again.

"You will forgive these small details," he apologized. "Since you have been so very kind as to help me in this calamity, I feel that I owe it to you, and to her memory, that you should know a little of my dear Mary's character and life." He bowed his head. "She went up to her room soon after dinner. Her maid, Christina, brought her a glass of milk about ten o'clock. She always drank a glass of milk just before going to sleep. Christina left her at a quarter past ten. She was then lying down and seemed, already, to have fallen asleep. Christina blew out the single candle with which the room was lighted."

"Was her maid the last person who saw Miss Gregor alive?" Dr. Hailey asked.

"The last." The old man raised himself in his chair. "I am glad that it was so, for they were old and dear friends. Christina closed my dear father's, the late Duchlan's, eyes. She has shared our joys and sorrows with us for more than thirty years."

Each time that he mentioned his father, Duchlan lowered his voice. That tribute was impressive; but Dr. Hailey could not forget what John MacCallien had told him about the late laird of Duchlan. The man had been a tyrant, strong-willed and stiff-necked, who had brooked no opposition to his will. He had been, in addition, especially in his later life, a very heavy drinker, and his carouses had brought both fear and shame on his family. Was it from these uneasy scenes that his son and daughter had drawn their reliance on one another? Doubtless they had had need of such comfort as they were able to get and bestow.

"Your sister did not use a paraffin lamp in her room?" he asked.

"No, sir." A faint smile appeared for an instant on the old man's lips. "Doubtless," he said, "you think that we live far behind these modern times, but it is a fact that Mary looked upon paraffin lamps with the anxiety which new inventions must always awaken in old minds. We were born and brought up in the age of candles, and that gentle form of illumination remained the most attractive to both of us. Our drawing-room was always lighted by candles and was always, I know, very much admired when so lighted, even by those who have grown accustomed to electricity. My son spoke recently of installing electric light in the castle; Mary begged that that innovation might be postponed until after her death."

This statement, like those which had preceded it, was made with a vehemence which detracted from its effect. Again the doctor had the impression that Duchlan was acting as a mere mouthpiece. Even from her death-bed his sister seemed to direct his thoughts and words. The temptation was great to ask him what his own opinion about the upbringing of children and paraffin lamps and electricity might be.

"Did your sister," he inquired, "leave Duchlan much during the year?"

"Never. Her life was here, in this house. Long ago, she used to travel sometimes to Edinburgh, and at very rare intervals she went to London for a week or so during the season. But latterly these excursions were wholly abandoned." Duchlan leaned back in his chair and closed his eyes. "Every detail of the management of this house and its surroundings was in her hands. Nothing was left to chance; nothing was overlooked or neglected. She was a wonderful manager, a wonderful director, a wonderful housekeeper. All she did, too, was done without haste or bustle, and without waste. I assure you that but for her admirable skill and foresight it would, long ago, have been impossible for me to have remained in the Castle. I should have been compelled to let my shooting every year and perhaps to have gone into permanent residence in one of the smaller houses on the estate. Mary had a horror of such a step which never ceased to disturb her."

The doctor took a silver box from his waistcoat pocket and, after a moment of silent deliberation, opened it and took snuff. He performed this act with much grace, but the vacant expression of his face remained unchanged.

"How was her death discovered?" he asked.

"It was discovered when the housemaid, Flora, took up my sister's early morning tea. My sister had apparently locked the door of her bedroom, a thing she had never done before. Flora got no reply when she knocked on the door. She called Christina, and then Angus, but they, too, failed to get any response. Angus came for me." The old man broke off and bowed his head for a moment. "My son had come back over night," he resumed. "He has been in Ayrshire on military duty. I roused him. We sent for a carpenter, who cut the lock out of the door. We sent also for Dr. McDonald of Ardmore. He came before the door was opened."

Duchlan lay back in his chair. His face, the skin of which resembled parchment, was pinched like the face of a corpse. He seemed to breathe with difficulty.

"You are quite sure," Dr. Hailey asked, "that Miss Gregor was not in the habit of locking her bedroom door?"

"Absolutely sure."

Duchlan's black eyes flickered as he answered the question. The doctor shook his head.

"So that," he said, "last night she reversed the habits of a life-time?"

The old man did not reply. He moved uneasily in his chair while his fingers began to drum on its arms. Suddenly he leaned forward listening. They heard a car drive up to the front door.

Chapter IV

Inspector Dundas

Inspector Robert Dundas was a young man with a shrewd expression. His manner of entering the smoking-room at Duchlan announced that he came to conquer. The mixture of cordiality and aloofness in the way he greeted the old laird indicated that he proposed to allow no consideration to interfere with the discharge of his duty.

He was not very tall, but his slight build made lack of height unimportant. Dr. Hailey thought of the word "wiry", for there was a hard quality as well as a quality of suppleness. Dundas's brow and eyes were girlish, but his mouth seemed well fitted to administer a bite. It descended at the corners and was furnished with lips of a singular thinness. Mr. McLeod, who knew the young man, introduced him to John MacCallien and the doctor, and Dundas informed each of these in turn that he was pleased to meet him. He did not look pleased.

"I lost no time, as you see, Fiscal," he said to Mr. McLeod.

His manner was quiet, with the pained restraint of an undertaker at work. But his blue eyes searched the room. They chilled when he learned what Dr. Hailey had already done.

"Before I go upstairs myself," he stated, "I should like to know who are at present living in this house." He turned to Duchlan and whipped a thin notebook out of his pocket. "I want a complete list, if you please."

The last remark was made in the manner of a doctor taking stock of symptoms, the significance of which can be understood only by himself. Duchlan bowed stiffly.

"I had better begin with myself," he said. "Then there is my son Eoghan and his wife. I have only four indoor servants…"

Dundas raised a manicured hand.

"One moment, please. You are Major Hamish Gregor, late of the Argyll and Sutherland Highlanders, and laird of Duchlan in the county of Argyll?" He wrote quickly as he spoke. "How old are you, sir?"

"Seventy-four."

"Older or younger than your late sister?"

"Older."

"What about your son? He's an officer in the Army, isn't he?"

"Eoghan is a Captain in the Royal Regiment of Artillery."

"On leave?"

"No. My son returned from Malta a month ago He had been there rather less than a year. He is now carrying out special duties in Ayrshire."

"I see. So he's only here for a day or so?"

"He arrived last night. I am not aware when he must return."

"Age?"

"Thirty-two."

"Is he your only son?"

"My only child."

"You are a widower, I believe?"

"I am."

"How long have you been a widower?"

Duchlan frowned, but after a moment his brow cleared.

"Since my son was four years of age."

"Twenty-eight years."

"Quite so."

"Has your sister lived with you during the whole of that period?"

"She has."

"So that she brought up your son?"

"Yes."

The busy pencil appeared to have been outstripped for Dundas asked no more questions until he had written during several minutes. Then he raised his head sharply.

"How long has your son been married?" he demanded.

"Three years and a few months."

"Any children?"

"One boy of two years."

"His wife's name? Full maiden name?"

"Oonagh Greenore."

"Irish?"

A faint smile appeared on Duchlan's lips.

"I believe so," he said gravely.

"Did Mrs. Gregor accompany her husband to Malta?"

"No, she remained here because of her son."

"Did she go to Ayrshire with him?"

"No."

"How old is she?"

"Twenty-four."

"Was he…" Dundas's fair head gleamed in the lamplight as he raised it in the quick, uncomfortable way that was apparently habitual—"was she on terms of affection with your late sister?"

Dr. Hailey moved uneasily in his chair, but he watched closely the effect of this question on the old man. Duchlan's black eyes flashed.

"I suppose," he said, "that I can pardon such a question by recalling the fact that you had not the privilege of knowing my sister."

"No offence meant, sir."

"So I have presumed." Duchlan passed his hand over his long chin. "My daughter-in law," he declared, "felt for her aunt the same respect and love which all who knew her felt for her."

Dundas wrote. "Relations cordial," he quoted from his memorandum in tones that set Dr. Hailey's teeth on edge. "So much can't be said in every case," he remarked reassuringly. "Very good. Now we can come to the servants. That was your butler, I take it, who admitted me."

"My piper, Angus MacDonald."

"Acting in the capacity of butler."

"Forgive me, Mr. Dundas, but you appear to be but ill-informed about Highland custom. Angus is first and foremost my friend, the friend of my family. He was piper to my father, the late Duchlan, who held his friendship an honour; should I predecease him, I pray God that he may serve my son. Our pipers stand remote from the class of domestic servants; but in these difficult times we are compelled to ask from them an extended range of service."

"Isn't it six of one and half a dozen of the other, sir?" Dundas remarked coolly. "I mean, piper or no piper, the old man is in fact acting as butler?"

"No."

The policeman shrugged his shoulders. He had the air of a modern jerry builder visiting a Gothic cathedral; there was no recognition of beauty, but in some sort, respect for age and mass, to be expressed later in exaggeration of both. Dundas, Dr. Hailey felt sure, would boast about his visit to Duchlan and embellish boasting with spurious detail. It seemed that Duchlan was not unaware of this probability for his face expressed a degree of ferocious anger that is seen only in the faces of men and carnivorous birds.

"Have the goodness, sir," he exclaimed, "to leave that alone which you do not and cannot understand. Confine yourself to your business."

"Very well. How old is your piper?"

"Sixty-eight."

"Married or single?"

"Single."

"The other servants?"

Duchlan considered a moment. His eyes were still glowing with anger, but he had himself in control.

"I employ the services of a cook and a housemaid," he stated. "They are sisters named Campbell. In addition, there is my son's old nurse, Christina, whose position is not that of a servant."

He paused, challenging Dundas to utter any syllable of comment. The policeman gazed at the carpet.

"Christina is sixty. She's a widow. Her name is Graeme. She has acted latterly as maid to my sister, as well as nurse to my grandson."

"Are the Campbells local people?"

"They are."

"Their Christian names?"

"Mary and Flora. Mary, my cook, is twenty-eight. Her sister is twenty-five."

The old man gave these facts and figures in tones of contempt. He sneered at the policeman and his notebook, baring his long teeth like a dog. But the doctor thought that, behind this mask of scorn, there was relief that the task of dealing with the murder had been committed to so narrow an intelligence.

Chapter V

The Sound of a Splash

An uneasy silence filled the room. Dundas broke it.

"There's one question," he remarked, "that I wish to ask before I go upstairs. It's this: Did you expect your son to return last night?"

"We expected him to return soon."

"Please answer my question."

"We did not know that he was coming last night."

"How did he come?"

"By motor-boat."

"What?"

Duchlan's eyes flashed again.

"He came by motor-boat."

"Is that the quickest way?"

"You must ask him that yourself."

Dr. Hailey accompanied Dundas to Miss Gregor's room. Before they entered the room the policeman told him that he proposed to conduct the investigation single-handed.

"I know very well, Doctor," he said, "how big your reputation is as an amateur detective. And I'm, of course, indebted to you for the preliminary work you've done here. I shall be honoured if you agree to stand by me during the examination of witnesses. But I mean to ride the horse myself. There must be no independent lines of inquiry."

He paused, having observed the flush which had risen to his companion's cheeks.

"Very well."

"Please don't be angry. Put yourself in my place. This is the chance of my life. I'll never get another if I fail. And I'm a solitary worker. Can't go in double harness. Can't concentrate if ideas are brought to me. My mind runs on its own scents, so to speak. So I say, 'Come with me, but don't confuse me.' And don't run on ahead of me. That's not being rude. It's being honest." The man's face was so earnest that the tactlessness of his address was discounted. The doctor smiled.

"I'm to have a seat on the bench, so to speak?" he asked in genial tones.

"Exactly. As a distinguished stranger."

"And if I decline that honour?"

"I'll be sorry. But not so sorry as if you had begun to work on the case independently of me."

Dr. Hailey nodded assent.

"I'm staying for another week at Darroch Mor," he said. "You may command my services at any time during that period."

"You won't come here at all?"

"No."

Dr. Hailey's habitual good-humour had reasserted itself. His large face expressed neither hostility nor contempt. It was not, perhaps, at any time an expressive face, but there was a gentleness in its aspect which conveyed its own message. The man compelled confidence and liking without moving a muscle.

"I do hope you'll make a great success," he said in quiet tones. "Nobody knows better than I do how much success in cases of this kind is conditioned by chance. It's like playing Bridge; a bad hand may discount the greatest ability."

"Oh, yes, one realizes that."

Dundas spoke in tones which suggested that his luck had not, so far, deserted him. But his manner had changed nevertheless. He opened a gun-metal cigarette-case and offered it with a smile that conveyed the suggestion of a wish to be friendly.

"I feel," he apologized, "that you may think I've been rude and ungrateful. It isn't that. Crime is your hobby; it's my business. If you fail, nobody's going to blame you; if I fail somebody else will be sent the next time." He paused. "And there's another point. If you work with me and we find our man, the credit will go to you, no matter how modest you may be. The public loves amateurs. Credit is the goodwill of my business. It's my only possession."

"I understand perfectly. Believe me, I didn't thrust myself in here."

Dundas nodded.

"What do you think of the case?" he asked suddenly.

The doctor met this advance with a smile which conveyed a gentle rebuke.

"My dear sir, if I told you shouldn't I be prejudicing your judgement?" he asked.

He smiled again when the detective's face reddened.

"All the same," Dundas exclaimed, "I'd like to know your opinion, that is, if you've formed any opinion at all."

Dr. Hailey shook his head.

"I haven't formed any opinion. When you arrived I was listening to Duchlan talking about his sister. The only clear idea I obtained from that recital was that Miss Gregor ruled this house with a heavy hand. Her brother appears to have allowed her to do exactly what she liked; he had no ideas, I think, except her ideas. Now that she's dead, he seems to be clinging to her ideas and precepts like a disciple who has lost his master. He can't endure the slightest criticism of them."

Dundas raised his eyebrows. It was clear that he saw no help in these personal details.

"I'm afraid," he confessed, "that my concern must be with those who wanted Miss Gregor out of the way, not with those who find it difficult to live without her."

They parted. The doctor descended the staircase. It was the first time, he reflected, that he had been dismissed from a case. But he meant to abide by his decision. He told Duchlan and the others frankly how the matter stood.

"Dundas is like that," Mr. McLeod said in tones of regret. "He always wants to do everything himself. So far, I'll admit, he's had the luck on his side."

"Let us hope it won't desert him."

John MacCallien rose to go. He held out his hand to Duchlan.

"You know how distressed I feel," he said. "This policeman, I'm afraid, is an additional burden."

"Thank you, John." Duchlan turned to Dr. Hailey. "Believe me, my gratitude is very real. I'm sorry that you have not been able to continue your inquiry." He shook his head as he spoke. But in spite of the melancholy expression on his face the doctor had the same impression he had experienced when taking leave of Dundas. The laird of Duchlan, no less than the policeman from Glasgow, was glad to see him go. Duchlan rose and glanced at the clock. Then he took a thin gold watch from his pocket and looked at that, too.

"Shall I send for the car?" he asked John MacCallien.

"No, please don't."

"Then may I walk with you as far as the lodge? I feel that I need air."

"My dear Duchlan, it's very late. Do you think you ought to venture out?"

"Ah, what hurts me is sitting here, alone."

The moon had come westward, and was high above their heads as they emerged from the Castle. In this light the sham medievalism of the building was tolerable largely because one could no longer see it. There had happened at Duchlan what happened all over the Highlands when the lairds became rich in the middle of the nineteenth century, namely, an attempt to turn the old bare house of the chiefs of the clan into a feudal castle on the English model. Turrets, balustrades, and the rest of the paraphernalia of baronialism had been heaped about a dwelling formerly humble and beautiful, to the profit of the local builder and the loss of the community.

The old man walked slowly and the journey to the lodge took a long time. John MacCallien tried, once or twice, to talk but failed to awaken any response. Dr. Hailey noticed that each time Duchlan stopped, and he stopped frequently, he turned and looked out, across the loch. On these occasions he seemed to be listening. Once, when a seabird screeched, he dropped his walking-stick. The doctor began to observe him and soon made up his mind that this excursion was predetermined. But to what was he listening? The night was still and without voice.

"My sister delighted in this walk," he told his companions. "She had travelled widely but maintained that the view from the north lodge was the most beautiful she had seen. I like to think that she may be watching us now."

He addressed Dr. Hailey. "We Highland folk," he said in low tones, "partake of the spirit of our hills and lochs. That's the secret of what the Lowlanders, who will never understand us, call our pride. Yes, we have pride; but the pride of blood, of family; of our dear land. Highlanders are ready to die for their pride."

It was gently spoken, but in accents which thrilled. Duchlan, clearly, was assured of the reality of those ideas on which his life was based. He had marched all the way to fanaticism; but, your fanatic, the doctor reflected, is ever a sceptic at heart.

They reached the lodge. The old man struck a match and looked at his watch.

"It's two o'clock," he announced, "or so I make it. What do you say, Doctor?"

"I'm afraid my watch has stopped."

John MacCallien held his wrist up to the moon.

"Yes," he declared, "just two o'clock precisely."

"I bid you good morning, gentlemen."

Duchlan bowed ceremoniously and turned back. They watched him until his figure could no longer be distinguished from the shadows.

John MacCallien was about to pass through the lodge gates when the doctor put his hand on his arm.

"I should like to see Duchlan reach home," he said.

"Oh, he's on his own ground, you know."

"Listen, my dear fellow. You go back to Darroch Mor and leave the front door on the latch for me. I'll follow as soon as I've satisfied myself that everything's all right."

"I'll come with you."

The doctor shook his head.

"Forgive me, if I say that I would rather go alone. And allow me to postpone explanations."

"My dear Hailey."

"I have good reasons for what I'm doing."

John MacCallien belonged to that rare type which is content to leave other folk to conduct their affairs in their own way. He nodded, took out his pipe, and began to fill it.

"Very well."

Dr. Hailey left him and hurried along the avenue after Duchlan. As he had foreseen, the old man was capable of walking fast when occasion required. He did not come up with him. When he reached the castle, he assured himself that Duchlan had not returned home; the light was still burning in the window of the study and the room was empty. Very cautiously, he approached the lighted window without, however, crossing the flower-bed which separated it from the carriage-way.

Where had the old man gone? He walked along the front of the house, passing from the carriage-way to the steep bank which he had seen from Miss Gregor's window. He descended the bank, keeping a sharp look-out to right and left. But he reached the burn without seeing anybody.

The stream broadened out above the jetty. It was high tide and the water was deep. He had an excellent view of the motor-boat. He raised his eyeglass to determine if there was anyone aboard and concluded that there was nobody. He thought of walking down the jetty and then decided against a course which must make him conspicuous to anybody standing among the trees on the far side of the burn. Doubts of the process of reasoning which had brought him back to the castle began to assail him; but when he recalled that process he put them away. Duchlan had fussed with his watch both before leaving the castle and at the lodge gate. He had been at pains to impress on the minds of his companions that two o'clock had struck before he left them. The inference seemed justified that he was anxious that some event, timed to occur at two o'clock, should not be laid to his account.

A twig snapped amongst the trees on the opposite side of the burn. Dr. Hailey turned and stood listening. He heard a window being opened. He crouched down. Footsteps approached and passed. Then the moonlight showed him a woman descending towards the jetty.

She walked slowly, seeming to linger at every step. He could see that she was young. As she approached the end of the jetty she stood and turned. The moon gave him a view of her face and he observed the tense, strained poise of her head. Suddenly she raised her arms and stretched them out towards the castle. She remained in this attitude for several seconds. Then her arms fell to her side and she turned to the water which shone and glimmered round the pier at her feet. A sound, like a subdued cough, which seemed to come from close at hand, made him turn his head and gaze into the shadows across the burn. A splash recalled him. The woman had disappeared.

Chapter VI

Oonagh Gregor

Dr. Hailey ran to the end of the jetty. The woman was struggling in the water a few feet away. He threw off his coat and jumped in.

She sank as he approached, but he dived and a moment later brought her to the surface. The moon gave him a glimpse of her face and he saw that she had fainted. He brought her to the bank. Then he laid her down and began artificial respiration.

He was not immediately successful and paused for a moment to breathe himself. He lit his lamp and glanced at the woman's face. She was beautiful, with jet black hair.

An exclamation broke from his lips. Two long bruises made semicircles round her throat. He bent to examine them. The purple colour was deep and fixed. The bruises had been inflicted at least twelve hours before. No doubt could exist that somebody had attempted to strangle this girl.

The discovery shook his nerve, but he realized the necessity of immediate action. He extinguished the lamp and set to work again. At last she breathed naturally. When he stopped to allow the rhythm of breathing to establish itself, he thought he heard footsteps behind him. But his lamp failed to reveal anybody. Her breathing was fitful and seemed ready to cease at any moment. He continued his work and laboured for what seemed a very long time before her distressed sighing was disciplined to regularity. Her pulse had acquired a larger volume. He illuminated her face once more and raised one of her eyelids so that the strong stimulus of the light might reach her brain. She moved and closed her eyes firmly, resisting him. A moan broke from her lips. A moment later he caught the words—"your sake" and "failure".

He patted her cheek, calling to her. After a moment she opened her eyes. She gazed vacantly into the darkness.

"I was so frightened."

She raised her hand as though inviting help. He took it and rubbed it. He felt her fingers tighten.

"I was so frightened…"

"Don't worry. You're all right now."

The vacant look in her eyes changed to fear. She withdrew her hand sharply.

"Where am I?" she cried in tones of great distress.

"You're all right."

"Oh, no, no." She caught her breath and then, with a swift gesture, pushed his hand away so that the beam no longer shone on her face.

"I was drowning?"

"Yes."

"You shouldn't have rescued me."

She clutched at him with both her hands. "I feel terribly weak…dreadful."

He took his flask from his pocket and opened it.

"Drink a little of this," he urged.

"What is it?"

"Brandy."

She obeyed him and the spirit kindled her anxiety.

"Why did you rescue me?" she moaned, then, suddenly and with bitterness: "Who are you?"

He told her. When he had spoken she remained silent for a few minutes. Then she said:

"I'm Oonagh Gregor. Eoghan Gregor's wife."

"So I guessed."

She offered no further explanation. He heard her begin to shiver and made her drink again from his flask.

"Are you strong enough to walk to the castle?"

"No. No."

"You can't stay here."

A sob broke from her lips. "Please don't ask me to go back there. I...I can't go back there."

"Why not?"

Her teeth chattered and her breath came in short gasps. He recognized that she was making a great effort to control herself.

"Please don't ask me, Dr. Hailey. I can't go back."

"Very well then, you must come to Darroch Mor, at once."

"Oh, no."

"I insist."

He stood erect as he spoke and, for the first time, realized how exhausted he was and how stiff. His wet clothes clung to his body inhospitably. He held out his hands to her, but she refused them.

"Please leave me," she cried. "Please go back to Darroch Mor yourself." Her voice failed. Her posture expressed utter dejection.

"Listen to me," he urged in gentle tones. "Whatever your motive in jumping into the water may have been, that attempt has failed. Providence, if I may say so, has preserved your life. And surely for a purpose. You cannot repeat the attempt because, if need be, I shall remain with you till morning. And I'm stronger than you are. In the morning I shall hand you over to the police if I think there is the least likelihood of your repeating your attempt."

"You don't understand. My life isn't worth saving. I promise you that it isn't worth saving."

"There's your son."

She cried out:

"Don't remind me of him."

"I must remind you of him."

"He'll forget. He won't remember. He won't know…" She broke off, wringing her hands.

"Would you leave him to strangers?"

"Strangers. It's I who am the stranger."

Dr. Hailey remained silent a moment then he said:

"I saw those bruises on your neck."

Her hands went up to the collar of her dress. She drew it more tightly round her neck. She did not answer him.

"A doctor can see at a glance that you were attacked by someone within the last twenty-four hours."

Still she offered no explanation. After a little while he urged her to tell him what had happened.

"If you're frank with me, I think I may be able to help you," he said. "Believe me, it's folly not to be frank in such cases as this."

"I would rather not talk about it."

Suddenly she raised her face to him.

"In a sense your knowledge of those bruises is a professional secret?" she asked.

"Possibly."

"Promise me you won't tell anybody about them."

He considered for a moment.

"Very well," he said. He extended his arm. "I insist on your walking. You mustn't sit still. It's as much as your life's worth."

She rose and, after a moment's hesitation, took his arm. He thought that her weakness was passing; a moment later she reeled and would have fallen if he had not supported her.

"I don't think I can walk."

"You must try."

He gave her his flask again and made her drink from it. They stumbled laboriously along the shore of the loch towards a clump of trees through which the carriage-way passed. When they reached the first of these trees he stood to allow her to breathe herself.

"I think you would comfort yourself," he told her, "if you confessed why you tried to take your life."

"No."

"Duchlan knew that you were going to drown yourself."

She started away from him and then caught at the trunk of a tree. In the silence which fell between them, he heard the screech owl keeping its vigil beside the castle.

"How do you know that?"

"He came down here a little time ago."

"He told you?"

"No. Nothing."

She sighed, expressing her relief. She took his arm again.

"It's my business to guess what people do not tell me," he said, "and that has become my habit. If your father-in-law knew what you were going to do, he must have approved, since he did not prevent. That can only mean that he associates you in some way with the death of his sister."

He paused. He was aware that she had listened to him with breathless attention.

"Well?"

"I can't tell you anything."

"You don't deny the justice of my reasoning."

"I can't tell you anything."

He considered a moment, wondering whether or not to try further to probe the secret. At last he said:

"I may be wrong but Duchlan impressed me as a man who would sacrifice anybody to his family pride. I fancy he has persuaded himself that his position as head of his family is a responsibility which must at all costs be discharged. He was prepared to let you drown. Your life constituted, I conclude, a danger to his family."

"Please don't go on. I…I can't bear it. Not just now at any rate."

She pleaded rather than protested. She was leaning heavily on his arm.

"Forgive me."

They reached the carriage-way and turned left handed towards Darroch Mor. After a few paces she stopped to breathe.

"Will you not leave me here?"

"No."

"If you only understood."

"Perhaps I do understand."

She seemed to summon all her courage. She began to walk again and slowly and painfully they came to the lodge where Duchlan had turned back.

"I can't go to Darroch Mor."

He thought that she was about to try to escape from him, but realized a moment later, when she sank down on her knees, how greatly he had overestimated her strength. He bent and picked her up and carried her some way in his arms.

"Can you walk a little now?"

"Yes, I think so."

She made an attempt but failed. Again he carried her and again found himself overcome.

"We stayed too long on the shore."

She did not answer. She did not seem to care what happened or where he took her, so long as he didn't take her back to Duchlan. After what seemed a long time, they came to the gate of Darroch Mor. She drew back suddenly:

"I can't come in."

She stood facing him; he could see that she was panic-stricken like a hunted creature.

"How can you stay out here?"

She shook her head.

"You don't understand."

"I refuse to leave you. Very soon Colonel MacCallien will come to look for me."

She caught at his arm, and held it in tense fingers.

"Were you alone when you rescued me?"

"Yes."

"But Duchlan was watching?"

"He may have been."

"Did he see you rescue me?"

"I don't know."

She glanced at the moon.

"If he was watching he must have seen. He'll know that we've come here."

"Perhaps."

She shuddered.

"He'll send Eoghan."

Suddenly she grew still, listening. They heard footsteps approaching from the direction of Duchlan.

Dr. Hailey turned and saw a tall man striding toward them. He flashed the beam of his torch on the man's face. The girl uttered a cry of dismay.

Chapter VII

A Woman Who Sees a Ghost

Her husband's arrival exerted a singular effect on Oonagh. She seemed to gather her wits and discipline them in an instant. When Eoghan demanded in tones in which anxiety and anger were mingled why she had left Duchlan, she answered:

"Because I had something to say to Dr. Hailey."

The words were spoken with a degree of assurance which was the more remarkable from the brightness of the moon. It seemed to the doctor that Gregor must observe the condition of his wife's clothing. But apparently he was too agitated to observe anything.

"It's dreadfully inconsiderate of you," he cried, "especially at such a time. My father roused me to come to look for you. He's terribly distressed."

"He knows that I wished to talk to Dr. Hailey."

"But not at this hour, surely!"

"Did your father tell you where to find me?"

"He said you might be here."

"He knew where I was."

Eoghan remained silent, gazing at his wife. He faced the moon and Dr. Hailey saw that his features expressed a deep melancholy.

"I should like you to come back with me now."

"No, Eoghan."

"What?"

"I can't come back to Duchlan."

A look of bewilderment appeared on the young man's face. "Why not?"

"I can't."

"You must come back."

She shook her head.

"Dr. Hailey is going to ask John MacCallien to put me up for the night."

"Oonagh—"

Eoghan tried to grasp his wife's arm. She shrank from him.

"Please don't."

"Surely, Doctor," he cried, "you can't approve of behaviour of this sort? We have sorrow enough at Duchlan…"

He broke off. Dr. Hailey considered a moment and then turned to him.

"I should like you both to come into the house with me," he said, "I have something to tell you." He glanced at Oonagh, whose face expressed a lively dissent. "I shall not try to persuade you against your will. All I want is to put you and your husband in possession of certain facts."

"I don't wish to hear them."

He realized that she feared the discovery of her attempted suicide and pitched about in his mind for some means of avoiding that discovery. There were none. He weighed the danger and took his decision.

"I have just rescued your wife from drowning," he told Eoghan in matter-of-fact tones.

"What!"

"It's as I say. The bank of the burn, under the castle, is very steep and it's easy, as you know, to slip on that steep bank. There's nothing to break the fall till the burn is reached and at high tide the water in the mouth of the burn is deep."

He spoke in challenging tones. He added: "Please don't ask any questions just now; I shall not answer them."

He watched the young man and saw his expression change from melancholy to fear. Eoghan's fists were clenched. Suddenly he caught his wife's arm, holding it in a strong grip. This time she did not shrink from him. They walked to the door of the house in silence. It was ajar. Dr. Hailey led the way into the smoking-room and switched up the light. An exclamation of dismay broke from Eoghan's lips when he saw his wife. He came to her and put his arm round her to help her to a chair. A fire was laid in the grate; he stooped and lit it. Oonagh's eyes followed every movement, but her face remained expressionless.

It was an interesting face in spite of its weakness. Even in her distress, the girl managed to convey a remarkable impression of vitality. Dr. Hailey glanced at Eoghan. There was vitality in his face too, but it was clouded by his melancholy. Oonagh, he thought, was one of those women who need to depend on a man's direction. Was this man capable of giving her the support without which her vitality must constitute a danger?

"As you know," he said, "I had an opportunity of inspecting Miss Gregor's body this evening. That inspection has convinced me that she was killed by someone possessed of great strength and using a weapon taken from a fishing-boat. That's the first fact that I wish to make known to you."

He sat down and put his eyeglass in his eye. Although his clothes clung to him rather dismally he had not lost his kindliness of manner.

"Why do you think the weapon was taken from a fishing boat?" Eoghan asked.

"Because I found the scale of a herring near the edge of the wound."

Oonagh raised her head sharply.

"That would mean that the scale had been on the blade of the weapon?"

"I think so. I don't see how it could have reached the place where I found it in any other way. There was only one scale, so I conclude that the weapon was wiped before being used."

The girl moved her chair nearer to the fire. He saw her knuckles whiten as she grasped its arms.

"Queerly enough," Eoghan said, "I bought some herring from a fishing boat on my way across the loch last night. They were pulling in the net when I passed them and I couldn't resist the temptation. The launch is full of herring scales."

He spoke calmly but his words exerted a strong effect on his wife, who bent closer to the fire as if to hide her uneasiness. A lambent flame revealed the tense expression on her face.

"Still, you didn't visit your aunt, did you?"

"Yes, I did."

"I understand, from what your father said, that he called you early this morning to help to break into Miss Gregor's room."

"Oh, yes. But I went to her room before I went to bed last night. Her door was locked."

Dr. Hailey waved his hand in a gesture which indicated that he would not at present concern himself with that aspect of the matter.

"The second fact I wish you to know," he said, "is that some time elapsed between the infliction of the wound and the death of Miss Gregor. During this time the murderer remained in the room. That is certain, because, had the weapon been withdrawn from the wound before death, a very much larger quantity of blood must have been spilt."

"Have you any idea," Eoghan asked, "how the room was entered?"

"Possibly by the door. The door was locked in the morning but…"

"It was locked when I tried it at eleven o'clock last night."

"Even so, you don't know when, exactly, the key was turned, do you?"

"I know," Oonagh said in quiet tones.

"What?"

She faced Dr. Hailey. He saw that excitement had returned to her eyes.

"I went to Aunt Mary's room just after ten o'clock," she said. "I knocked and then opened the door. Christina was just going to leave the room. I took her candle from her and went towards the bed where Aunt Mary was lying. When Aunt Mary saw me she sat up and began to gasp. I was frightened and went out and shut the door. I heard her get out of bed and run to the door. She locked the door. Christina had gone away."

Oonagh's voice had become louder but was still subdued. There was an assurance in her tones that carried conviction.

"How do you know Miss Gregor locked the door?" Dr. Hailey asked.

"Because I tried the handle. I thought that perhaps she was ill and that I ought to go into the room again."

"You are quite sure of that?"

"Absolutely sure. I tried the handle several times."

"Did you call to Miss Gregor while you were trying the handle?"

"Yes. She didn't answer me."

Dr. Hailey turned to Eoghan.

"Did you call to her when you tried the handle?"

"I did, yes. I got no answer. I thought she had fallen asleep."

"Aunt Mary seemed to be terrified of me," Oonagh stated. "I have never seen anyone look so terrified in my life."

"She wasn't easily frightened, was she?"

A smile flickered on the girl's lips.

"Oh, no." She added: "Until that moment I had been frightened of her."

"Do you think she was calling for help?"

"No, that's the strange thing. I think she was just dreadfully afraid. Panic-stricken. Like a woman who sees a ghost. She didn't try to call Christina back."

Dr. Hailey leaned forward.

"How were you dressed?" he asked.

"I was in my night-dress. I was wearing a blue silk dressing-gown."

Chapter VIII

Husband and Wife

The room grew silent. Oonagh pushed aside her heavy fringe, and revealed a high brow.

"Why did you go to Miss Gregor's room?" Dr. Hailey asked her.

The girl glanced at her husband before she replied.

"Aunt Mary and I had quarrelled before dinner. I wanted to talk to her."

"To make up your quarrel?"

"Yes."

The monosyllable came firmly.

Dr. Hailey nodded.

"Duchlan told me," he said, "that you had gone to bed before dinner because you weren't feeling well."

"I wasn't feeling well. But that was the result of my quarrel with Aunt Mary."

The doctor rose and took out his snuff-box.

"My position," he said, "is a little difficult. I told Inspector Dundas that I wouldn't try to double his work on the case. If I ask any more questions I'm afraid I shall be breaking that promise. My object in bringing you here, as you know, wasn't to get information but to give it. I wanted you both to realize that this case presents very great difficulties which will certainly tax the resources of the police to the utmost."

He took a pinch of snuff. Eoghan asked.

"Why did you want us to realize that?"

"So that your wife might feel able to return with you to Duchlan."

"I confess I don't follow."

Dr. Hailey glanced at Oonagh. She shook her head. He took more snuff to avoid making an immediate reply, and then said:

"I fancy it is better to tell the truth. Your wife was trying to drown herself when I rescued her."

Eoghan jumped up.

"What!" The blood ebbed out of his cheeks. "Is this true?" he demanded of Oonagh.

"Yes."

"That you tried to—to drown yourself?"

"Yes."

He turned fearful eyes to Dr. Hailey.

"I insist on knowing the whole truth. Why is my wife with you at this hour? How does my father know that she's with you?"

"I can't answer the last question. The answer to the first is that I saw her jump from the jetty, and ran to her help. It's possible your father may have observed us."

The young man strode to his wife and seized her hand.

"Why did you do it?" he cried.

There was anguish in his voice.

Oonagh remained bending over the fire, unresponsive and limp. When he repeated his question, she bowed her head, but she did not answer. The doctor sat down.

"I think I can supply the answer," he said. "Your wife feared that you had played a part in the murder of your aunt."

"I don't understand you."

"Her suicide was sure to be interpreted as a confession of her own guilt. She was shielding you."

Eoghan started.

"Oonagh, is that true?"

There was no reply. The doctor waited a moment and then said to Eoghan:

"It wasn't an unreasonable fear, perhaps. No more unreasonable, certainly, than the fear under which you are labouring at this moment, namely, that your wife's attempt to drown herself was a confession of guilt." His voice became gentle: "What's the use of pretence at a time such as this? The more deeply we love, the quicker must be our fear, seeing that each of us is liable, under provocation, to lose self-control. Why I told you about my examination of your aunt's wound was that you might realize that it cannot have been inflicted by a woman. Your wife did not kill your aunt. Your fear that she may have done so proves, surely, that you, too, are guiltless."

He paused. A look of inexpressible relief had appeared on Oonagh's face. She stretched out her hand to her husband, who grasped it.

"You have reasons, presumably, both of you, for your fears," Dr. Hailey added. "I can only speculate about these; I note, in passing, that you are no longer sharing a bedroom. Whatever your reasons may be, they do not invalidate my argument."

He turned to Eoghan:

"Take John MacCallien's car and drive your wife home. The door of the garage isn't locked."

Chapter IX

A Heat Wave

Dr. Hailey heard nothing officially about the murder of Miss Gregor for several days after his visit to Duchlan. But news of the activity of Inspector Dundas was not lacking. That young man, in his own phrase, was leaving no stone unturned. He had surrounded the castle with policemen; he had forbidden the inhabitants to leave the grounds on any pretext whatever; and he had commandeered motor-cars and boats for his own service. The household staff, or so it was reported, was reduced to a state of panic. Nor were his activities confined to Duchlan; everyone of the two thousand villagers of Ardmore lay under the heavy cloud of his suspicion.

"And yet," Dr. McDonald of Ardmore told Dr. Hailey, "he hasn't advanced a step. He has found no motive for the murder; suspicion attaches to nobody, and he possesses not even the remotest idea of how the murderer entered or left Miss Gregor's bedroom."

Dr. McDonald made this statement with a degree of bitterness which indicated how grievously he himself had suffered at Dundas's hands.

"The man's a fusser," he added. "Nothing must escape him. And so everything escapes him. He's always trying to hold a bunch of sparrows in one hand while he plucks them with the other."

The Ardmore doctor smiled at his metaphor.

"Lowlanders such as Dundas," he said, "always work on the assumption that we Highlanders are fools or knaves, or both. They invariably try to bamboozle us—to frighten us. Neither of these methods gets them anywhere because the Highlander is brave as well as subtle. Flora Campbell, the housemaid at Duchlan, asked Dundas if he was going to arrest all the herring in the Loch till he counted their scales. The fishermen call herring-scales 'Dundases' now."

"Sometimes that method succeeds, you know," Dr. Hailey said gently.

"Oh, one might forgive the method if it wasn't for the man. Not that he's a bad fellow really. One of the fishermen lost his temper with him and called him 'a wee whipper-snapper' to his face and he took that in good part. But you can't help feeling that he's waiting and watching all the time to get his teeth into you."

Dr. McDonald unscrewed his pipe and began to clean it with a spill of paper, an operation which promised badly from the outset.

"I smoke too much," he remarked, "but it keeps my nerves quiet. Dundas's voice is hard to bear when your nerves aren't as steady as they might be."

He withdrew the spill and tried to blow through the pipe. He looked rather uneasy but seemed to find comfort in his task.

"It's queer, isn't it," he said, "that however innocent you may be you aways feel uncomfortable when you know you're under suspicion?"

"Yes."

"Dundas possesses none of the subtlety which can set a suspected man at his ease and so loosen his tongue. Everybody, even the most talkative, becomes an oyster in his presence, because it's so obvious that anything you may say will be turned and twisted against you. Mrs. Eoghan, I believe, refused to answer his questions because he began by suggesting that she knew her husband was guilty. When he made the same suggestion to Duchlan the old man vowed he wouldn't see him again, and wrote to Glasgow, to police headquarters, to get him recalled."

"He won't be recalled because of that," Dr. Hailey remarked grimly.

"Possibly not. But complaints from lairds don't do a detective any good in this country. Scotland's supposed to be more democratic than England, but that's an illusion. I don't believe there's any place in the world where a landed proprietor has more influence. If Dundas fails he'll get short shrift. He knows that; his nerves are all on edge now and every day adds to his trouble."

Dr. Hailey took a pinch of snuff.

"Frankly," he said, "I rather liked him. If he was a trifle tactless, he was honest and good-natured."

"You're an Englishman."

"Well?"

"Highland people are the most difficult to handle in the world because they're the most touchy in the world. What they cannot endure is to be laughed at, and Dundas began by laughing at them—jeering at them would be a truer description. They won't forgive him, I can assure you."

Dr. McDonald nodded his head vigorously as he spoke. He was a big man, red of face and raw of bone, with a wooden leg which gave him much trouble, a man, as Dr. Hailey knew, reputed something of a dreamer but believed, too, to be very wise in the lore of his profession and in the knowledge of men. His blue eyes continued to sparkle.

"I promised not to interfere," Dr. Hailey said.

"He told me that. He hasn't much opinion of amateur methods of catching criminals."

"So I gathered."

Dr. McDonald's eyes narrowed. He leaned forward in his chair in order to move his leg to a more comfortable position.

"Did you see the old scar on Miss Gregor's chest?" he asked.

"Yes."

"What did you make of it?"

Dr. Hailey shook his head. "You mustn't ask me that, you know."

"Very well. But that's the clue that Dundas has fastened on. Who wounded Miss Gregor ten years ago? He thinks if he can answer that question his troubles'll be over. And the queer thing is that nobody can or nobody will tell him. He's got it worked out that the poor woman was probably at home here when she was wounded. And yet neither Duchlan nor Angus nor Christina seem to know anything about the wound."

Dr. McDonald paused. It was obvious that he hoped to interest his colleague, but Dr. Hailey only shook his head.

"You mustn't ask me for my opinion."

"There's another queer thing: Dundas, as I told you, has paid a lot of attention to the herring-scale you discovered. He found a second scale inside the wound. He argued that the weapon the wound was inflicted with must have come from the kitchen, and, as I said, he'd been giving the servants a fearful time. I believe he found an axe with fish scales on it, but the clue led him nowhere.

"His next idea was that Duchlan himself might be the murderer. He tried to work out a scheme on these lines.

Duchlan's poor, like all the lairds, so it was possible that he wanted his sister's money. The old man, I'm glad to say, didn't guess what was in the wind. He's a fine old man, is Duchlan, but his temper's not very dependable nowadays."

A second spill achieved what the first had failed to achieve. McDonald screwed up his pipe and put it in his mouth. It emitted a gurgling sound which in no way disconcerted him. He began to charge it with tobacco.

"Naturally," he went on, "this inquisition has refreshed a lot of memories. And a doctor hears everything. There's an old woman in the village who's reputed to be a witch as her mother was before her. I believe her name's MacLeod though they call her 'Annie Nannie'. Goodness knows why. She remembers Duchlan's wife, Eoghan's mother, well, and she told me yesterday that once the poor woman came to consult her. 'She looked at me,' Annie Nannie said, 'for a long time without speaking a word. Then she asked me if it was true I could tell what was going to happen to folk. I was a young woman then myself and I was frightened, seein' the laird's young wife in my cottage. So I told her it wasn't a true.' However, in the end she was persuaded to tell Mrs. Gregor's fortune. She says she prophesied evil."

Dr. Hailey shrugged his shoulders.

"Married women go to fortune-tellers when they're unhappy," he said. "Possibly Dundas might make something of that."

"Mrs. Gregor's death took place soon after that. It's a curious fact that nobody knows exactly what she died of. But her death was sudden. I've heard that it came as a great shock to the village because people didn't know she was ill. Duchlan would never speak about it, and nobody dared to ask him."

"Where was she buried?"

"In the family vault on the estate. So far as I know nobody was invited to attend the funeral. That doesn't necessarily mean much, because it's a tradition of the Gregor family to bury their dead secretly, at night. Duchlan's father's funeral, I believe, took place by torchlight."

"I would like," Dr. Hailey said, "to know whether or not Miss Gregor attended the funeral of her sister-in-law. If I were Dundas I should make a point of getting information about that."

McDonald shook his head.

"You would find it very difficult to get information. One has only to mention Duchlan's wife to produce an icy silence."

"Did she discuss her sister-in-law with the Ardmore witch?"

"Oh, no. She discussed nothing. She blamed nobody. She merely said that being Irish she believed in fortune-telling. She was very much afraid that her husband might hear of her visit, but he never did."

McDonald lit his pipe.

"Annie Nannie speaks very well of her client, and she's not given to flattery. By all accounts Duchlan's wife was a fine woman. 'It fair broke my heart,' she said, 'to see her sitting crying in my cottage, and her that kind and good to everybody.'"

The doctor took a pinch of snuff.

"It's curious that both father and son should have married Irish women," he said.

"Yes. And women so like one another too. Those who remember Eoghan's mother say she was the image of his wife. Mrs. Eoghan's very popular in the village, far more so, really, than Miss Gregor was."

"How about the servants at the castle?"

"They love her. Dundas has been going into that too; he's got an idea that the Campbell girls didn't like Miss Gregor and he's been trying to find out if either of them went to her bedroom on the night she was killed. There's nothing, as a matter of fact, to show that any of the servants went to Miss Gregor's room after Christina, her maid, had left it for the night."

"Is Dundas still hopeful of being able to solve the mystery?" Dr. Hailey asked.

"No." Dr. McDonald moved his leg again. "In a sense," he said, "I'm here in the capacity of an ambassador. Dundas wants your help; but he's too proud to ask for it—after what he said to you. He suggested that, as one of your professional brethren, I might carry the olive branch."

"I'm afraid not."

"I hope you won't stand too much on ceremony…You have him at your mercy."

"That's not the way to look at it." Dr. Hailey took a pinch of snuff. "If I go to Duchlan now I'll be compelled to work along Inspector Dundas's lines. I've no doubt they're good lines, but they are not mine. I should only confuse his mind and my own."

"I see. You insist on a free hand."

"Not that exactly. What I'm really asking is a free mind. I don't want to co-operate. You can tell Dundas that, if he likes, I'll work at the problem independently of him. Any discoveries I may make will belong to him, of course."

"He won't consent to that. He'll give you a free hand only so long as he's with you in all you do."

There was a moment of silence. Then Dr. Hailey made up his mind.

"Tell him," he said, "that I can't accept these terms. I'm an amateur, not a professional, and my studies of crime are undertaken only because they interest me. When I work alone my mind gropes about until it finds something which appeals to it. I follow a line of investigation often without knowing exactly why I'm following it—it would be intolerable to have to explain and justify every step. And Dundas would certainly insist on such explanations. The detection of crime, I think, is an art more than a science, like the practice of medicine."

Dr. McDonald did not dispute this idea; indeed, he seemed to agree with it. He went away saying that he would come back if Dundas agreed to the terms. Dr. Hailey joined John MacCallien under the pine trees in front of the house and sat down in the deck chair which awaited him. The day was insufferably hot and close, so hot and so close that even Loch Fyne seemed to be destitute of a ripple.

"Well?"

"Dundas sent him. But I can't work with Dundas."

John MacCallien nodded.

"Of course not. I was talking to the postman while you were indoors. He says that Dundas has got the whole place by the ears. There's a panic."

"So McDonald suggested."

"Dundas has found out that Eoghan Gregor is in debt. Eoghan's his aunt's heir, so you can guess what inference has been drawn. But there's the shut room to be got over. The man has had an inventory made of every ladder in Argyll."

"The windows were bolted. Nobody can have got into the room through the windows."

"No, so I supposed. But you know what Dundas and his kind are: detail, detail, till you can't see the forest for the trees."

The haze which veiled the loch about Otter and which blotted out the rolling contours of the hills of Cowal seemed to be charged with fire and suffocation. Even in the shade of the trees, a hot vapour lay on the ground. The doctor took off his coat and rolled up his sleeves.

"I never realized that it could be so hot in the Highlands."

He lay back and looked up at the clumps of dark green pine-needles above him.

"Did you know Miss Gregor well?" he asked his friend suddenly.

"Not very well. Since my return from India I've seen very little of her. My knowledge belongs chiefly to my youth. My father always spoke of her as a latter-day saint, and I suppose I adopted that opinion readymade."

He remained thoughtful for a few minutes, during which the doctor observed his kindly face with satisfaction. John MacCallien, he reflected, was one of those men who do not change their opinions gladly and who are specially reluctant to revise the teachings of their parents.

"My father," he added, "had the outlook of the nineteenth century on men and women. He demanded a standard of behaviour and made no allowances. Miss Gregor not only conformed to that standard, but exceeded it. Her horror of what was vaguely called 'impropriety' was known and admired all over Argyll. For example, I believe that she never herself spoke of a 'man' or a 'woman', but only of a 'gentleman' or a 'lady'. Ladies and gentlemen were beings whose chief concern it was to prove by their lives and manners that they lacked the human appetites."

"I know."

John MacCallien sighed.

"I suppose there was something to be said for that point of view," he declared. "But I'm afraid it was a fruitful begetter of cruelty and harshness. Anything was justified which could be shown to inflict shame or sorrow on the unregenerate. Besides, these good people lived within the ring-fence of a lie. They were not the disembodied spirits they pretended to be—far from it. Consequently their emotions and appetites were active in all kinds of hidden and even unsuspected ways." He paused and added: "Cruelty, as I say, was one of these ways, the easiest and the most hateful."

"Was Miss Gregor cruel?" Dr. Hailey asked.

"Do you know that's an extraordinary difficult question to answer. Offhand, I should say, 'Of course not'. But it depends, really, on what you mean by cruel. Her code was full, I'm sure, of unpardonable sins, sins that put people right outside the pale. On the other hand she could be extraordinarily kind and charitable. I told you that even tinkers and gipsies used to bless her. She was always bothering herself about people of that sort. Once, I remember, a child got pneumonia in one of the tinker's tents on the shore between here and the north lodge. She nursed it herself and paid for medical attendance. When the parish officer wanted to have it removed to the Poor's House at Lochgilphead she resisted him with all her might because she believed that these people cannot live within four walls. She was told that if the child died, its death would be laid to her charge, but that kind of threat was the least likely to influence her in any way. The case aroused a lot of interest in Ardmore. When the child got well everybody felt that she had saved its life."

Dr. Hailey nodded.

"I see. In that case her personal reputation was at stake, so to speak."

"Yes. And there was no question of sin." John MacCallien sighed. "She was merciless where sinners were concerned," he added, "if their sins were of the flesh. I fancy she might have found excuses for a thief— these tinkers are all thieves, you know."

"Provided he had not sinned?"

"Exactly. Mind you, that view wasn't confined to her. It was my father's also."

"Your father's view was shared by everybody else in this neighbourhood, wasn't it?"

"Yes. By everybody."

MacCallien sat up. He shook his head rather sadly. "When my brother and I were children," he said, "we often met Miss Gregor out driving. Our nurse, on these occasions, always told us to take our hats off and that became a burden. One day, just as the carriage was passing, we put out our tongues instead. I can still see the horror on the dear woman's face. She stopped the carriage, got out, and read us a lecture on good manners We didn't mind that so much but she wrote as well to our father. I remember thinking, while we were being punished, that she wasn't my idea of a saint."

He smiled faintly and then looked surprised when he saw how attentive Dr. Hailey had become.

"How old was Miss Gregor at that time?"

"She must have been quite young. In her twenties or early thirties, I suppose."

"What happened the next time you met her?"

"Oh, we took our hats off, of course."

"And she?"

"I fancy she bowed to us as she had done formerly. Funnily enough, though, I can't remember much about her after that."

"Did you know Duchlan's wife?"

"Oh, yes, rather." MacCallien's voice became suddenly enthusiastic. "She was an awfully good sort. We loved her. I remember my brother saying once that Mrs. Gregor would never have told our father if we had put our tongues out at her. She had a short married life, poor woman."

"Eoghan Gregor's wife is supposed to be like her in appearance, isn't she?" Dr. Hailey asked.

"Yes. I think with reason too, though a child's memory is always unreliable. I know that, when I saw Mrs. Eoghan for the first time, I wondered where I had met her before. And it's certain that I had never met her before. There must be some quality in the characters of Duchlan and his son which draws them to Irish women." He paused and then added: "Not a very robust quality perhaps."

"Why do you say that?"

"I'm afraid neither of these marriages has been conspicuously successful. I suppose the qualities which Miss Gregor represents are the dominants in all the members of her family. Duchlan's wife, like Mrs. Eoghan, was more concerned with men and women than with 'ladies' and 'gentlemen'."

"It must have been very difficult for her to have her sister-in-law always beside her, don't you think?"

Dr. Hailey frowned as he spoke. His companion nodded a vigorous assent.

"It must have been dreadful. No wife could hope to be happy in such circumstances. As a matter of fact, I believe Miss Gregor did all the housekeeping and management. Duchlan's wife was treated, from beginning to end, like a visitor. Goodness knows how she endured it."

"Was there much talk about the arrangement?"

"Any amount, of course. But nobody could interfere. People older than myself have told me that they saw the poor girl wilting before their eyes. I believe one woman, the wife of an old laird, did actually dare to suggest that it was high time a change was made. She was told to mind her own business. By all accounts Mrs. Gregor was splendidly loyal to her husband and wouldn't listen to a syllable of criticism or even of sympathy. But I haven't a doubt, all the same, that the strain undermined her constitution."

Dr. Hailey passed his hand over his brow.

"What did she die of?" he asked.

"Diphtheria, I believe. She died very suddenly."

Dr. Hailey spent the afternoon in a hammock, turning over the details of the mystery in his mind. He did not disguise from himself that he was disappointed at not having been allowed to attempt a solution; on the other hand such ideas as he had evolved offered no substantial basis of deduction. He discussed the subject again with his host after dinner but obtained no enlightenment.

"I've no doubt," John MacCallien said, "that Dundas has exhausted all such probabilities as secret doors and chambers. He was prepared, I feel sure, to tear the castle to pieces to find one clue. My friend the postman had it from Angus, Duchlan's piper, that he found nothing. There are no secret chambers, no passages, no trap-doors."

"And no other means by which the murderer can have entered the bedroom or escaped out of it?"

John MacCallien raised his head.

"We know that he did enter the bedroom and did escape out of it."

"Exactly. And miracles don't happen."

The doctor took a pinch of snuff. "This is the fourth time that I've encountered a case in which a murder was committed in what seemed like a closed room or a closed space. I imagine that the truth, in this instance, will not be more difficult to discover than in these others—"

A smile flickered on his lips.

"Most of the great murder mysteries of the past half-century," he added, "have turned either on an alibi or on an apparently closed space. For practical purposes these conditions are identical, because you have to show, in face of obvious evidence to the contrary, that your murderer was at a given spot at a given moment. That, believe me, is a harder task than proving that a particular individual administered poison or that an apparent accident was, in fact, due to foul play."

He broke off because they heard a car driving up to the door. A moment later Dr. McDonald came limping into the room.

"You've got your terms, Hailey," he said as he shook the doctor's hand. "Dundas owns himself beaten." He shook hands with John MacCallien, and then turned back to Dr. Hailey. "Can you possibly come to Duchlan to-night?"

Chapter X

"Duchlan Will Be Honoured"

Inspector Dundas received the two doctors in his bedroom, a large room situated near that formerly occupied by Miss Gregor and directly overlooking the burn. He was seated on his bed, when they entered, writing notes, and wore only a shirt and trousers. But he did not seem to be feeling the heat.

"It's good of you, Dr. Hailey," he said in grateful tones, "because I wasn't as polite as I might have been at our first meeting. Pride cometh before a fall, eh?"

"On the contrary, I thought your attitude entirely unexceptionable."

The doctor sat down near the open window and mopped his brow. Dundas, he perceived, had lost his air of assurance. Even his sprightliness of manner had deserted him. The change was rather shocking, as indicating a fundamental lack of self-confidence. The man had put all his trust in cleverness and thoroughness and when these failed, had nothing to fall back on.

"Perhaps you would like me to give you an account of what I've done," Dundas said. "A few facts have emerged."

He spoke wearily, without enthusiasm. Dr. Hailey shook his head.

"I should prefer to ask you questions."

"Very well."

The doctor rose and pulled off his coat; before he sat down again he glanced out at the sea, white under the full moon. The exquisite clearness of the north had returned with the falling of night, and the long rampart of Cowal lay like the back of some monstrous creature rearing itself up out of the shining water. He listened to the soft babbling of the burn at his feet, in which chuckles and gurgles were mingled deliciously. The drought had tamed this fierce stream till only its laughter remained. He followed its course round the house to the loch, marking where its water became transformed to silver. The sails of fishing-boats stained the silver here and there and he saw that several of the boats were lying close in shore, at the mouth of the burn. The sound of the fishermen's voices came softly on the still air. He turned to his companions:

"They seem to have shot a net out here."

Dr. McDonald looked out and turned indifferently away. "Yes."

"I had no idea they fished so close inshore."

"Oh, yes. The shoals of herring tend to come into the shallow water at night to feed. Ardmore has lived on that fact for more than a century. Lived well too. In the best days they used to get £2 or £3 a box and might take 200 boxes at one shot of the net. But not now. The old Loch Fyne herring that the whole country knew and enjoyed seems to have ceased to exist. It was blue and flat; the modern variety is much paler and much rounder."

"So that Ardmore has fallen on bad days?"

"Yes. And with Ardmore, Duchlan and his family. It isn't easy to pay rent if you're making no money."

"Has the depression produced any reactions?"

"Reactions?"

"Hard times tend to separate honest from dishonest men."

A faint smile flickered on Dundas's lips.

"You're thinking of the possibility that one of those fishermen may have climbed in here?" he asked. "That idea was in my own mind. But I feel sure now that there's nothing in it. Nobody could climb these walls."

Dr. Hailey sat down. He polished his eyeglass and put it in his eye.

"I'm afraid I wasn't only thinking of that," he confessed. "Boats, especially fishing-boats, have always attracted me. It used to be one of my boyish ambitions to spend a night with the herring fleet." He leaned forward. "McDonald told me that you observed the scar on Miss Gregor's chest."

"Yes. I tried to work on that clue but I got nothing. Nobody here knows anything about it."

"Isn't that rather strange?"

"Very strange. But truth to tell, doctor, the people here are impossible. They know nothing about anything. When I said to Duchlan that nobody could hide an injury of that sort, he met me with a shrug of his shoulders. What are you to do? The scar is very old. It may date back twenty years."

"Yes. But it represents what was once a severe wound. Long ago, somebody tried to kill Miss Gregor. Since I formed that opinion I've been trying to get information about the lady. I've made a discovery."

"Yes?" The detective's voice rang out sharply.

"Everybody seems to believe that she was a saint and nobody seems to know much about her."

"My dear sir," Dr. McDonald interrupted, "I knew her well. The whole neighbourhood knew her well."

"As a figure, yes. Not as a woman."

"What does that mean?"

"Who were her intimate friends?"

The Ardmore doctor nursed his leg with both hands. He looked blank.

"Oh, the lairds and their families."

"John MacCallien confesses that he used to see her out driving occasionally. He was taught to hold her in great respect. He knows next to nothing about her."

"He's a bachelor."

"Yes. But he goes everywhere. One of his friends told me yesterday that Miss Gregor was looked on as a woman apart. She was full of good works, but she gave her confidence to nobody. She had no woman friend, no man friend. In such a place as this, gossip is passed on from father to son and mother to daughter. It's quite clear that this woman lived her life in seclusion."

Dr. McDonald frowned. "She never impressed me in that way," he declared stubbornly. "On the contrary, there was nothing she was not interested in. Her intrusions in local affairs, believe me, could be most troublesome. Doctors were her special concern and she supervised their work, my work mostly, with tireless zeal. She called it 'taking a kindly interest', but it was sheer interference."

He spoke hotly. Dr. Hailey nodded.

"That's not quite what I mean, you know," he said. "That's impersonal work. The relations between the landed class and their people in this country are so well-defined that there was no danger of familiarity. Miss Gregor helped her poorer neighbours, I imagine, as she cared for her pets. They were remote from her life. Your Lady Bountiful is always the same; she spoils her dependents and avoids her equals."

"There's something in that," McDonald agreed. "I often noticed that the more dependent the person was, the more fuss Miss Gregor made. She got a lot of flattery from her pensioners."

"Exactly."

"Her nephew's upbringing had been the chief business of her life. I can still hear her clear voice saying: 'Doctor McDonald, the knowledge that a young life had been committed to my care overwhelmed me. I felt that I must live and work and think and plan for no other object than Eoghan's welfare in the very highest sense of that word!'"

"Are you not confirming what I've suggested? Miss Gregor's real life was here, in this house, between these walls." Dr. Hailey allowed his eyeglass to drop. "I've been asking myself where her interest was centred before Eoghan was born," he added. "Clever, active-minded women always, believe me, find something or somebody to absorb their attention."

Nobody answered him; Dundas's interest was wholly extinguished. There was a knock at the door. Angus, the piper, entered with a tray on which glasses tinkled together. The gilded neck of a champagne bottle protruded from a small ice-pail, like a pheasant's neck from a coop.

"Duchlan will be honoured, gentlemen," Angus announced, "if you'll accept a little refreshment."

He stood in the doorway awaiting their decision. Dundas signed to him to put the tray down on the dressing-table.

"Shall I open the bottle?"

"Yes, do."

Angus performed this office with much dignity. He filled the glasses on the tray and presented them to the three men. Dr. Hailey took occasion to glance at his face but found it inscrutable. The piper knew how to keep his thoughts to himself. When he had left the room Dundas remarked that a similar courtesy had not been extended to himself.

"I'm getting to know Duchlan," he declared. "This is his way of telling me what he thinks of me. Champagne isn't for a common policeman."

He laughed and flushed as he spoke. It was clear that, under his uncompromising manner, he was exceedingly sensitive.

"This is the hottest night of the year, you know," Dr. Hailey suggested amiably.

"Oh, it's been hot enough every night since I came here."

Dundas emptied his glass at a gulp, an offence, seeing that the wine was good. He made a joke about a farmer at a public dinner to whom champagne had been served, but failed to amuse his companions. Dr. Hailey sipped the liquor, watching the tiny clusters of bubbles on its surface, elfish pearls cunningly set in gold. The wine was excellently chilled and yielded its virtue generously.

"What do you make of Duchlan?" the doctor asked after a prolonged interval of silence.

"He's a Highland laird. They're all alike."

"Yes?"

"Pride and poverty."

"I understood that Miss Gregor was a rich woman."

The policeman's face brightened.

"Ah," he exclaimed, "you know that, do you?"

"John MacCallien told me."

"It's true. An uncle, who made money in business, left her a big sum about ten years ago; why, I don't know. Duchlan got nothing."

Dr. Hailey nodded.

"Has Duchlan helped you?"

"No, he has not."

"What about Eoghan Gregor?"

Dundas shrugged his shoulders.

"Another of the same. But I didn't expect help there after I found that the fellow had just gambled his money away." He leaned forward suddenly. "Eoghan Gregor was ruined on the day of his aunt's death. And his aunt has left him all her money."

He remained tensely expectant, watching the effect of his disclosure. Dr. Hailey denied him satisfaction.

"After all, his aunt brought him up, you know."

"Exactly. He knew that she would leave him her money."

"Wouldn't she have lent him money, if he had asked her?"

"I don't think so. Not to pay gambling debts at any rate. Miss Gregor, by all accounts, was a woman with most violent prejudices against gambling in any form."

Dundas glanced at Dr. McDonald for confirmation.

"She looked on every kind of game of chance as the invention of the devil," the Ardmore doctor declared. "I've heard her myself call playing-cards 'the Devil's Tools'. I'm sure that if she had suspected that her nephew indulged in gambling she would have disinherited him as a matter of principle."

Dr. Hailey nodded.

"I see."

"It came to this," Dundas declared. "Of the three questions that must be answered in every case of murder—Who? Why? How?—I may have found answers to two, namely Who? and Why?" He raised his right hand in a gesture which recalled a bandmaster. "But the third has remained obstinately unanswerable. There isn't a shadow of doubt that the door was locked on the inside. As you know, a carpenter had to be fetched to cut out the lock. He told me that he examined the windows and saw for himself that they were bolted. Dr. McDonald here arrived before the carpenter had completed his work to confirm these statements. In other words that room, with its thick walls and heavy door, was completely sealed up. You couldn't have broken into it without using great violence. And there's not a sign of violence anywhere."

The policeman rubbed his brow uneasily.

"Has the idea occurred to you," McDonald asked, "that the murder may have been committed in some other room?"

"What? But how was the body got into the bedroom in that case? I assure you that you can't turn the key of the door from the outside. I'm an authority on skeleton keys of all sorts. No skeleton key that was ever invented could pick that lock. And the end of the key doesn't protrude from the lock. The locks of this house are all astonishingly ingenious. I'm told they were the invention of Duchlan's grandfather, who had a passion for lock-making."

"Like Louis XVI."

Dundas looked blank: "I didn't know that Louis XVI. was interested in locks," he said in tones which proclaimed his innocence of any knowledge about that monarch.

"He was. And his interest set a fashion. I've little doubt that the Duchlan of those days acquired his taste for mechanics during a visit to London or Paris. Some years ago I made a study of these eighteenth-century locks. Many of them are extraordinarily clever."

"These here are, at any rate." Dundas rose as he spoke and brought the lock which had been cut from Miss Gregor's door for the doctor's inspection. He pointed to the keyhole. "Observe how the key enters at a different level on each side of the door. That precludes the possibility of picking the lock with a skeleton, or of turning the key from the outside with pliers. You would think there were two locks, indeed, instead of only one, but they're connected."

Dr. Hailey focussed his eyeglass on the piece of mechanism and then handed it back.

"I agree with you," he said. "It is absolutely certain that the door was neither locked nor unlocked from the outside."

"That means, remember, that Miss Gregor locked the door."

"I suppose so."

The detective shook his head.

"How can you, or I, for that matter, suppose anything else? Seeing that the windows were bolted on the inside."

Again he rubbed his brow. "My brain seems to be going round in circles," he cried. "What I'm really saying is that Miss Gregor inflicted that dreadful wound on herself, seeing that nobody was present in the room with her and that nobody can have escaped out of her room. And she certainly didn't inflict the wound on herself."

"She did not."

Dundas's face had become very solemn. This mystery, which had brought all his efforts to nothing, exerted, it seemed, a profoundly depressing effect on his spirits. He shook his head mournfully as the difficulties against which he had been contending presented themselves anew to his mind.

"What I don't understand," Dr. Hailey said, "is why the windows were shut at all. It was an exceedingly hot night—as hot or hotter than it is now. Nobody in such conditions would sleep with closed windows." He turned to Dr. McDonald: "Do you happen to know if Miss Gregor was afraid of open windows? I mean absurdly afraid?"

"I don't think so. I rather imagine that in summer she usually slept with her windows open."

"In that case she certainly meant to leave them open on the night of her death."

Dundas nodded.

"I thought of that too," he said. "No doubt you're right; but you'll have to supply an answer to the question why, in fact, the windows were shut. Why did she shut these windows on the hottest night of the year? If you can answer that question it seems to me that you'll have gone a long way towards the truth."

"You know, I take it, that Mrs. Eoghan Gregor visited the room immediately after her aunt had gone to bed?" Dr. Hailey asked.

"Yes, I know that. She told me herself. She said that Miss Gregor locked the door in her face."

"Isn't it probable that Miss Gregor shut the windows at the same time?"

"Why should she?"

"Perhaps for the same reason that she locked the door."

"Can you name that reason?" Dundas raised his head sharply as he spoke.

"Mrs. Eoghan Gregor thinks that her aunt was afraid of her."

"What, afraid she would climb in by the window?"

"Panic never reasons, you know. It acts in advance of reason, according to instinct. Instinct's only concern is to erect a barrier against the cause of the panic. A man who was in Russia during the Leninist Terror told me that when he escaped and returned to London he woke up one night and barricaded the door of his bedroom with every bit of furniture in the room. That was in his own home, among his own people."

Dundas looked troubled.

"Do you think," he asked, "that Miss Gregor had been living in expectation of an attack on her life?"

"Yes, I do." Dr. Hailey took a pinch of snuff. "Panic," he stated, "consists of two separate elements, namely, an immediate fear and a remote dread. It's not always conscience which makes cowards of us; sometimes it's memory. Having dreaded some contingency for years, we lose our heads completely when it seems to be at hand."

"But how can this woman have dreaded assassination for years?"

"She had been wounded, remember, years before."

The detective shook his head.

"Time blots out such memories."

"You're quite wrong. Time exaggerates them. One of the leaders of the French Revolution, who had known and feared Robespierre, lived till ninety years of age. On his death-bed, sixty years after the Revolution, he lay imploring his great-granddaughter not to let Robespierre enter his bedroom."

A knock on the door interrupted them. In answer to Dundas's invitation to come in Eoghan Gregor entered the room.

Chapter XI

Family Magic

Eoghan was pale and looked anxious. He addressed himself to Dr. McDonald.

"Will you please come to Hamish," he asked. "He's had another slight fit, I think."

He stood in the doorway, apparently unaware of the others in the room. Dr. McDonald jumped up and hurried away.

"That's unfortunate," Dundas remarked, in the tones of a man who resents any deflection of interest from his own concerns. He added: "A fit's the same as a convulsion, isn't it?"

"Of the same nature."

"The child's evidently subject to them. McDonald told me it had one a few days before Miss Gregor's death. He doesn't seem to think they're very serious?"

"No, not as a rule."

"Lots of children get them, don't they?"

"Yes."

Dr. Hailey found himself listening and recognized that, strong as was his interest in detective work, his interest in the practice of medicine was much stronger. He wished that Eoghan Gregor had invited him to accompany McDonald and felt a sudden, sharp disinclination to continue the work which had brought him to the house. It was with a sense of lively annoyance that he heard Dundas ask further if fits were a sign of nervous weakness.

"I have an idea that both Duchlan and his son are very highly strung," the detective suggested in those hushed tones which laymen always adopt when speaking to doctors about serious disease. "I don't mind confessing that I've been working along these lines. Duchlan, as you've probably heard, is a good laird, though a bit queer. His sister, Miss Gregor, seems to have had notions—what they call hereabouts Highland second-sight. That's the first generation. Eoghan Gregor's the second generation and he's a gambler with the temperament of a gambler. Then there's the boy, the third generation."

He paused expectantly. The doctor was in the act of taking a pinch of snuff and completed that operation.

"Fits in children," he stated coldly, "are usually caused by indigestion."

"Is that so?" Dundas was abashed.

"Yes. Probably the child has been eating berries or green apples."

"McDonald said he was afraid of brain fever."

Dr. Hailey did not reply. Listening, he fancied he heard a child's crying, but could not be sure. He thought that, but for the fact that this mystery so greatly challenged his curiosity, he would have abandoned the attempt to solve it. The picture of Oonagh Gregor, bending anxiously over her child, a picture that came and remained stubbornly in his mind, did not invite to revelations which might possibly add new sorrows to her lot. For an instant the futility of criminal investigations assailed her mind. What did it matter who had killed Miss Gregor, seeing that Miss Gregor was dead and beyond help? Then he recognized the source of that idea in his feelings towards Dundas. The hound is always so much less lovable, so much less interesting, than its quarry.

"I don't think," he said, "that I can go further to-night. I like to sleep on my ideas."

He rose as he spoke; but the expression in Dundas's eyes made him hesitate. The detective, as he suddenly realized, was in great distress.

"The truth is, doctor, that if I can't reach some sort of conclusion within the next day or two, I'll be recalled," Dundas said. "And up till now I've been going ahead from case to case. I'll never get another chance if somebody else succeeds where I've failed. I'm only speaking for myself, of course, but from that point of view there isn't a moment to be lost. I know, because I had a letter to-day from headquarters."

He took a folded sheet of paper from his pocket as he spoke and unfolded it. He read:

> "It's obvious that somebody entered Miss Gregor's bedroom, seeing that she didn't kill herself. Your report suggests that you're losing sight of this central fact in order to run after less important matters. Success can only be won by concentration. Ask yourself how the bedroom was entered; when you've found an answer to that question you'll have little difficulty, probably, in answering the further question: Who entered it?"

"That is exactly the method I have always found to be useless in difficult cases," Dr. Hailey said with warmth.

"But you see what the letter means: they're growing restive. The papers are shouting for a solution and they've got nothing to offer."

Dr. Hailey sat down again and leaned forward.

"My method is always to proceed from the people to the crime rather than from the crime to the people. And the person I take most interest in, as a rule, certainly in the present case, is the murdered man or woman. When you know everything there is to be known about a person who has been murdered, you know the identity of the murderer."

Dundas shook his head: "I feel that I do know the identity of the murderer. But that knowledge hasn't helped me."

The doctor rubbed his brow as a tired man tries to banish the seductions of sleep.

"Did you notice," he asked, "that Miss Gregor's room was like an old curiosity shop?"

"It seemed to be pretty full of stuff. Those samplers on the wall…"

"Exactly. It was full of ornaments that most people would have preferred to get rid of. And every one of those ornaments bore some relation to Miss Gregor herself. Are you interested at all in folk lore?"

Dundas shook his head.

"I'm afraid not."

"I am. I've studied it for years. One of the oldest and strongest beliefs among primitive peoples is that the virtue of a man or woman—his or her vital essence so to speak—is communicated in a subtle way to material things. For example, the sword a soldier has carried comes to possess something of his personality. We all make some use of the idea, I admit; but most of us stop short in that use at the point where the material thing serves as a symbol of the spiritual. A modern mother keeps and treasures her dead son's sword; she does not suppose that the sword contains or holds part of her son's personality. But there are still people, probably there always will be people, who do not stop short at that point. Things they or their relations have made or used acquire sacredness in their eyes so that they can't endure the idea of parting with them. The material becomes transmuted by a process of magic into something other than it appears to be. Miss Gregor, clearly, attached such importance to her own handiwork and to the possessions of her ancestors, that she would not willingly allow any of them to be taken out of her sight. Unless I'm very much mistaken that was the dominant note of her character."

He paused. The detective looked mystified though he tried to follow the reasoning to its conclusion.

"Well?" he asked.

"Her character was rooted in the past. It embraced the past, was nourished with it, as with food. But it reached out, also, to the future; because the future is the heir of all things. Her brother Duchlan was of her way of thinking. But could she feel sure that the next generation would hold by the tradition? What was to become of the precious and sacred possessions after her death? That thought, believe me, haunts the minds of men and women who have abandoned themselves to family magic. Duchlan's son, Eoghan, is the next generation. What were Miss Gregor's relations to her nephew?"

"She acted as his mother."

"Yes. So that another question arises: what were her relations to his mother? Duchlan's wife, don't forget, was Irish. That is to say she stood outside of the Highland tradition. If she had lived, and brought her son up herself, would he have inherited the authentic doctrine of the family? In other words, what kind of woman was Duchlan's wife? How did she fare in this place? What relations existed between her and her sister-in-law? I shall certainly try to obtain answers to all these questions."

"You won't obtain them. The old man is determined not to speak about his family. I told you that he professes to know nothing about the scar on his sister's chest. And his servants are as uncommunicative as he is."

"My dear sir, a laird is a laird. There are always people who know what is going on in big houses."

Dundas shrugged his shoulders.

"I haven't found any in Ardmore and I've spared no pains to find them."

Dr. Hailey took a note-book from his pocket and unscrewed the cap of his fountain-pen. He wrote for a few minutes and then explained that he had found that, if he kept a record of his thoughts about a case as these occurred to him, knowledge of the case seemed to grow in his mind.

"The act of writing impresses my brain in some curious way. When I write, things assume a new and different proportion."

He laid his pen down beside the champagne glasses and leaned back.

"Detective work is like looking at a puzzle. The solution is there before one's eyes, only one can't see it. And one can't see it because some detail, more aggressive than the others, leads one's eyes away from the essential detail. I have often thought that a painter could make a picture in which one particular face or one particular object would be invisible to the spectator until he had attained a certain degree of concentration or detachment. This room of Miss Gregor's, for example, seems to us to be a closed box into which nobody can have entered and from which nobody can have emerged. The consequence of that idea is that we cannot conceive how the poor lady was murdered. Yet, believe me, the method of her murder is there, written plainly in the details we have both observed. When I write, I attain a new point of view that is not attainable when I speak. For example…"

He leaned forward again and extended his note-book. "I've written here that you found Duchlan and his household exceedingly reticent about past events. When you told me that I merely wondered why it should be so. Now I can see that, in all their minds, a connection must exist between the present and the past. It follows, doesn't it, that the scar on the dead woman's chest is the clue to a great family upheaval, the effects of which are still being acutely felt, so acutely, indeed, that even murder is accepted as a possible or even probable outcome."

"That's possible, certainly."

"I'm prepared to go farther and say that it must be so."

Dundas plucked at his shirt with uneasy hands.

"It's hard to believe," he objected, "that anybody has been waiting for twenty years to murder that poor old woman, or that a man like Duchlan has sat with his hands folded during that time in face of such a danger."

"That isn't what I mean. The beginning of murder, like the beginning of any other human enterprise, lies deep down in somebody's mind—not necessarily in the mind of the person who actually kills…"

"What?"

"We know very little of Miss Gregor's character, but there's no doubt that she was a self-centred woman with a highly developed faculty of domination. People, and especially women, of that type arouse strong opposition. That takes various forms. Weak natures tend to flatter and be subservient; stronger natures are exasperated; still stronger natures resist actively. But though these types of behaviour differ, they have the same first cause, namely, dislike. The subservient flatterer is an enemy at heart and understands perfectly the feelings of the violent opponent. In other words, everybody in this house hated Miss Gregor."

"My dear sir!"

"I know, you're thinking of Duchlan and Eoghan. I believe that both of them hated her."

"Why?"

"Because she was hateful."

Dundas shook his head.

"You'll get no support for that idea in Ardmore."

"Possibly not. The point I was trying to make is that murder has been on the cards for years, so to speak. You get the idea exactly in the popular phrase, 'It's a wonder nobody has murdered him!' which means: 'I feel inclined to murder him myself.' That inclination is the link between the old wound and the new, and the reason why nobody will talk. It's a subject that doesn't bear talking about."

The detective shrugged his shoulders. He raised his hand to his mouth and yawned. Speculations of this kind struck him, evidently, as sheer waste of time. He repeated that he had cross-examined every member of the household about past events.

"Angus and Christina were my chief hope," he complained, "but they seem to think it a deadly sin even to suggest that Duchlan's sister may have possessed an enemy. I simply couldn't get a word out of either of them."

"What do you make of them?"

Dundas shrugged his shoulders.

"I suppose," he said with a bitter smile, "that they belong to a superior order of beings who mustn't be judged by ordinary standards. I'm a Lowland Scot and we all think the same about these Highlanders. They struck me as dull, prejudiced people, without two ideas to rub together. Angus talks about Duchlan as if he was a god. As for Christina, her mind doesn't seem to have grown since its earliest infancy."

He passed his hand over his corn-coloured head. His eyes expressed irritation and perplexity, the immemorial trouble of the Saxon when faced by the Celt. Dr. Hailey thought that a less happy choice of a man to deal with this case could scarcely have been imagined.

"Did they deny all knowledge of the early wound?" he asked.

"Absolutely."

"That only means, probably, that they had no direct knowledge of it."

"Goodness knows what it means."

"I think it should be possible to persuade them to refresh their memories."

Dr. Hailey turned sharply as he spoke. Dr. McDonald had entered the room and was standing behind him. He rose to his feet.

"I'd like you to come and see this boy," McDonald said. "It's one of those puzzling cases that one finds it difficult to name." He hesitated and then added: "It may be only a passing indigestion. On the other hand it may be brain. I've acted so far on the assumption that it's brain."

Dr. Hailey promised Dundas that he would come back in the morning. He took his hat and followed McDonald to the door. He shut the door. When they reached the foot of the stairs leading to the nursery, he remembered that he had left his fountain-pen behind him and told his companion.

"I'll go back for it," McDonald said.

McDonald ran back along the lighted corridor. Next moment Dr. Hailey heard his own name called in accents which proclaimed distress and horror. He strode to Dundas's room.

The detective was lying huddled on the floor beside the bed. There was an ominous stain on his corn-coloured hair.

Chapter XII

The Second Murder

Dr. McDonald was on his knees beside the man, trying apparently to feel his pulse. He raised frightened eyes as his colleague came into the room.

"He's dead!"

"What?"

"He's dead!"

Dr. Hailey glanced round the room and, seeing nothing, looked again as though aware of a presence that defied human senses. Then he touched the stain on the yellow head. He started back.

"His skull's broken," he cried, "broken like an eggshell. Was the door of the room shut?"

"Yes."

"We met nobody in the corridor. There's no other door on the corridor. There's nowhere anybody could hide."

Dr. Hailey satisfied himself that Dundas was dead. Then he walked to the opened window. The night was very still. He listened, but could hear nothing except the gurgle of the burn below the window and the less sophisticated mirth of small waves on the shingle. The herring-boats were still lying at anchor near the shore. He looked down at the smooth wall which fell even farther here than under Miss Gregor's window, because of the sharp fall of the ground towards the burn. Nobody had come this way.

McDonald had risen and was standing gazing at the detective's body. His cheeks were white, his eyes rather staring. Every now and then he moistened his dry lips.

"There's no sign of a struggle," he said in a hoarse whisper.

Dr. Hailey nodded. The champagne glasses stood where they had been placed and, though the bottle had descended somewhat into its pail, it had not been disturbed.

"You heard no cry?"

"I heard nothing."

"How long do you suppose we were absent from the room?"

"Half a minute. Not more."

"These oil lamps throw long and deep shadows, you know. And we weren't looking for possible assassins…"

As he spoke Dr. Hailey stepped out into the corridor. He lit his electric lamp and directed the beam to right and left. The corridor ended at a window which looked out in the same direction as the windows of Dundas's bedroom, and there was a space of about a yard between this window and the bedroom door—a space evidently big enough to serve as a hiding-place. He extinguished his lamp. The rays of the paraffin lamp near the stairhead, feeble as they were, effectively illuminated the space under the window. He called Dr. McDonald.

"You would have seen anybody there," he said.

"Of course. Nobody could hide there."

"He must have hidden somewhere!"

The doctor's tones were peremptory, like the tones of a schoolmaster cross-examining a shifty pupil.

"Of course. We passed nobody."

"Nobody."

Their eyes met. Each read the growing horror in the other's eyes. They glanced to right and left.

"It's only a question of making a careful enough search," McDonald said. "We've overlooked something of course. Our nerves…"

He broke off. He gazed about him. His mouth opened but no words came to his lips. He walked to the window, looked out, and came back again to his companion.

"Shall I shut the door?" he asked.

"There's nobody here."

"There must be. If we leave the door open he may get away."

McDonald shut the door. He began to prowl round the room like a caged animal. His eyes, Dr. Hailey thought, held the expression which is characteristic of caged animals. He was waiting, expecting. But he was also without hope. He looked into the wardrobe and under the bed and again into the wardrobe. After that he locked the wardrobe door.

"I feel that we aren't alone," he declared in challenging tones.

He kept fidgeting with his necktie. Dr. Hailey shook his head.

"I'm afraid it's useless," he declared.

"Don't you feel that there's somebody beside us?"

"No."

McDonald pressed his hand to his brow.

"It must be my nerves. One doesn't see, though…It's such a long fall to the ground, and I heard nothing."

He continued to make rambling, disjointed comments. His face had lost its accustomed expression of cheerfulness;

it revealed the deep agitation which fear and horror were arousing in his mind. "I think," he cried suddenly, "that we ought to go down below and make sure that no ladder or rope was employed."

"Very well."

Dr. Hailey walked back to the dead man and examined his injury again. Then he accompanied his colleague. They found Duchlan and his son waiting for them at the head of the stairs.

"It's good of you to come, Dr. Hailey," Eoghan Gregor said. He noticed the pallor of Dr. McDonald's face and stiffened. "Is anything wrong?"

"Dundas has just been murdered."

Both father and son recoiled.

"What?"

"His skull has been broken…" McDonald faltered over this medical detail and then added: "Hailey and I are going down to…to investigate the ground under the window."

Duchlan seemed to wish to ask some further questions but desisted. He stood aside to allow the doctors to pass. He followed them downstairs and was followed in turn by Eoghan. Dr. Hailey asked them if they possessed an electric lamp and was told that they did not.

Eoghan led the way to the place immediately under Dundas's window. Dr. Hailey lit his torch and swept the bank with the strong beam. The beam showed him nothing. He turned it to light the front of the house and saw that there was a french-window immediately under Dundas's bedroom.

"What room is that?" he asked Duchlan.

"The writing-room."

"You heard nothing?"

"Nothing."

Duchlan put his hand on the doctor's arm.

"I thought I saw something gleam out there just now, to the left of the boats," he said.

"Really?"

The old man stood gazing seawards for a few minutes and then turned again.

"Moonlight is always deceptive," he declared, "and never more so than when it shines on water."

"Yes."

"It seems impossible that anybody can have reached that poor young man's bedroom. Eoghan and I must have seen anybody who tried to descend the staircase."

The doctor nodded. "Nobody left the room," he declared in positive tones.

"Nor entered it."

"No."

Duchlan drew a sharp breath.

"They say there are places in Loch Fyne," he declared inconsequently, "where the sea has no bed. Bottomless deeps about which our local lore is prolific of uneasy tales."

His voice fell to a whisper. "I've heard my father, the late Duchlan, speak of swimmers, half-man, half-fish, whose mission it was…"

He broke off. The awe in his tones sufficiently declared the nature of the fear which was compelling him. He gazed seaward again, expecting, apparently, a further glimpse of the shining object he had already seen.

"The Highland superstition is a byword in the Lowlands," he added after a few minutes. "They mock and jeer at us. But so might blind men mock at those possessed of sight. If our scientists were blind they would, believe me, furnish indisputable proof that sight is no more than an illusion of the simple."

"What was the object like which gleamed?" Dr. Hailey asked in impatient tones.

"Like a fish. A leaping salmon gleams in that way, in moonlight; but this was bigger than any salmon. And it did not leave the water."

"You saw it once only?"

The old man nodded.

"Yes, only once. I've been watching to see if I could catch another glimpse of it, but it has disappeared."

He spoke in tones which left no doubt that he believed that what he had witnessed was no mere reflection of the moon's light on the water. The doctor watched the play of emotion on his features, and realized that he had already reached his own conclusions about the murders. He turned to Eoghan and McDonald and asked them if they had observed anything.

"Nothing," Eoghan said.

"And you, doctor?"

"I've seen nothing at all."

McDonald's voice was unsteady. He stood gazing at the facade of the house as if he expected to gain enlightenment from it. Suddenly he turned and raised his hand to his eyes. He pointed to the herring-boats.

"If they're not all asleep they must have seen something," he declared.

Dr. Hailey was busy with his lamp. He turned the beam on the wall.

There was no sign of any attempt to climb the wall. He walked for some distance to right and left and repeated his examination. The grass was innocent of any mark such as must have been imprinted on it had a ladder been used to reach the window. He turned to Duchlan who was standing beside him.

"The Procurator Fiscal told me that he examined the ground under your sister's window?" he said.

"He did, yes. I was with him. We had the advantage of bright sunlight on that occasion and also of the fact that there's a flower bed under the window. We found absolutely nothing. Neither footprint nor ladder-print."

"There seems to be nothing here either."

"Nothing."

They stood facing each other in silence. The murmur of voices came softly to them from the herring-boats. Dr. Hailey turned and descended the bank to the shore. He hailed the nearest of the boats and was answered in the soft accents of the Highlands.

"Did you see anybody at that lighted window up there?"

"I did not. We've been sleeping. It was your voices that wakened us."

"Did you hear anything?"

"No, sir."

Dr. Hailey felt exasperated at the man's calmness and told him what had happened. The news was received with a stream of exclamations.

"I thought your look-out man might have seen something at the window."

"We have no look-out man when we anchor in-shore. But we're light sleepers, all of us. As I told you, it was your voices wakened us. There was no cry from the bedroom. Not a sound at all whatever."

They returned to the house and entered Duchlan's study. Dr. Hailey told Eoghan Gregor that he wished to see his little boy before they dealt further with the case of Dundas, and he and McDonald left father and son together and climbed the stairs to the top floor of the house. Oonagh met them at the top of the stairs.

"He's had another attack," she cried in anxious tones.

She paused an instant before the word "attack". Dr. Hailey realized that she had meant to say "fit". That short word carried too great a burden of fear. She led the way into a big room, the walls of which were covered with texts from the Bible. The little boy was lying down; as he approached the bed an old woman in cap and apron, who had been bending over the child, stood up and moved aside to let him pass. Her broad, deeply-wrinkled face was streaked with tears. Dr. Hailey lifted the ice-bag from the child's brow and looked into the wide-open eyes. He lit his lamp and flashed it, suddenly, on the small face. When the patient winced, he nodded reassuringly.

"What about the signs?" he asked McDonald.

"They're all negative."

"Kernig's?"

"Yes."

Dr. Hailey patted the hand which lay, closed, on the coverlet beside him. He asked the child to tell him his name and got a clear answer: "Hamish Gregor of Duchlan". Even the babes in Duchlan Castle were taught, it seemed, to set store on their territorial right.

"Who taught you your name?" he asked.

"Aunt Mary."

He bent and drew his nail lightly across the child's fore-arm, a proceeding watched with careful eyes by the nurse. After a short interval a red wheal appeared on the skin where he had stroked it. The wheal became, rapidly, more marked and acquired a pallor in the middle, which suggested that the arm had been lashed with a whipcord. Both Oonagh and the nurse exclaimed in dismay.

"What does it mean?" Oonagh asked.

"Nothing."

"What?"

"It's a sign of a certain type of nervous temperament, that's all. The attacks belong to the same order. They'll soon pass off though they may return." Dr. Hailey exchanged a smile with his patient, who was now viewing the wheal with astonishment. He added: "There's absolutely nothing to fear, now or later."

Oonagh thanked him with a sincerity that admitted of no question. She seemed to have changed since the night on which he had rescued her but he did not fail to observe that she was strung up to a high pitch. He wondered if it was from her that the child had inherited its weakness, but decided that, in all probability, Dundas's view was the correct one. This girl was physically healthy even if her mind was being severely tried. She listened with an admirable self-control to his direction about the treatment of her boy and emphasized these directions for the guidance of the old nurse.

"You've noticed, I suppose," Dr. Hailey said to the nurse, "that the child bruises easily, and sometimes more easily than at other times."

"Yes, doctor, I have." The old woman's grave, attractive face darkened. "I call him 'Hamish hurt himself' whiles because he always seems to be covered with bruises. There's bruises that come of themselves, too, without his hurting himself. I didna know that it was his nerves."

Her voice was soft and urgent like a deep stream in spate. Its tones suggested that she was only half convinced. Duchlan's descriptions of his servants as friends was evidently fully justified.

"He'll grow out of it."

The nurse hesitated a moment. Then the blood darkened in her withered cheeks.

"I should tell you, doctor," she said, "that Hamish has been losing ground lately. He seems that lifeless and depressed. I think whiles it's as if he was frightened of something or somebody. Children are mair sensitive like than old folk."

She broke off and glanced at Oonagh as if she feared that she had exceeded her right. But the girl nodded.

"I've noticed that too," she said. "He seems what we call in Ireland 'droopy'."

"Children," Christina repeated, "are mair sensitive than auld folks. They seem to ken when there's anything against them. They're fashed and frightened, like. It doesna do to say that there's nothing in that. What means have we of knowing all that passes through a child's mind?"

She spoke gently without a trace of disrespect. It was obvious that anxiety alone dictated her thoughts.

"I'm afraid," Dr. Hailey agreed, "that we have very small means."

"Aye, verra small means. You, that has the skill, kens that them turns is comin' from the nerves, but what is it that's workin' on the nerves? That's what I would like to ken."

The doctor shook his head.

"That's very difficult to say," he confessed. "Rheumatism sometimes causes this kind of nervous irritability. But undoubtedly other causes exist. I saw a case once that was certainly due to a severe fright and I saw another case which I was able to trace to nervous exhaustion brought on by anxiety. That poor child was terrified of its father, who was a drunkard."

A quick flush spread over the old nurse's cheeks.

"Highland folks," she said, "believes that there's more causes of trouble than any skill can find."

She spoke cryptically but with great earnestness. Dr. Hailey saw a faint smile pass across McDonald's lips. Was this a veiled reference to the relations existing between Eoghan and his wife? Oonagh's eyes suggested that she thought so.

"Do you believe," he asked Christina, "that the feelings of older people are known and understood by children?"

"Aye, that I do, doctor. What's more, I believe that you can poison a mind the same as you can poison a body."

When they left the nursery, McDonald put his hand on his companion's arm.

"You see what Highland people are," he declared. "We haven't changed."

"It isn't only Highland people, you know, who are superstitious about nervous ailments," Dr. Hailey said. "Mankind as a whole is afraid of them. People who bruised easily were looked upon with veneration in the Middle Ages. There are thousands of records of men and women who could, at will, produce the stigmata of the Cross on their hands and feet and brows. It was supposed that these people were in intimate touch with divine beings. Others bore blemishes that were popularly ascribed to the touch of the Devil or the influence of the Evil Eye. It seems, for example, to be true that the real reason why Henry VIII got rid of Anne Boleyn so quickly was that he observed such blemishes on her skin as were reputed to be borne only by witches. He was more superstitious than any of your Highlanders."

They returned to the smoking-room to Duchlan and his son. As they did so, Angus the piper came to the door. He announced that a young fisherman wished to speak to the laird.

"Show him in, Angus."

A tall fellow in a blue jersey appeared. He carried a tam-o'-shanter in his hand. When he had half-crossed the room he stood and began to fidget with his cap in the fashion of a woman unpicking a seam. Duchlan greeted him cordially.

"Well, Dugald, what has brought you here to-night?" he asked, and then before the lad could reply introduced him as the brother of "my two good friends and helpers, Mary and Flora Campbell".

Dugald recovered his self-possession slowly. He stated that he had been told by his friends that the laird was anxious to meet a fisherman who had not been asleep during the last hour and who had therefore been in a position to see what was happening at the castle.

"I wass in the farthest out of the boats," he added, "and I wass not sleeping. I could see the house all the time."

Angus brought a chair and the young fellow sat down. Dr. Hailey asked him:

"Were you looking at the house?"

"Yess, I wass."

"What did you see?"

"There wass a window with a light in it. A big man came to the window and then, after a long time, a little man."

"You didn't see their faces?"

"No, sir. Because the light wass behind them. The moon wass shining on the windows but it wass not so bright as the light in the room."

The doctor nodded his agreement with these just considerations.

"Quite. Now do you remember which of the two men whom you saw remained longest at the window, the big man or the little man?"

"The big man, sir."

Dr. Hailey turned to his companions.

"I looked out of the window after I reached the room. I was feeling very hot and remained at the window a little time. So far, therefore, we seem to be on solid ground." He addressed the fisherman: "Can you describe what you saw of the little man?"

"I saw him at the window. He went away again in a moment."

The doctor leaned forward.

"You noticed nothing peculiar about his coming or going?"

"No, sir."

"Think very carefully, please."

"No, sir, I noticed nothing at all. He came and he went, like the big man before him."

"There was no cry?"

"I did not hear any cry."

"Was that the only window on the floor that was lighted?"

"Yes, sir."

"You're quite sure?"

"Yes, sir."

"What do you say, Duchlan?"

The old man inclined his head.

"He's quite right. I was here with Eoghan. The nursery window doesn't overlook the sea."

Dr. Hailey put his eyeglass in his eye.

"You said the moon was shining on the house? Did you see anything unusual on the wall or the roof?"

"No, sir, nothing at all."

"Do you think that, if somebody had climbed up to the window by means of a ladder, you would have seen him?"

"Oh, yes, I would."

"In spite of the lighted window?"

"Yes. If a cat had climbed up to the window I would have seen her. There wass no ladder."

"You can swear to that?"

"I can swear to it."

"Tell me, Dugald," Duchlan asked, "did you see anything float by your boat about the time when the wee man was at the window?"

A look of fear crept into the lad's eyes. He raised his eyebrows and then contracted them sharply.

"No, laird."

"Something that shone."

"No, laird."

Dugald plucked more vigorously at his tam-o'-shanter. The fear in his eyes had deepened. It was evident that he was well aware of the tales about the fish-like swimmers. He looked inquiringly at Duchlan.

"I thought," the old man said, "that I saw something gleam near one of the boats. But you can't be sure in the moonlight."

Dugald's uneasiness was increasing.

"I saw nothing, laird, nothing at all, whatever. But Sandy Dreich he said that to-night would be a bad night for us because we passed four women when we wass going down to the boats. And, sure enough, there's been no fishin'. Sandy, he saw a shoal a wee bit out from the burn and we shot the net. But there wass nothing in the net."

This information was given with extreme seriousness. It was so received by Duchlan. Laird and fisherman appeared to be in agreement about the probable cause of the poor fishing.

"Is it unlucky," Dr. Hailey asked, "to meet women when you're going to your boats?"

"Yess, sir; there's many as turns back when that happens."

The doctor turned to Duchlan:

"The fishermen of Holy Island, on the Northumbrian coast, won't go out if anybody speaks the word 'pig' in their hearing. They never speak that word themselves. All the pigs on Holy Island are creatures—'craturs' as they call them."

The old man inclined his head gravely. He offered no comment, and it was clear that he thought the subject undesirable in present circumstances.

Angus was told to give the fisherman a drink. When he had gone Duchlan roused himself from the lethargy into which he seemed to have fallen.

"You yourself can testify, Dr. Hailey," he asked, "that nobody entered the room after you had left it?"

"I can."

"So that both door and windows were as effectually sealed as if they had been locked and bolted?"

"It seems so."

"As effectually as were the windows and door of my poor sister's room?"

"Yes."

The old man straightened in his chair.

"Can you suggest any explanation of those two tragedies?" he demanded.

"None."

"They're exactly alike?"

"Yes."

"In conception and execution, exactly alike?"

"Yes."

"The same hand must have struck both blows?"

"It seems so."

Silence fell in the room; they glanced at one another uneasily.

"On the face of it, it's impossible that murder can have been committed in either case," Duchlan said at last.

His voice faded away. He began to move uneasily in his chair. The habit into which he had fallen, of ascribing so many of the events of his life to supernatural agencies, was doubtless the cause of the fear which was expressed vividly on his features.

"It will be necessary," Dr. Hailey said, "to recall Mr. McLeod. I may be wrong but I feel we have no time to lose. What has happened twice may happen a third time."

That thought had, apparently, been present to the minds of his companions. Dr. McDonald glanced uncomfortably about him while Duchlan wiped his brow. There was alacrity too in Eoghan's manner of promising to go at once to the police office in Ardmore.

Chapter XIII

"A Curse on this House"

Dr. Hailey spent the next morning examining the ground under Dundas's window. The hot weather had hardened the turf so that it was idle to expect that it would reveal much; it revealed nothing. The hardest lawn must have taken some imprint from a ladder that bore a man's weight. He stood looking at the blank slope with eyes that betrayed no feeling; then his gaze moved over the grass, down to the burn; and beyond the burn, to the loch. He shook his head and returned to the castle, where he found Mr. McLeod, newly arrived from Campbeltown, awaiting him. The Procurator Fiscal seemed to be deeply moved by the new tragedy.

"What is this manner of death, doctor," he asked, "which can pass through locked doors?" His tones accused; he added, "Duchlan tells me that you and McDonald hadn't left the poor man more than a minute before he was killed. Is that so?"

"I don't think that a minute elapsed between our leaving him and his death."

Mr. McLeod's big face grew pale. "You're saying that Dundas was struck down, not that he was murdered," he exclaimed in tones of awe.

They had entered the study. The Procurator Fiscal sat down and bent his head. When he had remained in that posture of humility for a few minutes he stated that he had sent to Glasgow for help.

"They'll send their best, depend on it."

"I hope so."

"Poor Dundas!" he moralized in unsteady tones. "This case was to have made his name. How little we know, Dr. Hailey, of the secret designs of Providence." He paused and then added: "I have heard it said that there is a curse on this house."

A kind of paralysis seemed to have affected him, for he sank lower in his chair. He kept nodding his head and mumbling as if he was repeating chastening truths to himself and registering his acceptance of them. Dr. Hailey got the impression that he was greatly afraid lest his own life might be taken at any moment.

"I spoke to Duchlan as I came in," Mr. McLeod said. "He tells me he thought he saw some bright object on the water a few minutes after Dundas met his death."

"Yes."

"He told you that, too, did he?"

"Yes."

Dr. Hailey's tones were not encouraging.

"It's very strange if it's true." Again the worthy man wiped his face. "There's queer stories about Loch Fyne as you may know. The fishermen tell very queer stories sometimes."

"So I believe."

Mr. McLeod roused himself.

"Aye," he exclaimed with warmth, "it's easy to say you don't believe in old wives' tales. But these men are shrewd observers with highly developed and trained senses. Who knows but what they may be able to see and hear and feel more than you or I could see or hear or feel? All the time they are watching the face of the water, which is the mirror of the heavens."

The doctor assented. Mr. McLeod, he observed, was divided, in his fear, between his natural credulousness and his acquired ideas. These ideas were based on gloomy reflections about the trivial character and brief duration of human life derived from the minor Hebrew prophets. No wonder the man found whisky essential to his well-being!

He left him and went up to Dundas's bedroom. The body had not been moved. A shaft of sunlight touched the yellow hair. It was easy to discount the panic of McLeod and the others, but not so easy to escape from the influences which had wrought that panic. He picked up one of the notebooks which the detective had filled with details of his investigation. It made melancholy reading. The pages were crowded with negative observations; everything had been eliminated, door, windows, walls, ceiling, floor. The last note was not without pathos: "It will be necessary to begin again."

He put the book back in its place and polished his eyeglass. He held the glass above the dead man's head where the skull was fractured and marvelled again at the strange, savage violence of the blow. The bedroom, assuredly, did not contain any weapon capable of inflicting this grievous injury. He had already examined such pieces of the movable furniture as might have been made use of. The murderer had carried his own weapon, or rather two weapons; an axe, perhaps, in the case of Miss Gregor, a bludgeon or a knuckle-duster in this case. The first weapon, had it been employed in the second case, must have split Dundas's skull from vault to base. Again he turned to the window and again surveyed the bank between the house and the burn. Autumn was dressing herself in her scarlets and saffrons; already the air held that magical quality of light which belongs only to diminishing days and which seems to be of the same texture as the colours it illuminates. He marked the fans of the chestnuts across the burn, pale gold and pale green. The small coin of birch leaves a-jingle in the wind, light as the sequins on a girl's dress, the beeches and oaks, wine-stained from the winds' Bacchanal, the rowans, flushed with their fruiting. A man might easily from this place throw a tell-tale weapon into that fervent tangle or into the burn even. But no, he had searched diligently and knew that no weapon lay hidden in any of these places. He turned back to the room. He bent forward and then strode quickly to the dead man's side.

The light had revealed a gleam of silver among the golden hair. He recognized another herring scale.

Chapter XIV

A Queer Omission

The discovery of the herring scale on Dundas's head sent Dr. Hailey down to Ardmore to McDonald. The doctor's house stood on a spur of rock overlooking the harbour. As he ascended the path, which mounted in zigzags to the house, he had a view of the whole extent of this singular natural basin with its islands and bays. The bulk of the fishing-fleet lay at anchor, far up, opposite the town, but skiffs, in pairs, were dotted over the whole expanse of water. He marked the clean, dainty lines of these vessels in excellent accord with their short, raked masts. They looked like young gulls in their first grey plumage, lively, eager. A small coaster was fussing in from the loch. He lingered to watch it enter the narrow mouth of the harbour. As it passed, the fringes of seaweed round the islands were lifted and small waves broke on the shores. The smell of boats and seaweed and fish rose to his nostrils. Soft voices reached him across the still, hot air. He ascended higher and turned again. From this point the drying poles, on which a few herring-nets hung like corpses on a gallows, had a macabre appearance, as of some great ship in irretrievable wreck. But the colour of the nets made very comfortable contrast with the pine-wood on Garvel point, across the bay.

The house was built of red sandstone and had a red roof which stood up sharply against the hill behind it. The windows looked out on the harbour, but their longest view was limited everywhere by rocks and heather, a patchwork of purple and green and grey, very bare and desolate, even in sunlight. He rang the bell and was invited to enter by a young woman whose high colour and dark, shining hair were in the tradition of Highland beauty. She showed him into a big room and only then announced that her master had not yet returned from his morning round.

"But I'm expecting him back at any moment now, so perhaps you'll be able to wait."

She went away immediately, without hearing his answer. He walked to the bookshelf which filled one side of the room and glanced at its contents. McDonald, it seemed, was a reader of catholic taste, for here were most of the classics of European literature, especially of French literature: Balzac, Flaubert, de Maupassant, Montaigne, Voltaire, Saint Beuve. He pulled out one or two of the volumes. They looked distinctly the worse of wear. There were no medical books on any of the shelves. The owner of the library, clearly, was a romantic, though he had tempered his enthusiasm with other fare. Dr. Hailey found it difficult to reconcile his knowledge of the man with the man's books. The room was comfortable as men understand that word; it was supplied with big chairs and the apparatus of reading and smoking. A shot-gun, of rather old-fashioned type, whose barrels were shining with oil, stood in one corner. A vase on the mantelpiece was piled high with cartridges. The walls bore pictures of boats, all of them, evidently, the work of the same artist, all equally undistinguished. Dr. Hailey examined one of them. It was signed by McDonald himself.

He sat down and took a pinch of snuff. The medical profession, he reflected, is full of men who wish, all their lives, that they had never entered it. Yet very few of these doctors succeed in making their escape because, though they possess the temperaments of artists, they lack the necessary power of expression or perhaps the necessary craftsmanship. A practice makes too many demands on time and strength to be bedfellow with any enthusiasm. Since McDonald painted pictures, the odds were that he wrote novels or poetry. It was unlikely that his accomplishment in writing was better than his accomplishment in painting. Why had he not married?

A second pinch of snuff went to the answering of this last question, but before it had been answered McDonald himself strode into the room.

"Annie told me that a very tall man was waiting for me," he exclaimed. "I thought it must be you." He shook hands. "Well, anything new?"

"Not much— There was a herring scale on Dundas's head."

"Good heavens! So the same weapon was used in both cases?"

Dr. Hailey shook his head.

"I don't think that's probable," he said, "though of course the head of an axe might cause such an injury."

McDonald's tone became undecided. He stood in the middle of the floor frowning heavily and tugging at his chin. At last he shook his head.

"These fish scales are mysterious enough," he declared, "but the real mystery, it seems to me, isn't going to be solved by them or by any question of weapons. Until you can explain how these two bedrooms were entered and how escape from them took place you are necessarily working in the dark."

Dr. Hailey considered for a moment.

"It's obvious," he said, "that Duchlan has made up his mind that the murders are due to supernatural agency."

"He was certain to do that in any case."

"Quite. And consequently the temptation, from the murderer's point of view, to supply evidence of such supernatural agency must have been strong. That evidence would tend to paralyse his pursuers."

"I don't follow. What evidence of supernatural agency has he supplied?"

"The fish scales."

McDonald stared.

"What, herring scales on Loch Fyne side! How can they be evidence of supernatural agency?"

"Duchlan thought he saw something which gleamed in the moonlight floating away from the mouth of the burn after Dundas was killed."

The Ardmore doctor whistled.

"So that's it, is it?"

"That?"

"The swimmers. Every time anything which can't be explained happens on Loch Fyne side, it's the 'swimmers' who are to blame. They disturb the shoals of herring and so produce bad catches or they call the fish out of the nets at the moment when the catch seems to be secure. You can point out that such losses are due to carelessness till you're black in the face. Nobody believes you. What can mere men do against such beings?"

Dr. Hailey nodded.

"Ardmore lives by the chances of the sea," he said.

"Most superstitions, as you know, are embodiments of bad luck. In agricultural districts the demons blight the crops and dry up the wells…"

"Exactly."

"The point for us is that these fish scales may have been introduced deliberately into the wounds with the object of suggesting that no human hand was concerned in these murders. If so, we may be able to find our man by a process of elimination. The use of superstition as a cloak for crime is evidence of a fairly high order of intelligence."

"I see what you mean. The servants, for example, would not think of doing that."

Dr. Hailey nodded. He leaned back in his chair. "How long have you attended the Duchlan family?" he asked.

"More than ten years."

"And yet you were unaware that Miss Gregor had been wounded?"

"I was. I've never examined Miss Gregor's chest." McDonald strode to the window and back again. "She often suffered from colds and two years ago had a severe attack of bronchitis, but she would never allow me to listen to her breathing. Duchlan told me, before I saw her the first time, that she had a great horror, amounting to an obsession, of medical examinations and that I must do my best to treat her without causing her distress."

"So he knew about the scar? Dundas said that he denied all knowledge of it."

"It's possible, isn't it, that she had made the same excuses to her brother that she made to her doctors. Duchlan may have believed that she really was averse from any examination."

Dr. Hailey nodded.

"That's true. But you'll admit that it's strange she should have sustained a wound of such severity without allowing anybody in the house to find out that she had sustained it." He wrinkled his brows. "I still think that, when she locked her door, she was the victim of panic. Is there a portrait of Duchlan's wife at the castle?"

"I've never seen one."

"I looked for one in all the public rooms and in some of the bedrooms. I didn't find it. For a man who clings to his possessions so tenaciously, that's a queer omission. Every other event of Duchlan's life is celebrated in some fashion on his walls."

McDonald sat down and drew his wooden leg forward with both hands.

"What are you driving at?" he asked.

"I'm beginning to think that Duchlan's wife was concerned in the wounding of Miss Gregor. That would explain the absence of her portrait and the wish to hide the scar. It might explain Miss Gregor's panic at sight of Eoghan's wife. Both father and son, remember, married Irish girls. Mrs. Eoghan's sudden appearance in her bedroom may conceivably have recalled to the old woman's mind a terrible crisis of her life."

"Miss Gregor, believe me, was a level-headed woman."

"No doubt. But shocks of that sort, as you know, leave indelible scars on the mind, so that every reminder of them induces a condition of nervous prostration."

"Very well," McDonald moved his leg again and leaned forward: "What happened after she locked her bedroom door?"

"I think she shut and bolted her windows. It's only reasonable to suppose that the windows were open on account of the heat."

"And then?"

"Then she was murdered."

The country doctor sighed. He repeated: "Then she was murdered," adding in weary tones: "How? Why? By whom?"

He raised his kindly grey eyes to look his colleague in the face. Dr. Hailey dismissed his questions with a short, impatient gesture.

"Never mind that. Come back to Mrs. Eoghan. She told me that she went to her aunt's room in a blue silk dressing-gown, because, having quarrelled with her aunt before dinner, she now wished to make up her quarrel. A similar order of events may have occurred in the case of Duchlan's wife."

McDonald's face had become troubled.

"You don't suggest, do you," he demanded in tones of impatience, "that that fearful wound was inflicted by a girl?"

"No." Dr. Hailey shook his head. "You go too fast, my friend. Leave the room out of the picture for a moment, entirely out of the picture. Here's a more interesting question: was the quarrel between Mrs. Eoghan and Miss Gregor of the same nature as the quarrel between Duchlan's wife and Miss Gregor? The answer depends, obviously on Miss Gregor. There are women, plenty of women, who cannot live at peace with the wives of their men-folk, women who resent these wives as interlopers, women whose chief object it becomes to estrange their husbands from them, sometimes even to alienate their children. Was Miss Gregor one of these women?"

A prolonged silence followed this challenge. McDonald's uneasiness appeared to grow from moment to moment. He kept shifting in his chair and moving his wooden leg about in accord with the movements of his body. A deep flush had spread over his face.

"She was one of those women," he said at last.

Chapter XV

The Real Enemy

McDonald rose and stood in front of the empty fireplace.

"As a matter of fact," he said, "I have reason to know that Mrs. Eoghan's life at Duchlan was made impossible by Miss Gregor's jealousy. Almost from the moment when Eoghan went away to Malta, his aunt began to torment and persecute his wife. The burden of her complaint was that little Hamish, the heir of Duchlan, was not being properly brought up."

The doctor paused and turned to find his pipe on the mantelpiece behind him. He put the pipe in his mouth and opened a jar of tobacco.

"My information comes from Mrs. Eoghan herself," he stated. "I suppose I can count myself one of the only two friends she possessed in this neighbourhood."

He extracted a handful of tobacco from the jar and began to fill his pipe, proceeding with this task in a manner the deliberation of which was belied by his embarrassment. Dr. Hailey saw that his hands were shaking.

"The whole atmosphere at Duchlan, believe me, was charged with reproof and every day brought its heavy burden of correction. Miss Gregor inflicted her wounds in soft tones that soon grew unendurable. She never ordered; she pleaded. But her pleas were so many back-handers. She possessed the most amazing ingenuity in discovering the weak points of her antagonist and a sleepless persistence in turning them to her advantage. Things came to a head a month ago."

His pipe was full. He lit it carefully.

"A month ago, little Hamish had a fit. I was sent for. I haven't had as much experience of nervous ailments as you have had and I confess that I was frightened. I suppose my fear communicated itself to the child's mother. At any rate she told me that she felt sure the trouble had its origin in the state of her own nerves and that she had made up her mind to leave Duchlan. 'Eoghan's work in Ayrshire is nearly finished,' she said, 'and I've told him that, if he won't make a home for me after that, I'll leave him.' I could see that she was at the end of her resources. I tried to calm her; but she was past being talked round. When I came downstairs from the nursery Miss Gregor was waiting for me. 'It's his mother, poor child,' she lamented. 'My dear Oonagh means well, of course, but she's had no experience. No experience.'"

He dropped his pipe and stooped to pick it up.

"I can hear her voice still," he declared. "She shook her head slowly as she spoke and tears came into her eyes. 'We've done everything that love can do, doctor,' she told me. 'But I'm afraid it's too true that our efforts have been resented. Eoghan's father is deeply distressed. I cannot tell you what I feel. As you know I've looked on Eoghan and loved him as my own child.' Then the suggestion for which I was waiting was offered: 'Couldn't you use your authority to insist that dear Oonagh must have a complete rest. She has sisters and brothers who will be so glad to see her, and she needn't feel a moment's anxiety about dear Hamish. Christina and I will devote ourselves to him.' What could I say? I told her that such plans must wait till the child was better."

He paused. Dr. Hailey, who was watching him closely, asked:

"How did she receive that opinion?"

"Badly, that's to say, with an exquisite resignation. 'Of course, doctor,' was what she said, 'we must all bow to your discretion in a matter of this kind. You alone are possessed of the knowledge necessary to a decision. But I do feel that I have a duty to place before you those personal considerations which no doctor can be expected to learn for himself.' In other words: 'If you're on the side of the enemy, I shall make it exceedingly unpleasant for you.' I saw the promise of that in her eyes. And she knew that I saw it."

"You stood your ground, though?"

There was eagerness in the doctor's tones.

"Yes. That old woman roused my fighting instinct. There was a whine in her voice that made my hair bristle. She used to pronounce the word 'dear', 'dee-ah', and she always pronounced Mrs. Eoghan's name 'Una' although she had been corrected hundreds of times. Behind her stubborn nature there was a kind of impishness, a wicked quality, which took joy in hurting the people she didn't like. You looked at the saint or the martyr and you knew that a little devil was watching you out of her swimming eyes."

McDonald's face was red. He shook his head.

"If there had been another doctor here, he would have been sent for. But there isn't. She had to put up with me. Each time we met I felt that her dislike was growing. And she couldn't dislike without disapproving. People who got into her black books were soon described by her as 'not the right thing', a phrase which she knew how to use so that it conveyed an impression of moral obliquity. I was certain I should not have long to wait for some proof of her wish to punish me…"

Dr. Hailey held up his hand.

"A moment, please. Did you continue to visit Hamish?"

"Yes."

"And to refuse to allow Miss Gregor to interfere?"

"I refused to agree that Mrs. Eoghan should leave the child and go to Ireland. One day I said that I thought a child's mother was always the best nurse who could be obtained for him. Miss Gregor winced when I said that, and just for one instant I was sorry for her."

"I see."

McDonald's nervousness increased. He tried to relight his pipe and then abandoned the attempt.

"A week later, three weeks ago," he said, "I heard a knock at this door one night just when I was going to bed. I opened the door. Mrs. Eoghan was standing behind it."

A deep silence fell in the room. It was broken by the pleasant sound of blocks and tackle, the hoisting of sails. Dr. Hailey nodded without offering any comment.

"The girl was in a terrible state, weeping, hysterical, half-crazy. She fell into the hall when I opened the door. I picked her up. Her clothes seemed to have been flung on anyhow. I carried her in here and put her in that chair," with a sudden, jerky gesture he indicated the chair in which Dr. Hailey was seated. "She told me she had left Duchlan for ever. Later on, when she had recovered a little, she told me that she had had a violent quarrel with Miss Gregor. She said Hamish had had another turn. 'Aunt Mary accused me of ill-using him…killing him. I lost all control of myself.'"

"Did it surprise you," Dr. Hailey asked, "that she should have lost control of herself?"

"No, no. What surprised me was that she had endured Miss Gregor so long."

"I didn't mean that. Do you think her a hysterical type?"

McDonald hesitated.

"Not hysterical; highly-strung. She has an extremely quick intelligence and a great honesty of mind. Miss Gregor's hypocrisy exasperated her to delirium. She didn't care what happened. She told me that she didn't care what happened." He covered his eyes with his hand. "I lit the fire here because the night had grown chilly. I boiled the kettle and made tea. After a while she grew calmer and described what had happened. They had all gone to bed. The nurse had called her because Hamish seemed to be breathing badly. She had hurried upstairs to find Miss Gregor giving the child a dose of sal volatile. You can imagine the rest. I had said that stimulants were not to be given."

"Miss Gregor had suggested a dose of sal volatile?"

"Yes. That morning. Mrs. Eoghan ordered her out of the nursery. She obeyed but roused her brother and brought him upstairs to fight her battle for her. Duchlan was clay in her hands; like most cowards he has a cruel streak in his nature."

McDonald broke off. His uneasiness was increasing. He put his pipe down and stood staring in front of him at the pictures on the wall opposite. "Naturally Mrs. Eoghan quoted my order. She demanded that I should be sent for. Duchlan said: 'It seems to me, and your aunt agrees with me, that Dr. McDonald has been sent for quite often enough lately.' There was no mistaking what he insinuated. She wouldn't defend herself. She left them and came here."

"I see." Dr. Hailey moved in his chair. He looked up and saw that his companion was still gazing at the pictures. The muscles of McDonald's neck stood out rigidly; his arms were stiff.

"Miss Gregor had prompted that remark?"

"Of course. She did all her brother's thinking for him. Mrs. Eoghan realized that the prompting hadn't stopped at Duchlan…"

"What?"

"Miss Gregor wrote regularly to Eoghan."

"And yet Mrs. Eoghan came here. Surely that was playing directly into the enemy's hands?"

Dr. Hailey kept his eyes averted without knowing exactly why he did so. A prolonged silence followed his question. At last McDonald said:

"I fancy Eoghan had written his wife an unkind letter."

"Blaming her for sending for you?"

"Accusing her perhaps of being in love with me."

Dr. Hailey sat up.

"Do you mean that she was leaving her husband and child when she came here?" he exclaimed.

"She was."

They heard another sail being hoisted. The sound of row-locks came up to them from the harbour and then, suddenly and intolerably, the hoot of a steam-whistle.

"Why did she come to you?" Dr. Hailey asked.

"For advice and shelter." McDonald turned and picked up his pipe. His uneasiness seemed to have left him. He lit the tobacco and began to smoke.

"Naturally," he said, "you want to know how much truth there was in Miss Gregor's suggestion. So far as Mrs. Eoghan is concerned the answer is: None at all. But that isn't the answer in my case. I want to tell you," he turned and faced his companion as he spoke, "that I fell in love with Mrs. Eoghan almost as soon as I met her. Her husband was then in Malta. She was hungry for friendship and help and I gave her both. I'm not a child. I knew what had happened to me. And I knew that it was hopeless, in the sense that Oonagh was genuinely in love with her husband. But knowledge about the causes of pain does not help you when you're compelled to bear it. What did help me was to try to smooth her way for her…"

He shook his head.

"She thought that I was acting solely from professional motives. They were there all right, mind you, those professional motives; the girl's nerves were frayed, jagged. But Miss Gregor wasn't so unsuspecting. I had dared to call her behaviour in question. I was an obstacle in her way. Worse, I was a danger. As I told you just now, she hated me." He drew a deep breath. "Do you know, Hailey, there was something big in that wicked old woman's character? I couldn't help admiring her. The busy way she set about discrediting my motives—first in her own mind, then in Duchlan's. What persistence! And mind you, I had sympathy for her too. Eoghan was her child. She meant to hold him and his for ever. I saw that in her little, quick brown eyes. I had more than Highland pride and Highland craft against me. More than a will as strong as buffalo hide. Motherhood, hungry, unsatisfied, implacable was the real enemy. Deep called to deep. I knew her and she knew me. Only one mistake she made and that's not strange in a woman. Oonagh wasn't in love and hadn't guessed, hadn't dreamed what my feelings were. There's the misfortune that nobody could cure. I'm the only doctor in a radius of twelve miles. Oonagh kept sending for me for herself or Hamish and I could plead my duty against my scruples. The old woman's eyes saw every move. When Eoghan came back from Malta the tension reached breaking-point; only his going to Ayrshire prevented a break. He didn't accuse Oonagh then of running after me, but that was in the back of his mind, where his aunt had put it. But he blamed her for her want of gratitude to his people and for her slackness in Hamish's upbringing. They weren't on speaking terms when he went away. The day he went away she sent for me and told me she was afraid of what she might do."

Chapter XVI

Inspector Barley

His confession seemed to release Dr. McDonald from bondage. His manner, until now gloomy and reserved, changed.

"I've been frank with you, Hailey," he said, "because, sooner or later, you're bound to hear about the suspicions which Miss Gregor instilled into so many minds. I want you to know the truth. Oonagh belongs to Eoghan. Not for a single instant has she swerved from her loyalty to him. Her coming here was a gesture, a protest made when her fears for Hamish and her distress that her husband should have seemed to take sides against her had brought her to the edge of a breakdown."

He seated himself as he spoke and once more arranged his leg in front of him.

"The end of the story, happily, was better than the beginning. I was trying to persuade her to let me take her back to the castle when a car came to the door. It was the old nurse, Christina, who had been sent as a peacemaker, because Duchlan and his sister were genuinely afraid by that time. The old woman was terribly distressed. You saw her last night. She fixed those queer, black eyes of hers on Oonagh's face and told her that Hamish was crying for his mother. I don't know, there was something in her voice, some tone or quality, that made that appeal irresistible. You saw the child's face; heard his voice. Oonagh's resistance broke down at once. Then the old woman comforted her, promising that her troubles would soon be at an end. You couldn't help believing her. But she's a retainer of the Gregors. I felt that, in her heart of hearts, she shared Miss Gregor's suspicions of me. Queerly enough, she awakened a sense of guilt which I hadn't experienced in any of my dealings with Miss Gregor."

He shook his head.

"I wasn't wrong. She had read my secret. She put Oonagh in the car and came back to this room for a shawl that had been left behind. I was outside at the car, and when she didn't return, I followed her to find out if anything was amiss. She turned and gazed at me just as she had gazed at Oonagh, but with very hostile eyes. 'Whom God hath joined together,' she said in solemn tones, 'let not man put asunder.' Then she picked up the shawl and hurried away."

"Do you know what happened," Dr. Hailey asked, "after Mrs. Eoghan got home?"

"Oh, yes, they received her with relief if without cordiality. That feeling soon passes. What remained was the knowledge that she had disgraced them publicly—the unpardonable sin. I called on the child next morning. Miss Gregor was in the nursery; she told me that Mrs. Eoghan was in bed with a headache."

"She had yielded to them?"

McDonald's eyes narrowed. He shook his head.

"I don't think that is how I should put it. Oonagh isn't an Irishwoman for nothing. She was biding her time. I realized that the real battle would be fought when her husband came back. But I knew also that the period of waiting for that event would be greatly distressing to Oonagh. She's one of those women who can't act alone, who needs a friend to advise her and help her to gather her forces." He raised his right hand, holding the palm horizontal and keeping the fingers extended. "I suppose we all depend to some extent on the feelings which animate us at any given moment. It's only on high emotional planes that we're heroes." He lowered his hand. "Down here is weakness and hesitation. I think the truth is that she came to me for strength. She told me, a few days later, that she only lived when she was talking to me." He leaned forward. "Mind you, it wasn't my strength she wanted; it was her own. I helped her to command her own strength."

Dr. Hailey nodded: "I know. Humanity as well as chemistry has its catalysts."

"Exactly."

Dr. Hailey rose to go. "Am I at liberty to tell the new detective from Edinburgh what you've told me?" he asked.

"Yes."

He held out his hand. Suddenly he turned back.

"Do you know why Eoghan came back so hurriedly from Ayrshire?"

McDonald's face lost its eagerness: a slow flush rose to his cheeks.

"I suppose he came to borrow money. But Oonagh had sent for him."

"To take her away?"

"Yes."

"He refused?"

Dr. Hailey asked the question in the tones of a man who knows the answer.

"I don't know."

"Eoghan's like his father, isn't he?"

McDonald shook his head.

"In some ways. Not in all ways. For example, he isn't superstitious. The terrible logic of the Irish clashes with that Highland element."

"When I met him," Dr. Hailey said, "I realized that he was a difficult man to know. I formed no very clear idea of his character except that he was in love with his wife."

"I have no very clear idea of his character."

"Has his wife?"

"She's in love with him."

Dr. Hailey sighed.

"Sometimes," he confessed rather sadly, "I wonder what that means. Do lovers really see one another truthfully? Isn't it rather their own illusions that they see?"

There was no answer. McDonald passed his hand wearily across his brow.

"Perhaps lovers see everything and forgive everything," he said.

When Dr. Hailey left McDonald he walked up the harbour to the manse. This was a big square house standing back from the road among scrubby trees that looked terribly wind-worn. He rang the bell. The door was opened by a small girl who stated that her father was at home. A moment later a short, stout man in clerical dress came into the hall. He advanced to the door, dismissing his daughter with a genial gesture.

Dr. Hailey explained who he was and was immediately invited to come in. The Rev. John Dugald led the way to his study and shut the door. He moved a big arm-chair by its back and urged his visitor to sit down. After a glance at the formidable array of volumes with which all the four walls were lined the doctor complied.

"What can I do for you?" the minister asked in rich Highland accents. His good-humoured face was grave, but his eyes gleamed with excitement.

"I want you to tell me about Dr. McDonald."

"Really?" With an effort the Rev. John stifled his curiosity. "McDonald is not a member of my congregation," he said. "He's not a member, indeed, of any congregation. But I have always found him to be a good man, aye and a skilful man too. When my wee boy had bronchitis last winter, he saved his life."

Dr. Hailey inclined his head.

"I'm sure he's a good doctor. My concern, frankly, is with his personal character. His character as a man."

"That's a hard question, sir." The minister considered for a few moments. "If you had asked me that question six months ago," he said, "I would have replied that McDonald was a poet and an artist who had lost his way and become a doctor. I would have said that his only interest was his books and his writing."

He broke off. A troubled look appeared on his face.

"And now?"

"Now it's different. There have been rumours. Stories."

"Such as?"

The Rev. John moved uncomfortably.

"I'll be frank with you. The village has begun to talk about the doctor's intimacy with Mrs. Eoghan Gregor. And not the village only."

He leaned forward. His right hand descended to find his pipe on the top of a wooden coal-box which stood beside his chair.

He put the pipe in his mouth.

"The late Miss Gregor was one of my people," he said. "She came to me a few days ago in the greatest distress to ask my advice. It appears that she had surprised her niece walking on the shore, after dark, with McDonald. What troubled her was whether or not she was bound in duty to report to her nephew."

"I see. What did you advise?"

"I advised her to see Dr. McDonald and talk to him."

"Well?"

"She then told me that she was scarcely on speaking terms with him."

Dr. Hailey frowned.

"The suggestion being that McDonald was so deeply in love with Mrs. Eoghan that no plea was likely to be listened to?" he asked.

"Yes."

"What did you advise in those circumstances?"

"I felt that I could not take the responsibility of giving any advice. But I offered to see the doctor myself. That offer was not accepted, and Miss Gregor went away saying that she must consult her own conscience."

"Were you the only person to whom she confided this information?"

The minister shook his head.

"I don't think so."

"In other words a systematic attempt was being made to blacken Mrs. Eoghan's character?"

There was no reply. Again Dr. Hailey leaned forward.

"Tell me," he asked, "whether or not you're inclined to believe the suggestion conveyed?"

"I'm not inclined to believe it."

"You trust McDonald?"

"Yes, and Mrs. Eoghan."

The doctor nodded. Then he asked:

"And Miss Gregor?"

Silence fell in the room. At last the Rev. John said:

"Miss Gregor, as I've told you, was one of my people. I believe that she felt herself justified in what she did and said. At least I hope so. But it has always seemed to me that there was a quality in her character difficult to reconcile with Christian ideals. I've often tried to define that quality in my mind. I can't say I have succeeded. She was not a hard woman; she was not an ungenerous woman. But there was something…"

He broke off. Dr. Hailey rose and held out his hand.

"Jealousy," he remarked, "is neither hard nor ungenerous except in certain directions."

The detective sent from Glasgow to replace Dundas had arrived when Dr. Hailey returned to the castle. He was with Duchlan in the study. He jumped to his feet the moment the doctor entered the room and thrust out his hand like a man snatching a child from danger.

"Dr. Hailey, I presume. My name is Inspector Barley. Thompson Barley."

He seized the doctor's hand and wrung it; at the same time a broad smile exposed his strong, stained teeth.

"Delighted to make your acquaintance, doctor," he cried. "Even at such a tragic" (he pronounced the word traagic) "*contretemps*. Duchlan here has just been telling me of your goodness. What a calamity! What a calamity!" He waved his hand in a gesture which reproached the gods. "What a calamity!"

Dr. Hailey sat down at the table. This most un-Scots-like Scot interested him. Barley, who wore a black-and-white check dust-coat of terrific pattern, looked like a shop-walker and spoke like a decayed actor in a Strand public-house, but he detected another quality and warmed to it. Inspector Barley possessed pleasant grey eyes; his brow was fine, square and massive and he had eloquent hands. What a pity that he had dyed his hair with henna!

"I am going to venture to ask you," Barley cried, "for an outline of the case. After that I hope that we may co-operate in everything." He turned to Duchlan, bowing as he turned. "Doubtless, sir, you are well aware of the great distinction which attaches to Dr. Hailey's name, both in medical and in criminological circles? But let me tell you that it is only among the *élite* of both these professions that his true worth is understood and appreciated. Only among the *élite*."

He gave his head a strong downward movement as he repeated the last sentence. His mouth at this moment was slightly open and his face had a vacant expression which, paradoxically, expressed a great deal. Duchlan gazed at him with lively astonishment.

"No doubt."

Inspector Barley swung round again to face the doctor. He listened with gravity to the story of the two murders, offering no comment, but bowing occasionally as he took a point. His face remained inscrutable. The fact that his features were somewhat broad and coarse and that he wore a bristling moustache added a grotesque touch to his ceremoniousness. When Dr. Hailey finished he leaned back in his chair and closed his eyes.

"Most mysterious. Most mysterious," he exclaimed in quick tones that wholly discounted the meaning of his words. "Apparently murders of a new *genre*. Of a new *genre*. But probably not. Murder, as you know, changes its form only in unessentials. *Plus ça change, plus c'est la même chose*."

His French accent was better than his English and went some way towards explaining his gestures. He rose and walked to the fireplace, seeming to glide across the carpet. He stood with his back leaning on the mantelpiece.

"It must have struck you, of course, Dr. Hailey," he exclaimed, "that there is one person who certainly had the opportunity of murdering poor Dundas."

He paused. He glanced in turn at each of his companions. Neither spoke, though Dr. Hailey frowned.

"I mean Dr. McDonald, who returned alone to Dundas's room to get your pen."

A sound like a groan punctuated the silence.

Duchlan's head had sunk on to his chest. He swayed for an instant and then slipped from his chair.

Chapter XVII

"What an Actress!"

Inspector Barley, like Napoleon, who, as he said, he admired *à outrance*, knew the value of time. It took him only a few minutes to ascertain from Oonagh that Dr. McDonald had visited her child on the night of Miss Gregor's death, a visit which, as Dr. Hailey felt bound to acknowledge, had been overlooked in all the earlier investigations.

"McDonald has made no secret, of course, of his frequent visits," the doctor declared. "And, as I told you, he was present when the door of Miss Gregor's room was forced."

"Quite. No doubt the circumstance is unimportant." Barley bowed to Oonagh, who was seated in an arm-chair, apologizing to her, apparently, for the interruption of her narrative. "Pray continue, Mrs. Gregor."

The girl glanced at Dr. Hailey and then lowered her eyes. She repeated the account she had already given of her behaviour on the night of her aunt's murder in tones which were so low as to be nearly inaudible. She looked exceedingly ill at ease. There were dark lines under her eyes and she kept drawing her hand across her brow.

"In my humble judgement, and you will correct me if I am mistaken," Barley exclaimed when she had finished, "your account amounts to this. You had gone early to bed because you were feeling indisposed. You were summoned about 9 o'clock by the nurse Christina, because your small son had become ill again. Dr. McDonald was sent for and after he went away you wished to report the result of his visit to your aunt, Miss Gregor, who had meanwhile gone to bed, where she was being attended as usual by your nurse, Christina. For some reason unknown to you, Miss Gregor received your well-intentioned visit to her bedroom with dismay and locked the door of the room in your face."

He leaned back in his chair and thrust his thumbs into the armholes of his waistcoat. "Am I right?"

"Yes."

"Dr. McDonald had left the house before you paid your visit to Miss Gregor's room?"

The blood ebbed slowly out of Oonagh's cheeks.

"He remained with Hamish while I paid my visit," she said with an evident effort. "Because Christina had gone to my aunt."

"And then?"

"He was waiting for me at the top of the stairs. We came downstairs together."

"To the study?"

"Yes. Dr. McDonald wanted to give me some directions about the treatment."

Barley swept the room with his eyes, fixing his gaze finally on the ceiling.

"This room is situated immediately under Miss Gregor's room, is it not?" he asked.

"Yes."

There was a moment of silence. Then the detective rose to his feet and pointed his finger at the girl.

"I put it to you," he cried, "that Dr. McDonald accompanied you to Miss Gregor's bedroom?"

"No."

"Take care, Mrs. Gregor."

"He did not accompany me to Miss Gregor's bedroom, Christina will tell you that he did not."

Her eyes were unflinching; her beauty shone with the strength of conviction which animated her face. Barley caught his breath in a gasp of admiration.

"What an actress!" he exclaimed insolently.

He sat down again and appeared to remain unaware of the vigour with which his rudeness had been resented. He dismissed Oonagh with a wave of his hand, then suddenly rose and opened the door for her, bowing as she went out. He rang the bell and returned to his chair.

"Dr. McDonald did accompany her to her aunt's room," he said, "you shall hear."

Angus, the piper, answered the bell. Barley ordered him to sit down in tones so gracious that the Highlander appeared to think himself insulted. His solemn face expressed a lively resentment.

"Did you see Dr. McDonald on the night your mistress was murdered?" the detective asked.

"Yes, sir, I did."

"Where?"

"In this house, sir."

"Where, in this house?"

Angus turned and indicated the door with a gesture superb in its mingling of deference with scorn.

"I opened the front door to him."

"Did you see him after that?"

"I did not, sir. The doctor told me not to wait up for him because Mistress Gregor or Christina would let him out of the house."

"Did you hear him going away?"

"I did not. My room is at the other side of the castle."

"Did anybody hear him going away?"

Angus hesitated. He smoothed his kilt with his big red hand.

"Christina told me that she heard him going down the top flight of stairs, but she did not hear him going down the second flight to the hall."

Barley started and strained forward.

"What do you mean?"

"Dr. McDonald has a wooden leg, sir."

"Ask Christina to come here immediately."

When the door shut, the detective no longer attempted to hide his jubilation. He began to walk up and down the room with his hands clasped behind his back and his head and shoulders thrust forward. He paused at every few steps to throw out a remark, much as turkeys pause to gobble.

"Wooden leg! You didn't tell me that. But, of course, it's a detail…My dear doctor, I believe that the solution of this mystery cannot now be long delayed. The solution may be displeasing, distressing." He shrugged his shoulders. "*Que voulez-vous?* What a point: that thumping of the wooden leg on the wooden stairs! The old woman listening. Hearing the 'thump, thump' down to the first floor. Then silence. A silence more eloquent than words." He came to Dr. Hailey and stood in front of him. "The husband is coming home: there is a story to tell him." He shook his head. "Don't forget that Miss Gregor was Eoghan's foster-mother. *In loco parentis.* Women can endure least of all, in my humble judgement, to see the men they have mothered betrayed in their absence."

He stopped speaking because the door of the room had opened. Christina came hobbling into the room. She was dressed in cap and apron. She glanced at Barley in a manner that was quite frankly hostile and then seated herself on the edge of the chair which he offered her. He came to the point in an instant.

"You heard Dr. McDonald going downstairs from the nursery on the night your mistress was murdered?" he asked.

"Yes, I did."

"Did you hear him go down to the hall?"

"I did not."

"Tell me exactly what you heard."

The old woman clasped her skinny hands in her lap and looked at them attentively.

"I heard him go down to the floor below," she said.

Barley began to nod his head vigorously.

"That means he didn't go down to the ground floor. You couldn't have helped hearing his wooden leg on the stair if he had gone down to the hall."

"I was not listening." The old woman shook her head. "Very likely he did go down to the hall. I had shut the door of the nursery."

A quick frown gathered on Barley's brow.

"A wooden leg makes a deal of noise on a wooden floor," he exclaimed.

"It does, if you are near it."

"Why did you tell Angus that you only heard the doctor go down one flight of the stair?"

"Because I only heard him go down one flight. After that I shut the nursery door."

Christina's face was grave but Dr. Hailey fancied that he detected a grim smile lurking among its wrinkles. The Highlander, he reflected with some satisfaction, has his own sense of humour. Barley did not try to hide his annoyance at the check he had received; but he did not, in his annoyance, abate his eloquence.

"You heard him go down to the first floor. You returned to your duties. *Ca va bien.* Angus, the piper, has told us that he had already gone to bed. The question is: Who locked up the house after the doctor had gone away?"

"I do not know."

"The doctor stayed with the child, did he not, while you went to put your mistress to bed?"

"He and Mistress Eoghan Gregor stayed with Hamish."

"Now be careful how you answer this question: Did Mrs. Eoghan Gregor come to Miss Gregor's bedroom?"

"Yes, and then I went back to the nursery, where the doctor was waiting."

Barley bowed over his waistcoat. He raised his hand in the manner of the conductor of an orchestra.

"What happened," he asked, "when Mrs. Eoghan Gregor entered Miss Gregor's bedroom?"

"I did not see what happened."

"But you were there?"

"I was. But I went away. Mrs. Eoghan took the candle from me at the door. I wished to go back to Hamish."

"Did you hear Mrs. Eoghan come out of Miss Gregor's room?"

Christina shook her head.

"I did not."

"What happened after you returned to the nursery?"

"Dr. McDonald went away down the stair."

"Mrs. Eoghan Gregor says that Miss Gregor ordered her out of her bedroom and locked the door behind her?"

"Yes."

"She told you that?"

"Yes."

Once again Barley gesticulated.

"Dr. McDonald, for all you know to the contrary, may have gone to Miss Gregor's room?"

"Mrs. Eoghan did not say that. She said…"

"Yes, I know what she said." The detective swept away the repetition he did not wish to hear. "Now tell me," he continued, "did you hear Mrs. Eoghan shutting the front door after the doctor left the castle?"

"I did not. I heard Mr. Eoghan's motor-boat coming into the jetty."

"What, so Mr. Eoghan arrived just when Dr. McDonald was going away?"

"Yes, he did."

"Did they meet?"

Christina shook her head. "I do not know if they met."

Barley dismissed her and addressed Dr. Hailey.

"I admit," he exclaimed, "that I have not proved all that I had hoped to prove. But something has undoubtedly accrued from my investigation. Something!" He bit at his words as they escaped from his mouth. Suddenly he took a small comb from his pocket and combed his moustache in short, quick strokes that made it bristle. After the comb he produced a pipe, dark and well-seasoned, which he polished lovingly on the side of his nose.

"Point one," he stated, pointing the stem of his pipe at his companion. "Dr. McDonald is the only person who can possibly have murdered Dundas. Point two. It may very well be that Dr. McDonald entered Miss Gregor's bedroom. We have only the word of Mrs. Eoghan that he did not do so, and her word, in my humble opinion, is suspect. Point three. A link establishes itself between these two associations. What did Miss Gregor know? Here is a young wife, left by her husband in circumstances which doubtless were uncongenial. Her boy is ill. She summons the local doctor who calls at frequent intervals. Acquaintance ripens into a warmer emotion. *A côte de l'amour* " The pipe made a great circle. "Your Celtic temperament is nothing if not ardent.

Emotion rises to full tide in a day, an hour. Nothing else seems to matter. Ah, this is the very quintessence of love!"

The man raised his eyes ecstatically. They were loosely set and moved with a tipsy roll that was full of surprises. Evidently he attached importance to a lyrical quality which he supposed his nature to possess for he quoted some lines about love, the authorship of which he did not disclose. His voice tripped along and stopped and tripped along again like an old maid trying to cross a crowded thoroughfare.

"But there was Miss Gregor to mar these stolen sweets," he went on. "That austere, puritanical nature doubtless burned with cold fire at the spectacle of this doctor and his patient…"

"I feel sure," Dr. Hailey interrupted, "that Mrs. Eoghan's feelings for McDonald were merely those of an anxious mother…"

"Look at the facts. What does our immortal bard tell us?"

"'Facts are chiels as winna ding'."

"Mrs. Eoghan had fled by night to McDonald's house. Isn't that enough to justify what I've said? 'Love flows like the Solway.' Do you think that Miss Gregor's shrewd eyes had overlooked what was so plainly to be seen?"

"No, but…"

"Oh, my dear Dr. Hailey, your knowledge of that lady is clearly less accurate than it should be. As for me, I've been at pains, at great pains, to inform myself about her. A puritan, believe me, of the most rigid school. In her long life she never touched a playing-card or entered a place of public amusement. How do I know that?"

He stopped. His wide nostrils dilated.

"I have a friend in Glasgow who knew the Gregor family well many years ago. A retired Army man. Excellent family. Delightful, most cultured man. Once upon a time, he told me, he persuaded Miss Gregor—she was a girl in her twenties then—to accompany him to see Sir Henry Irving playing in *Hamlet*. When they reached the theatre the first thing she saw was a notice, 'To The Pit'. After that nothing would induce her to enter the building. That's Miss Gregor for you. What mercy were Mrs. Eoghan and McDonald likely to receive from such a woman?"

Dr. Hailey did not reply. His silence was instantly interpreted as consent. Barley's face stiffened with new gravity.

"The eternal triangle!" he announced magnificently. "With a woman of the hew-Agag-in-pieces-before-the-Lord type in the middle of it. Are not these the lively ingredients of tragedy? Put yourself in McDonald's position, in Mrs. Eoghan's position. Would you not have feared greatly both the husband who was returning and the woman who was waiting to inform him whenever he did return? Believe me, it's that fear which must hold all our attention."

Another gesture called the heavens to witness. Dr. Hailey remained silent.

"As a psychologist," Barley assured him, "you cannot but be aware of the demoralizing effect of fear even on the strongest characters. It corrodes, as rust corrodes iron. It demoralizes. Fear is one of the nursing mothers of crime. Like greed. Like jealousy. McDonald was afraid; Mrs. Eoghan was afraid. They were mice in the presence of the cat. The time was approaching when the cat would pounce…"

He threw himself back with staring eyes and open mouth. His thoughts seemed to coil round his head like smoke.

"In addition," he added, "there was Dundas. Dundas the mole, digging, digging under the surface, piling fact upon fact. What had Dundas discovered? What was he going to tell?"

"I don't think," Dr. Hailey said, "that Dundas had discovered anything. He admitted himself that he had reached a blank wall."

"Dundas, my dear Dr. Hailey, was one of those remarkable men who delighted...delighted to throw dust in the eyes of their rivals. Can it be doubted that he saw a rival in an amateur of your outstanding reputation? No doubt exists in my mind that he called you in only when he already felt sure of success. To employ McDonald as his go-between was entirely in keeping with character."

"It may be so. But I understood him to say that any suspicions he entertained were fixed on Eoghan Gregor, not on McDonald. As I told you, Eoghan has undoubtedly suffered heavy financial losses."

Barley shook his head. He filled his pipe quickly and lit it with an astounding deftness.

"Delightful fellow, Dundas," he exclaimed, "and most honest in all his dealings. But secretive, jealous, *difficile*." He spread out his hands. "My cards, as you see, are on the table. His were under it." Once more the moustache-comb did service.

"'The proof of the pudding is in the eating?' Very well. I shall follow my theory and you, my dear Dr. Hailey, shall be judge of the result. Let us recall Mrs. Eoghan."

Chapter XVIII

Secret Meetings

Dr. Hailey found it impossible not to admire Inspector Barley. The man possessed an extraordinary quickness of mind and an excellent imagination which never appeared to escape from the control of his reason. His dramatic instinct, on the other hand, and the thickness of his social skin, enabled him to launch his formidable questions in a way that served his purpose admirably. Either those whom he was examining became resentful or they lost their composure; he knew how to profit by both happenings. His comb, and his method of polishing his pipe on his nose, supplied the element of vulgarity which is necessary to the success of every charlatan.

It was disturbing, nevertheless, to see Oonagh placed at the mercy of such a man. When her cross-examination began the doctor was already sorry for her. Before it had continued many minutes he had become her partisan, for the key-note of the examination was the insult already levelled at her: "What an actress!" Barley continued to discount in advance the sincerity of expression which was the girl's defence.

"I wish you to understand, madam," he gushed, "that the intimate and delicate character of the questions which I am about to put to you is conditioned by no vulgar curiosity. I beg of you, dismiss that unworthy suspicion wholly from your mind. The occasion is so serious, so fraught with momentous consequences, that there is enough justification, in my humble opinion, for any question however embarrassing its nature."

He paused; the sound of his words buzzed about their ears like a May-time swarm. Then, when he judged that the effect he wished had been obtained, he asked quietly:

"What were your relations, madam, with Dr. McDonald?"

Oonagh's lips quivered. A flush of lively resentment mounted to her cheeks. She glanced at Dr. Hailey in the manner of a woman attacked by a bully, who looks to a decent man for help. Then her eyes darkened, and she braced herself to fight.

"What do you mean?" she asked in tones which attacked him.

Barley was much too wide awake to give battle on that ground. He rose to his feet and drew himself up.

"Believe me, madam," he cried, "I am ready, willing, to discount every slander that has been uttered against you. But how can I do that if you refuse me the information I ask for? You know as well as I do that your friendship" (he emphasized the word) "for Dr. McDonald has given rise, in this house and outside of it, to talk, to speculation, perhaps to calumny."

"Dr. McDonald has been very kind to my little boy."

Oonagh measured her words; her face had recovered its calmness of expression. Dr. Hailey realized with a pang that that calmness must soon be disturbed once more. How beautiful the girl looked in her adversity! Barley sat down with the suddenness which characterized all his actions.

"There are only four people who can have killed your aunt," he stated. "Duchlan, the piper Angus, Dr. McDonald and your husband—for that terrible blow was certainly not struck by a woman. Duchlan is a weak old man: I exclude him. There remain Angus, the doctor, and your husband. But we're not dealing only with the murder of your aunt. There's the murder of Dundas to be considered. The only man who can possibly have murdered Dundas, *the only person* who had access to him at all, at the moment of his death is McDonald. In my humble submission, McDonald had access also to your aunt on the night when she was murdered. And the two murders appear to be the work of the same hand."

He broke off and pointed at the girl.

"Why should McDonald have murdered your aunt?" he cried in loud tones.

"I don't know any reason why he should have murdered her."

"Think again, madam."

Oonagh remained silent with her lips tightly pressed together. But her cheeks were losing their colour.

"Miss Gregor was aware of an equivocal relationship existing between yourself and the doctor!"

The challenge was spoken in the tones of a man who offers a suggestion. But its effect was that of an accusation against which there is no defence. The girl wilted visibly.

"Am I right?"

"My aunt misunderstood everything."

The detective's practical mind pounced like a cat.

"Have the goodness to describe the circumstances which your aunt misunderstood," he demanded.

She hesitated a long time before she replied. Then she said:

"I was unhappy in this house. Dr. McDonald was the only friend to whom I could turn for advice. I saw a good deal of him."

"Here?"

"Here and elsewhere."

"Ah!" Barley leaned forward. "You mean that you had private, secret meetings with him?"

"We met privately."

"In the grounds?"

"On the shore. Dr. McDonald has a boat of his own."

Dr. Hailey saw a gleam of triumph in the detective's eyes.

"Miss Gregor surprised one of these meetings, eh?"

"She saw us talking to each other on one occasion."

"I put it to you that she threatened to tell your husband what she had seen?"

There was no reply. Suddenly Oonagh raised her head.

"I've told you," she declared in candid tones, "that my aunt misunderstood everything. She was ready to find evil in all I did, because she wanted to have control of my child and I would not give her control. Dr. McDonald has never been other than my good friend. If I had to meet him secretly that was only because it was impossible to meet him openly without arousing my aunt's suspicions, or rather giving her the means of making trouble between my husband and me."

"Why should you want to meet Dr. McDonald?"

"He was my only friend."

"What, when you've got your husband!"

"Eoghan was not here."

"He was in Ayrshire. One can write to Ayrshire."

"He would not have understood. Eoghan has always had great faith in his aunt. She brought him up."

Barley's face assumed a grave expression. He smoothed his dull, dyed hair with a careful hand.

"May I ask upon what subject you consulted Dr. McDonald?" he demanded in sarcastic tones.

"I thought of leaving my husband. He tried to persuade me not to do that."

"Most excellent advice, undoubtedly. Most excellent advice. *Les femmes n'ont d'existence que par l'amour.*" Barley filled his mouth with the quotation, the equivocal character of which seemed to give him great satisfaction. He paused for a moment and then said: "You thought of leaving your husband because you didn't hit it off with his relations? You'll forgive me, madam, if I say that, in my humble opinion, that is no reason at all for a step of so reprehensible a character?"

"I decided not to leave him."

Oonagh was losing her nerve and no longer seemed capable of offering effective resistance to the detective's bombardment. She plucked at the neck of her dress, creasing the thin fabric in several places. Barley was quick to follow up his success.

"Your explanation is not one which commends itself to reason or to experience," he declared. "Those who seek advice, seek it openly. But I'm prepared to believe that your final decision was to remain with your husband. It is, if I may say so, the final decision of most women in similar circumstances. You know, doubtless, that a doctor who is involved in a divorce suit with the wife of one of his patients is invariably expelled from the medical profession."

He paused to allow this grim truth to sink in.

"When Miss Gregor surprised your *tête-à-tête* with the doctor, she became possessed of the means of ruining him as well as you. Dr. McDonald, at that moment, knew that his existence as a professional man was hanging in the balance. I venture to think that when, on the night of the murder, he heard the sound of your husband's motor-boat approaching across the loch, he realized that the balance had been determined against him." Again the minatory finger was extended. "Why, may I ask, did your husband return at that hour and in that fashion?"

Oonagh shook her head.

"I think," she said, "that you had better ask him that question yourself."

"No, madam. I must ask that question of you. Of you, who, as I have been informed, had already served an ultimatum upon your husband."

"I don't understand."

"You had threatened to leave him unless your terms were agreed to."

"I had told him that I wanted a home of my own."

Barley's body stiffened.

"The Emperor Napoleon used to say that attack is the best form of defence," he exclaimed in tones which suggested that he was speaking of an old friend. "I suggest that you were pressing this demand for a home of your own in order to offset the charge which Miss Gregor had made against you?"

"No."

"You've just admitted that you did demand a home of your own."

"Every mother wants that, surely?"

"No doubt. But you had formerly consented to live here. Your demand for a home of your own was made only when there was danger, great danger, that you might forfeit your right to any home at all, to your husband, to your child."

A sweep of Barley's arm, like a spearman's thrust, speeded this accusation. Oonagh's face grew pale.

"I've always wanted a home of my own," she exclaimed. "Always, since the day I married Eoghan."

"I suggest, on the contrary, that you were quite happy here until you became intimate with McDonald." He thrust out his head towards her. "Do you deny that you offered yourself to McDonald and were refused by him?"

Oonagh jumped up. Her eyes were wild with pain and resentment.

"How dare you?" she cried in tones which betrayed the anguish he had inflicted on her.

Barley bared his teeth.

"You ran away to McDonald in the middle of the night, remember," he said. "Duchlan told me that. And then you allowed yourself to be brought back again. It was after that humiliation, was it not, that your demand for a home of your own became insistent?"

Chapter XIX

Accusation

Dr. Hailey had made a few notes during Barley's cross-examination of Oonagh and felt a strong inclination, when the examination ended, to raise some objection to the theory upon which the detective was working. But a glance at the triumphant face of his companion made him decide to postpone the realization of this wish. Barley was transported already to regions of self-congratulation where no whisper of doubt or criticism could penetrate. His eyes were half-closed; his mouth was held slightly open; and his head was poised on one side. He remained in this condition of ecstasy for some minutes and then woke up and combed his moustache.

"We're getting close to the truth, my dear doctor," he said. "I feel it." He frowned and shook his head. "It's most distasteful to me, believe me, to have to question these charming people in this way. But *que voulez vous? Que voulez vous?* Now I must deal with Eoghan Gregor. What a tragedy that it should be necessary to question a young man in his exalted station about the fair name of his wife!"

He rang the bell and flung himself down in an arm-chair, apparently limp with regret.

"I've studied your methods, doctor," he stated. "Most admirable; but scarcely applicable perhaps to the present case. My method as you see is different. You proceed from character to event; I follow a lead, using all my powers of imagination as I go. It seems to me that, in cases where the issue is complicated, you're bound to win; but where there are definite physical obstacles, such as these locked rooms, I have the better of you. 'A nod's as good as a wink to a blind horse'. Opportunity counts for more than character when one person has the chance to kill and the other has not."

He remained in his limp attitude. After he had enunciated his philosophy, he sighed deeply several times. But when Eoghan entered the room, he became immediately as alert as ever.

"Come in, come in," he cried. "Let me see, you're Major Gregor, aren't you?"

"Captain."

Eoghan's indolent good looks had not deserted him. He glanced at Barley and, for a moment, betrayed a flicker of amusement. Then the air of melancholy which he wore with excellent ease removed him from that profane contact.

"I've just been telling Dr. Hailey with what reluctance I'm pursuing this present quest." Barley apologized. "But, 'needs does as needs must'. Let me say that if you resent any of the questions which it is my duty to address to you, you will be within your rights in refusing to answer them."

This with many bows and flourishes.

Dr. Hailey duly noted the difference between the method used in dealing with Eoghan and that used with Oonagh, and felt bound to agree that the characters of husband and wife were Barley's complete justification. Eoghan would be less on his guard if he supposed he was dealing with a fool; Oonagh's weakness was her nervousness.

"Very well," Eoghan said.

"The question I am most concerned to ask you is this: Why did you return so suddenly from Ayrshire?"

"Because I wanted to borrow some money from my father."

"What? You had to come back by motor-boat to do that?"

"I always travel to Ayrshire by motor-boat at this time of year. It's much the quickest way."

"Might you not have written?"

"No."

"You had no other reason for your sudden visit?"

"No."

"Believe me, I don't wish to push my quest beyond reasonable bounds," Barley declared, "but I am compelled to ask for more enlightenment that you seem disposed to accord to me. *Suaviter in modo, fortiter in re.* I have reason to think," he paused suddenly and dramatically, "that you were not entirely easy in your mind about your domestic and family affairs."

Eoghan shook his head. "You're mistaken."

"About your wife's relations with your aunt, and arising out of that, about her relations with yourself."

"Nonsense."

The first note of irritation sounded in Eoghan's voice. Dr. Hailey saw the detective react like a dog making a point.

"Your wife," he said, "has told me that she was scarcely able to endure the interferences of your aunt."

"Indeed."

"Further, that she sought counsel with Dr. McDonald of Ardmore whether or not she should leave you, supposing that you refused to take her away from here."

"Don't be idiotic," Eoghan exclaimed in tones which declared his growing uneasiness.

"My dear sir, if you suppose I'm trifling, or bluffing, you're making a grave mistake. A mistake, I'm afraid, which you will soon have occasion to correct. Your wife has declared unequivocally that she did think of leaving you. Place that fact in the forefront of your mind. The reason she has given is that you had failed to provide her with a home of her own. Very well, it is now necessary for me to ask you when your wife made her first complaint about this failure on your part."

Barley spoke slowly, giving each word due weight. He kept his eyes fixed on Eoghan's face.

"What has this got to do with my aunt's death?" the young man demanded.

"A great deal, believe me."

"What?"

"No, I refuse to be bounced. You must answer my question, or bear the consequences of refusing to answer it." Barley leaned back in his chair. He repeated: "When did your wife first complain about your failure to provide her with a house?"

Eoghan moved uneasily in his chair. He glanced at Dr. Hailey and then let his gaze stray about the room. The doctor had the impression that he was calculating, coolly, the probable effects of different answers. At last, he appeared to reach a decision.

"My wife mentioned quite recently," he stated, "that she thought the time had come for us to set up our own home."

"What does 'quite recently' mean?"

"A fortnight ago."

A gleam of triumph shone in Barley's eyes.

"Do you know that your wife ran away from this house one night?" he asked.

"Yes."

"Who told you?"

"She told me herself."

Eoghan imparted the information in surly tones. But these had no effect on the detective.

"Did your aunt inform you also?" he asked.

"Yes."

"By letter?"

"How else could she inform me?"

Barley nodded. "You told your wife that your aunt had informed you?" he demanded.

"No, sir."

"At any rate, your wife knew that you knew?"

"That doesn't follow, does it?"

Eoghan was recovering his self-possession. It was evident that he had no idea of the object of Barley's questions. Like his wife he had committed the mistake of underestimating his opponent's capacity; like her he was surely destined to pay for his error. Dr. Hailey reflected that the manner of a fool, when it covers the thought of a wise man, is an advantage of incalculable worth.

"I think it does follow," Barley said. "I formed the opinion, after seeing your wife, that she knew how bitterly your aunt disliked her. She was well aware that your aunt would not fail to report to you anything disadvantageous to herself."

"What are you driving at? What does it matter whether or not my wife knew that my aunt had reported the incident?"

"If she knew, her confession to you was made only because she was compelled to make it."

"Well?"

Barley leaned forward.

"Your wife desired to patch up her quarrel with you. She was in a weak position. She adopted the usual method of women in such circumstances. She attacked you because you had not provided her with a home of her own. At the same time she confessed openly what could not, in any case, be hidden. But there was one piece of information, the one essential piece of information, which she did not give."

Silence fell in the room. Eoghan tried to look indifferent but his face betrayed him. He made a small gesture with his right hand.

"I'm afraid," he declared, "that your speculations about my wife's ideas and motives possess very little interest for me."

"On the contrary."

"What do you mean?"

"The essential piece of information which your wife withheld from you was that, when she ran away from this house, it was with the intention of offering herself to Dr. McDonald. McDonald refused her."

Eoghan's cheeks had grown pale. His hands, which rested on the arms of the wooden chair where he was seated, began to twitch.

"Leave my wife out of the discussion," he ordered, in hoarse tones which betrayed the violence of his feelings.

"Impossible. I am very much afraid that it will soon be my duty to accuse your wife of aiding and abetting the murder of your aunt."

"What!" Eoghan jumped up from his chair.

"Of aiding and abetting Dr. McDonald of Ardmore."

A single stride brought the young man to the detective. He seized Barley by the shoulders and fixed his eyes on his face.

"I swear to you that you're wholly mistaken," he cried. "Oonagh had nothing whatever to do with my aunt's death. Do you hear?"

"Have the goodness to unhand me, sir."

"Not until you swear that you'll drop that grotesque accusation."

Barley took a step back, leaving the young man standing alone.

"Sit down," he ordered in tones which revealed a side of his character hitherto undisclosed. His eyes flashed with anger. But Eoghan did not obey.

"I wish you to know," he said, "that it was I who killed my aunt. I'm prepared to give you an account of the murder."

Chapter XX

Eoghan Explains

Eoghan's tones were so steady, his manner so insolent in its calmness, that even Barley was shaken. He recoiled, and then, collecting himself, sat down and assumed his most judicial attitude.

"Do I understand," he asked, "that you are accusing yourself of the murder of Miss Gregor?"

Eoghan's face had become paler; but he kept so excellent a self-control that this was scarcely noticeable. He bore, Dr. Hailey thought, a remarkable likeness to his father; the harshness of Duchlan's face, however, was softened by a quality which derived no doubt from his Irish mother. The young man looked like an eighteenth century nobleman a little the worse for wear, but with his pride untarnished. His rather girlish cheeks and mouth accentuated, if anything, the firmness of his expression and the cold resolution in his eyes.

"Let me remark at once," Barley declared, "that you made this confession when you heard that I suspected your wife. *Post hoc ergo propter hoc*, may not be good logic in every instance; but the temptation so to regard it in this case is very great." He waved his hand in a gesture of dismissal. "I do not believe that you murdered Miss Gregor."

"No?"

"No, sir."

"Do you expect me to supply you with proofs?"

"Yes, since only the strongest possible proof is going to convince me."

"My aunt has left me all her money. And I need money very badly."

"What does that prove?"

"That her death came most opportunely. Not a minute too soon, believe me."

"Why do you say that?"

"Because it's true. My father, as it happens, has no money. I could not have borrowed from him. And the debts I must meet immediately run into thousands—many thousands."

"Surely you could have borrowed the money from your aunt?"

"Oh! no. My aunt looked on gambling as a deadly sin."

"My dear sir, people's opinions are necessarily conditioned by circumstances."

"Not my aunt's opinions."

"Everybody's opinions. It was Napoleon who said that men are always and everywhere the same."

"Napoleon didn't know my aunt."

Not a flicker of a smile accompanied this statement. Barley gasped, biting at the air in the manner peculiar to him.

"May I say," he remarked, "that, in my humble opinion, the occasion is unsuitable, most unsuitable, for jesting." He leaned forward as judges sometimes lean from the Bench. "May I ask how you entered your aunt's room?" he demanded.

"By the door."

"I have reason to believe the door was locked."

"What reason?"

"Your wife stated that she heard Miss Gregor lock the door."

"Are you prepared to take her word on that point?"

Barley frowned. "Why not?"

"You haven't taken her word on any other point, have you?"

Eoghan raised his eyebrows as he asked this question. The effect on Barley was all that he could have wished. The man scowled and then flushed angrily.

"I must beg leave," he cried, "to accept or reject according to my instinct and experience."

"That means, doesn't it, according to your theory of the crime?"

"It does not. I have no *a priori* theory. I look for facts and am guided by what I find."

"I can only repeat that I entered the bedroom by the door."

"How did you leave the bedroom?"

Eoghan flicked a speck of dust from the sleeve of his shooting coat.

"By the door."

"What!"

"It's obvious, isn't it, that I didn't leave by the window?"

"The door was locked on the inside," Barley stated.

"How do you know?"

Dr. Hailey saw Barley start; but the fellow had excellent nerves.

"There are five witnesses to prove that: Angus, the carpenter who cut away the lock, Dr. McDonald, the maid who took up your aunt's tea, and yourself."

"On the contrary there are no witnesses at all. The door was held shut by a small wedge which I placed under it. The maid naturally thought it was locked; she's young and unsuspecting. When she called me I confirmed that. Angus never tried the door at all. He's old and believes what I tell him. Why should the carpenter disbelieve when I sent for him to cut the lock away? Why should McDonald disbelieve? After the lock was cut out I pulled out my wedge. Then I found an opportunity to turn the key in the lock."

He shrugged his shoulders slightly as he finished his account.

"With what weapon did you kill your aunt?" Barley demanded in husky tones.

"The wood-axe from the kitchen."

Eoghan raised his eyelids and gazed at the detective. "I got it when I took some herring I had bought down to the larder."

The shot told. It was evident to Dr. Hailey that Barley had been keeping the matter of the herring scales up his sleeve for use as a final argument. He threw up his head like an angry horse.

"Were these the methods adopted by you," he demanded in tones of bitter sarcasm, "when you killed my colleague Dundas?"

"Not quite."

"What, you suggest you committed that crime also?"

"It's obvious, isn't it, that both crimes were committed by the same person?"

"You waste my time, sir. You did not kill Dundas." Barley rose and dismissed the young man with a gesture. But Eoghan did not seem inclined to go away. He took a small gold cigarette-case from his pocket.

"May I smoke?"

"I have no more questions to ask you."

He lit a cigarette.

"I think you may have more questions to ask me, however," he said, "when I point out to you that Dundas's bed was provided with a feather mattress and an eiderdown.

One of the Duchlan feather mattresses; one of the Duchlan eiderdowns."

There was a ring of triumph in his voice as he spoke. Dr. Hailey felt the blood rise to his own cheeks. Both McDonald and he had looked under the bed after the murder; neither of them had looked in it.

"What do you mean?"

"My aunt possessed the deepest, the most voluminous feather mattresses in a county which holds the world's record in that respect. Her eiderdowns, as you must have seen, are of equal merit. One can lie on such a mattress, under such an eiderdown, without causing so much as a ripple on the bed's surface, provided one has time to settle down and arrange oneself. And I had ample time."

A look of lively horror filled Barley's eyes. He gasped, but no longer solemnly; Dr. Hailey saw that his hands were wet.

"What happened? What did you do?" he cried in tones that showed how small a measure of self-control remained to him. Eoghan took his cigarette from between his lips and looked at the lighted end critically.

"Hit him on the back of the head with a lead sinker," he remarked coolly. "Did it as soon as Dr. Hailey left the room. Only one arm needed, and that was tucked nicely away under the eiderdown before Dr. McDonald got to the room. One got a bit cramped, of course. Still…"

He broke off and replaced the cigarette in his mouth. He added: "Dundas, unlike yourself, Mr. Barley, was on the right track."

He rose as he spoke. His cigarette-case, which he had omitted to return to his pocket, fell clattering to the floor. He stooped down to pick it up.

At the same instant Dr. Hailey sprang from his chair and hurled himself on the stooping figure.

Chapter XXI

Cheating the Gallows

The two men rolled together on the floor. Barley sprang to the help of his companion and between them they secured Eoghan. When that had been accomplished Dr. Hailey put his hand in the young man's pocket and took out a revolver.

"Fortunately," he stated, "I saw the bulge it made in his pocket."

Eoghan's face had become flushed and his collar and necktie were dragged out of place; but he did not appear to have lost his self-control.

"Now that you've got my pistol," he said, "you can leave me."

Barley, who was holding down his shoulders, shook his head.

"Certainly not, sir." He addressed himself to Dr. Hailey. "Search all his pockets, if you please. He may have other weapons hidden about his person."

Dr. Hailey was looking after the pistol. He put it down and passed his hands quickly over the young man's body. Then he signed to the detective. Eoghan was allowed to rise.

"You forget, perhaps," he said in unruffled tones, "that as an officer in the Army I'm entitled to carry a pistol."

"But not to use it," Barley exclaimed.

"How do you know that I was going to use it?"

"It's enough, sir, that we have no assurance that you were not going to use it. Are you not a self-confessed assassin?"

The young man shrugged his shoulders. He rearranged his collar.

"What I can never understand about the police," he remarked, "is the tender care with which they surround people whom they know they will have to hang very soon. Why prevent a poor devil from doing himself in, if he has the courage?"

Nobody answered him. He strode to Barley and stood facing him.

"May I ask that you will not tell my wife anything about what I have told you," he requested, "until my arrest has taken place?"

"Why not?"

"Good gracious, man, surely it's better to save people unnecessary suffering! If she knows I'm likely to be arrested she'll move heaven and earth to save me. And she can't save me."

Barley shook his head.

"I make it a rule," he declared, "never to make promises which I may not be able to keep. The chances are that it will not be necessary to tell your wife, but it's too early yet to be sure."

Eoghan shook his head.

"If you people would only adopt the decent and merciful methods of the Army," he exclaimed, "what a lot of distress would be saved."

Nobody answered him. He turned to Dr. Hailey.

"You know that Oonagh suspects that I killed Aunt Mary," he challenged.

"I think she did suspect you."

"Take it from me her feelings haven't changed. She knows about my debts. There was only one way of paying these debts, and not to be able to pay them meant expulsion from the Army."

He broke off and lit another cigarette. Then he added:

"Tell Mr. Barley about Oonagh. It will help him to understand her character and her relations with me."

There was a note of pride in his voice which was unmistakable. He turned to Barley.

"Do you want me here any longer?" he asked.

Barley had returned to the fireside. He looked uneasy and doubtful about his duty.

"Technically you've given yourself up," he stated. "But it remains to be decided whether or not I accept your story. I have not yet accepted it. Far from it. You must remain in the castle till my decision shall have been taken." His manner had become dictatorial; but his mouth was as full as ever of phrases. He waved his hand; Eoghan walked out of the room.

"Do you really suppose, my dear doctor, that he meant to shoot himself?"

"Yes."

Barley took the pistol and opened it.

"It's loaded, anyhow." He emptied it and put the cartridges in his pocket. "It's just possible, I suppose, that he may have murdered his aunt and Dundas. Believe me, your apparently impossible crime always admits of several different explanations. On the other hand the law, as you know, holds confessions suspect. Murderers, cold-blooded murderers at any rate, are not prone to confess their crimes."

"No."

Dr. Hailey considered a moment, and then told Barley about Oonagh's attempt to drown herself and her husband's subsequent visit to Darroch Mor.

"I have no doubt," he added, "that Duchlan knew what was afoot. I don't think Eoghan Gregor knew."

"But this is tremendously important, my dear sir." Barley began to walk up and down the room. "If Duchlan knew, and I share your view that he must have known, then it follows that he had counselled this tragic act. Why should he do that?" A gesture executed with both hands consigned the house of Gregor to bottomless deeps. "Manifestly, because he knew that his daughter-in-law was guilty of playing a part in the murder of his sister. That knowledge, in my humble opinion, would exert on the old man an influence tending to awaken all his most inhuman qualities. He's as proud as Lucifer. He's as cold-blooded as a fish. If the girl was guilty let her drown. Better that than a trial and a public condemnation. Anything to save the sacred name of Gregor!"

Dr. Hailey nodded.

"I reached more or less the same conclusion. Eoghan also gave me the impression of suspecting his wife. I must add, though, that his wife seemed to suspect him. I believe myself that her attempt to drown herself was prompted by the determination to shield him."

"In view of her relations with Dr. McDonald, I confess that that question scarcely interests me. Women do not shield with their lives husbands whom they have already discarded. On the other hand, if Duchlan knew that she was accessory to his sister's murder, her fate was sealed. With his son's name at stake that old man would not spare her; from his point of view she was better drowned than hanged."

He clapped his hands. "I shall question the old man. I had meant to send for Dr. McDonald, but Duchlan shall come first. Now I understand why he nearly fainted when I said that McDonald was the only man who could have murdered Dundas."

That idea formed the basis of the first questions which Barley addressed to Duchlan. The old man looked pale and more wasted than usual but his eyes had not lost their quickness. He seated himself like a king about to give an audience and disposed his hands on the arms of his chair according to his habit. His head kept moving backwards and forwards. The detective showed him a deference which he had not accorded to any earlier witnesses.

"My investigations," he explained, "have made it necessary that I should inquire closely into the behaviour of your daughter-in-law both before and after the death of your sister." He paused. When he spoke again his voice had assumed a grave tone. "I have reason to believe that you were a witness of certain incidents which you have not, so far, seen fit to mention to the police."

"For example?"

"Mrs. Eoghan Gregor was in the habit of meeting Dr. McDonald at night on the shore."

Duchlan closed his eyes. The wrinkles in his face deepened as his muscles contracted. He looked like a mummy recalled suddenly to affliction.

"You are aware that your daughter-in-law met Dr. McDonald in this way?"

"Yes."

"You were the witness of one, or more, of these meetings?"

"Yes."

"Was Miss Gregor with you on these occasions?"

"Yes."

Barley leaned forward.

"Was your presence observed by your daughter-in-law and the doctor?"

The old man bowed his head.

"Yes."

"That was the reason why Mrs. Eoghan retired to her bedroom at such an early hour on the day before your sister was murdered?"

"My sister felt it to be her duty to warn my son's wife. Unfortunately her kindness was misunderstood and resented."

Duchlan spoke in low tones, but his voice was perfectly clear. It was obvious that he suffered greatly in being forced to recall the incident. But Barley was inexorable.

"I'm afraid," he stated, "that I must ask for details. For instance, did Miss Gregor utter any threat?"

"She said that, as Eoghan's nearest relation, she must tell him about what was going on."

"Ah."

"As a matter of fact she had already written to Eoghan, hinting that things were not in a satisfactory state. She took that action, believe me, after long and most anxious consideration and after very many attempts to recall my daughter-in-law from the dangerous course on which she was embarking."

"I see." Barley closed his eyes and nodded gravely. "*Facilis est decensus Averni, sed revocare gradum,*" he quoted insolently.

The rest of the quotation was lost in his moustache. Duchlan sighed.

"We had both done all that lay in our power to preserve Oonagh from disaster," he said. "The time for warning had evidently gone by, though in my weakness, as I now recognize, I was prepared to accord one further chance."

"You were against telling your son?"

"Perhaps I feared to tell him." The old man glanced up rather timidly. "My son is quick-tempered. And he is devotedly attached to his wife."

"Miss Gregor over-ruled your fear?"

"She anticipated it. I was not aware that she had written to Eoghan. When I heard that she had done so I recognized the wisdom of her action."

Dr. Hailey had been leaning back in his chair. He intervened to ask:

"When Miss Gregor wrote to your son did she know about the meetings with Dr. McDonald at night?"

"No. In point of fact neither she nor I knew about these meetings until the night before she met her death. What we did know was that my son's wife was in constant communication with the doctor."

"So the question on the fatal day," Barley exclaimed, "was whether or not a definite accusation was to be made as soon as your son returned?"

"Yes."

"And whereas you favoured mercy, your sister was determined to punish?"

"Please don't express my dear sister's attitude in that way," Duchlan pleaded. "Goodness and mercy abounded in her heart. Her one, her only concern, believe me, was the welfare of this misguided and rebellious girl. She felt, I think, that her own influence was exhausted; Oonagh had defied her and made cruel and untrue accusations against her. My dear Mary wished that the strength of the husband might be made available to rescue the wife. Naturally her thought and care went out, too, to Eoghan, for she had been more than mother to him, and to Eoghan's child, exposed meanwhile to these lamentable influences."

Barley shook his head.

"No mother, in my humble judgement," he declared, "can endure the thought that her child is to be taken away from her."

"You misunderstand, sir. My dear sister's plan was not to remove Hamish from his mother's custody, but to place his mother under some measure of restraint. She felt that if Oonagh could be influenced by herself, the girl's good qualities of courage and cheerfulness might be developed in such a way as to effect a change of character."

Barley shrugged his shoulders and spread out his hands. Then his business-like manner reasserted itself.

"Did your daughter-in-law complain to you or your sister," he asked, "that her husband had failed to provide her with a home of her own?"

"She did, yes. She made many bitter and unjust complaints against Eoghan. These, as you can imagine, were very difficult to bear and it needed all my dear sister's self-restraint and kindness of heart to bear them. We pointed out to her that she was fortunate in possessing a good and kind husband whose sole desire it was to make her happy and to make provision for her boy. The pay of an Army officer is small. Eoghan's resources were slender and had it not been that his aunt and I, but especially his aunt, gave him some financial help…"

Barley interrupted with a sudden gesture.

"So," he exclaimed, "your son and his wife were dependent to some extent on your sister's bounty?"

"To a very great extent. The pay of a Captain in the gunners approximates to £1 a day. Eoghan's personal expenses absorb all that. My daughter-in-law has been living here at the expense of myself and of my dear sister." Duchlan paused and raised his eyes. "Not that we have ever begrudged her anything for her good."

"You made your son no regular allowance?"

The old man raised his hand and moved it in a circle which indicated and presented his estate.

"How could I? You've seen these heather hills. What is there to yield an income? Believe me, it has been as much as I could do to make ends meet these many years. When Eoghan told me he was going to marry, I had to warn him that he must make provision for his wife out of his pay. Then my dear Mary came to his rescue. She possessed a considerable fortune of her own."

Barley's face expressed both doubt and some indignation.

"It appears to me," he said, "that your late sister made a mistake in her manner of giving. Your daughter-in-law must have felt like a charity boarder in this house. Does she, tell me, possess any means of her own?"

"Oh, no. None."

"What did she do for pocket money, pin money, whatever it's called?"

"My dear sister allowed her to buy her clothing at certain shops…"

"What, do you mean to say she had *no* money that she could call her own?"

"I think Eoghan sent her such sums of money as he could spare."

"Her position was worse than that of your servants?"

Duchlan did not reply for a few minutes. Then he said:

"She had no expenses so long as she remained here with us."

"I see." Barley leaned forward suddenly. "Tell me please: At what period of her stay did your daughter-in-law begin to complain of her husband?"

"She has never seemed to be really satisfied. But these last weeks have been much more trying than any earlier period."

"Since she became friendly with McDonald?"

"Yes, I think so."

"It was during the last few weeks, was it, that she began to demand a home of her own?"

Duchlan inclined his head.

"After she ran away from this house," he stated in low tones. "That evening saw the crisis of her relations with my sister. She told my sister that she would never again be indebted to her for a crust of bread. She said she was going away to earn her own living by any means that offered, even if it meant going into domestic service."

"Did she talk in that way after she came back?"

Barley asked the question in tones which thrilled with excitement. He thrust his body forward as if he feared to miss a syllable of the reply.

"Not quite in that way. After she came back she expressed a determination to have a home of her own, with her husband and child."

There was a short period of silence. The cackle of a seagull fell unseasonably on their ears. Then Barley waved his hand.

"It boils down to this, I venture to think," he remarked, "namely, that Miss Gregor suspected your daughter-in law and was determined to expose her to her husband, doubtless from the highest motives. That, believe me, was likely to be a serious affair both for Mrs. Eoghan and for Dr. McDonald. As Mrs. Eoghan is not possessed of any private means, her position as a divorced wife, deprived of her child, must have been sufficiently melancholy. As for the doctor, he ran a great risk of being removed from the Medical Register and so completely ruined. It's obvious therefore that both the woman and the man had strong motives for wishing that your sister might be removed from their paths."

Duchlan did not reply. Even his fingers were still. The detective rose and struck his hands together.

"I suggest," he declared in tones that were menacing, "that it was these considerations which led you to suggest to your daughter-in-law, after the murder of your sister, that she had better take immediate steps to cheat the gallows?"

"What! You accuse me…"

"Pardon me, Duchlan, but the facts as I know them admit, in my humble opinion, of no other explanation. You believed that your daughter-in-law was party to the murder of your sister by Dr. McDonald. His fate did not concern you; hers did. She is your son's wife, the mother of your only grandson, of the heir to Duchlan. You knew very well that if she drowned herself there would be silence not only about her share in the crime but even about the manner of her death. There is no Coroner's Court in Scotland. Moreover, only you knew about her meetings with Dr. McDonald. So long as she lived there was the dreadful fear that these relations might continue and so be discovered. Her death promised safety for everybody, for you and your son and your son's son, for your house and your name."

The silence fell again and deepened so that the chiming of a clock in the hall outside was an intolerable burden. Duchlan's head began to nod like the head of one of those cunning ivory toys which react for long periods to the slightest touch.

"Your daughter-in-law," Barley added, "yielded to your compulsion. Acknowledgment, surely, of her guilt."

Chapter XXII

Torture

When Duchlan had gone away, Dr. Hailey gave the detective an account of his interview with Dr. McDonald.

"You can, of course, question him yourself if you wish," he added, "but I think that if you do, you will waste your time. He admitted quite frankly that he had fallen in love with Mrs. Eoghan; he denied and went on denying, that she has ever, in any degree, given him encouragement."

"Did he?" Barley's expression showed how much importance he attached to such a statement. "It's curious, if he's telling the truth, that Mrs. Eoghan should have tried to drown herself; indeed, that these murders were committed at all. Innocent people never commit crimes to escape from unjust accusations."

"I agree. But innocent people sometimes sacrifice themselves to preserve those they love."

"Why should Mrs. Eoghan have thought that her husband had killed his aunt?"

"I feel sure she did think so."

"Yes, but why, why?"

"If one loves one fears. There was a strong motive, remember."

Barley frowned.

"That's saying that she believed her husband capable of murder."

He stared at Dr. Hailey as he spoke. When the doctor shook his head he frowned again.

"It may mean that, of course. But does it necessarily mean that? Knowing that a strong motive exists one may be seized by a dreadful fear, a fear that does not shape itself in words, scarcely even in thoughts; that is a feeling rather than an idea. And one may act on that feeling…"

"Still, the basis of the idea is murder."

"No, I think the basis of the idea is sympathy, the knowledge of human nature which we all derive from the fact of our own humanity. Is there a single crime that you or I might not commit in certain circumstances? You remember: 'But for the grace of God there goes John Bunyan.' I feel sure that only very stupid or very vain people are so entirely sure of themselves as to believe themselves immune from temptation. Saints and sinners have more in common than is usually supposed."

Barley leaned back in his chair. His face assumed a gracious expression.

"Your method, believe me," he declared, "is rich in attraction for me. If I could believe that Mrs. Eoghan cared for her husband, I might even be persuaded. But what are the facts?" He shook his head. "Can you doubt, speaking as man to man, that she cared for McDonald? Does a woman run away at night to a man in whom she is not specially interested? Does she meet that man in secret? Women, believe me, are not easily got rid of when their affections are engaged. But she was shrewd. If she couldn't have the doctor, she did not mean to lose her husband. Remember that Miss Gregor's death served the purposes of three different people: It rescued Dr. McDonald, it saved Eoghan Gregor, and it gave back her husband and child to the woman."

"Even so, McDonald struck me as being an honest man."

Barley did not reply. He had made up his mind to question Dr. McDonald and was not the man to be turned from such a resolution.

Assuming his singular dust-coat, which made him look like a chess-board, he drove to Ardmore with Dr. Hailey during the afternoon. They found the doctor at home. He took them to a small room at the back of the house, which smelt faintly of iodoform. The room contained a number of glass cases full of instruments and numerous jars in which lints and gauzes were stored. Though the cleanliness and order of this surgery were beyond reproach, it had a desolate aspect. The spirit somehow was lacking.

Dr. McDonald opened a drawer in the desk which occupied the end of the room and took out a box of cigars.

"You'll smoke, Inspector?"

"No, thank you." Barley sat down on a leather-covered couch and crossed his legs. He got to business immediately, explaining that the questions he was about to ask were likely to tax both memory and observation.

"Let us go back, in the first place, to the night of the murder of Miss Gregor. You were, I understand, summoned on that night to see Mrs. Eoghan Gregor's little boy?"

"Yes, I was."

"About what time?"

"About half-past nine."

"Did Mrs. Eoghan Gregor receive you?"

"She was in the nursery. The child had had another of his hysterical attacks and was rather weak. I…"

"Excuse me interrupting you, but how was Mrs. Eoghan Gregor dressed?"

"She wore a blue dressing-gown."

"Was the maid, Christina, in the nursery?"

"Yes. But as soon as I arrived she went away to attend to Miss Gregor. She came back before I left."

"So that you and Mrs. Eoghan Gregor were alone?"

"With the child, yes."

"Did Mrs. Eoghan seem to be unduly excited?"

McDonald raised his head sharply. A look of anxiety appeared on his face.

"She was distressed about the child."

Barley thrust out his hands.

"I shall be frank with you," he declared. "Duchlan has just told me that Mrs. Eoghan and her aunt quarrelled violently during the evening, for which reason Mrs. Eoghan retired early to bed. What I want to know is whether or not Mrs. Eoghan discussed this quarrel with you."

"She told me that she was upset with the attitude her aunt was adopting towards her."

"Did she tell you that her aunt accused her of being in love with yourself?"

Barley's voice rang out. But the impression he produced was less than he seemed to expect. McDonald nodded.

"She told me that, yes."

"That Miss Gregor was determined to impart all her suspicions to her nephew on his return?"

"Yes."

The detective thrust his head forward:

"That meant ruin both for Mrs. Eoghan and yourself?" he demanded.

"Possibly, if Eoghan Gregor believed his aunt."

"Have you any reason to suppose that he would not have believed her?"

McDonald wiped his brow.

"Eoghan Gregor," he said in quiet tones, "is in love with his wife, and she is in love with him."

"Nevertheless his wife was meeting you each evening after dark?"

"Did Duchlan tell you that too?"

"He did."

"It's not true. We met on one or two occasions only, because Mrs. Eoghan wished to ask my advice." Suddenly McDonald's voice rang out: "You can have no idea of the torture inflicted on that poor girl by her father-in-law and her aunt."

"Torture! Torture!" Barley exclaimed in tones which rebuked such extravagance of language.

McDonald rose and began to stump about the room. His powerful body seemed too big for its narrow limits. Dr. Hailey was reminded of a young tiger he had seen pacing its cage at the Zoo.

"Yes, torture," he cried. "That's the only word that applies. You didn't know Miss Gregor; I did. A woman without a flicker of compassion; devoured by jealousy and family pride. She had not married, I believe, because the idea of losing her name of Gregor of Duchlan was intolerable to her. It may seem a grotesque idea, but I am convinced that it was her instinct to be the mother as well as the daughter of her race. Fate, as it happened, had allowed her to realize that instinct in the case of Eoghan. Mrs. Eoghan, however, robbed her of its complete fulfilment. She dared to assert her wifehood and her motherhood. Eoghan loved her more than he loved his aunt. It was obvious that as soon as the slender thread of Duchlan's life was broken, Miss Gregor's reign at the castle would end for ever." McDonald paused and then added: "Unless, in the meanwhile, husband and wife could be estranged from one another and separated permanently. In that case Hamish would fall into his aunt's hands just as his father had done before him. Miss Gregor would remain the mistress of Duchlan."

He turned as he spoke and faced his accuser. Barley was too good a student of human nature not to be impressed, but he was also a practical man, well able to judge of the motives underlying any process of reasoning.

"You are telling me, remember," he warned, "that neither you nor Mrs. Eoghan could expect any mercy from Miss Gregor. That is exactly what I believe myself."

"What does that prove?"

"It supplies a strong motive for the crime which, as I believe, you committed between you."

The doctor started.

"What? You think I murdered Miss Gregor?"

"With the help of Mrs. Eoghan."

McDonald's face darkened. He wiped his brow again. Dr. Hailey saw him glance out of the window as though an impulse to escape had come to him. Then he began to laugh.

"You must be crazy. Crazy! How do you suppose I got into the woman's bedroom?"

He wiped his brow again. He sat down and disposed his leg with the most attentive care.

"By the door."

"What? Do you mean to say you don't know that the door was locked?"

"Eoghan Gregor says it was not locked."

The doctor stared. He repeated in tones of bewilderment:

"Eoghan says it was not locked? Why I saw the carpenter cut out the lock."

"Did you try the handle?"

"No."

"So your knowledge is at second-hand."

"The carpenter tried the handle."

"He told you that?"

"Good gracious, no, I saw him do it. He tried it several times."

Barley blinked his eyes. "That, however, was in the morning. What I am suggesting is that the door was unlocked when you left the nursery at the end of your visit on the night before?"

"It was locked then too. Mrs. Eoghan heard her aunt lock it."

"Forgive me, Mrs. Eoghan's evidence is of no value on that point."

McDonald laughed again. "I see. It's a case of heads I win, tails you lose, is it?"

"My dear sir, Miss Gregor was murdered. Somebody, therefore, entered the room and escaped from it. And human beings do not pass through doors and windows. It's easier, in my humble opinion, to assume that Mrs. Eoghan and yourself have given an untrue account of your doings than to believe that the laws of nature have been set aside."

"How do you suggest that I killed the old woman? With my wooden leg?"

"No, sir. I believe that Mrs. Eoghan brought an axe from the kitchen. The servants had gone to bed."

"I see." The doctor drew a deep breath. "And the herring scale that was found in the wound, where did that come from?"

"Possibly from the blade of the axe."

"You have still to explain how the door locked itself on the inside, haven't you?"

"I believe I can explain that too."

Barley had recovered his suavity; like a huntsman whose quarry has turned at bay, he seemed to be making ready to deal a final blow.

"I shall be surprised," he declared, "if positive proof is not soon forthcoming that you did murder Miss Gregor.

Very greatly surprised! I go farther than that. I know where to look for that proof and I know that, when I do look for it, I shall find it."

He spoke with complete conviction.

Dr. Hailey experienced a sense of bewilderment, which, he saw, was shared, fully, by McDonald. How could it be proved that the doctor had entered the bedroom? Or that he had escaped from it again without passing through the door?

"There's one further point," Barley said, "on which I am seeking enlightenment. Do you remember who was the first to enter Miss Gregor's room after the lock had been cut from the door?"

"I was."

"Were the blinds in the room drawn?"

"Yes."

"Did you open them?"

"Yes."

"Very well. Now tell me, was the amputation which made it necessary for you to wear a wooden leg a high or a low amputation?"

"A high amputation."

"So that you walk with difficulty?"

"Oh, no."

"I mean you're always in some danger of slipping or falling?"

McDonald shook his head. He raised his wooden leg from the floor, using both hands in the work.

"As you see," he remarked, "I wear a special shoe in this foot. These nails in the sole are guaranteed to grip anything."

On the way back to the castle, Barley asked Dr. Hailey if he had noticed that no mention of the murder of Dundas had been made by McDonald.

"Every moment I expected to hear him advance that second murder as proof of his innocence."

"Why?"

"Because guilty people always overstate their cases."

"I see. Does that mean that you harbour some doubts about his guilt?"

"Not doubts exactly. I believe my case is good; good enough to secure a unanimous verdict from any jury. But it's a case in logic rather than in personal conviction. Frankly, McDonald doesn't seem to me to fill the part assigned to him."

"I agree with you."

"And the same applies to Mrs. Eoghan?"

"Yes."

"And yet the choice undoubtedly lies between them and Eoghan Gregor. And we know now that Eoghan Gregor lied to us."

"About the locked door?"

"Exactly. The carpenter did try the door." Barley lay back on the cushions and combed his moustache. "I left a message that he was to be called to the castle. We shall hear his own story."

"You didn't ask any questions, I noticed," Dr. Hailey said, "about Mrs. Eoghan's flight to McDonald's house?"

"No. He would have told me what he told you. Frankly, since I've seen him, I feel less sure about the circumstances of that flight. I begin to think that he is in love with her. In that case it's certain that he didn't reject her."

"And therefore unlikely that she offered herself."

Barley shook his head in his most emphatic manner.

"No, no; that doesn't follow. Women in love seldom or never count the cost, and therefore act as a rule with extreme rashness. But it's quite another matter with men in love. A man, happily, never loses his social sense, no, not even when he seems to be ready to abandon himself. The ages have branded it upon the male mind that work that is service must have first place. McDonald, I believe, suggested the secret meetings which afterwards took place. But he sent Mrs. Eoghan home that night. He was not ready to immolate his professional being."

Chapter XXIII

Footprints

The carpenter awaited them. He was a tall lean man with big features and clear, bright eyes. He made short work of the idea that the door had not been locked when he opened it.

"It was locked," he declared. "I tried the handle mysel'. What is more I tried to force the lock. But that's not possible with these doors. I dare say that you knew that Duchlan's father was a locksmith."

Barley nodded. "You're prepared to swear, are you," he asked, "that the key had been turned on the inside?"

"I am."

The detective dismissed the man and told Angus to bring a pair of bellows from the kitchen. Then he invited Dr. Hailey to accompany him.

"I promised you positive proof of McDonald's guilt," he said. "And will now furnish it. I warn you to be prepared for a surprise. As you've just heard, Eoghan Gregor's story is a fabrication."

They left the house and walked to the flower-bed which lay under the window of Miss Gregor's bedroom. The detective took the bellows from the piper.

"Observe," he said, "that Miss Gregor's room is immediately above the study. Also that the earth in this bed is quite dry. Mr. McLeod, the Procurator Fiscal, examined the bed on the morning after the murder and found it undisturbed." He turned to Angus: "Am I right?"

"Yes, sir. I was with Mr. McLeod, sir, when he examined the ground. It looked exactly as it looks at this moment."

"Very well."

Barley applied the snout of the bellows to the surface of the earth and began to blow gently. As he blew dust was driven away in semi-circles, leaving a more or less even surface. He continued to work for a few minutes and then stood erect. There was a puzzled look on his face.

"Well?" Dr. Hailey asked.

"You see, there's nothing. Frankly I don't understand it." He glanced up at Miss Gregor's window. An exclamation broke from his lips. He pointed to an iron spike sticking out from the wall just above the window.

"What's that?" he demanded of Angus.

"It was put there long ago to carry a sun-blind, sir. But Miss Gregor did not like the blind."

"You could reach it from the window-sill?"

"Yes, sir."

The detective measured the distance from the spike to the ground with his eye. Then he stepped on to the border and applied his bellows to a spot immediately under the spike. A few vigorous strokes of the bellows revealed a footprint under the loose dust of the surface. A moment later a second footprint, on which the marks of heavy nails were clearly visible, was disclosed. Barley stood back and pointed to these signs.

"You see. Footprints, one of which is studded with nails."

A gleam of triumph shone in his eyes. He turned to Dr. Hailey.

"You saw McDonald's shoe," he exclaimed. "Do you doubt that this print was made by it?"

"No. There's no doubt that it was made by it."

"Notice: right under the spike. He had a piece of rope apparently. He must have dropped only a short distance because these footprints are not deep. I feel sure that, as soon as he landed, he climbed into the window of the smoke-room; there are no other footprints. No doubt she was waiting for him there, ready to throw a few handfuls of loose earth on his tracks."

Dr. Hailey nodded: "It must be so, of course," he said. "I congratulate you."

They returned to the house and mounted to Miss Gregor's room. Barley climbed out on the window-sill and satisfied himself that the spike was within reach.

"We may as well complete our job," he declared, "by inspecting the spike from above. The iron is rusty and it's long odds that the rope he used has left some trace of its presence."

This expectation was confirmed. Looking down from the window of the little pantry, which served the nursery on the top floor, Dr. Hailey had an excellent view of the upper surface of the iron spike. The thick rust on the surface had been broken away at one place and the metal was visible.

"Are you satisfied, now, that a rope was used?" Barley asked.

"Yes."

"That must be the explanation, because, as you see, nobody can possibly have reached the spike from above, the drop is too great. Nobody reached it from below because there are no signs of the use of a ladder. It was reached therefore from the window-sill, which as I've just proved, is easy."

Barley leant against the dresser, which occupied one side of the room, and on which were standing jugs of milk and dishes of various kinds.

"What I think happened was this," he said. "When Mrs. Eoghan realized that her aunt was determined on her ruin and the ruin of her lover, her first idea, as you know, was to run away. But neither she nor McDonald has any money. He saw the folly of that course. Did he not exert himself to get the girl home again when she escaped to his house? From what you told me about that incident, I think it's a just inference that he had become thoroughly alarmed by her violence and by the reactions to her violence in this house. He was specially afraid of Miss Gregor, whose character he knew only too well. But to get rid of a headstrong woman with whom one has become compromised is no easy task. *Facilis est decensus Averni, sed revocare gradum, hic labor, hoc opus est!*"

The quotation broke gorgeously from his lips. He swept the air with his hands, making the plates behind him rattle.

"Mrs. Eoghan could summon him whenever she wished, because of her child. She compelled him in addition—and perhaps he needed no compulsion—to visit her unofficially in his boat. He learned that matters were going from bad to worse here. Then came discovery, and the immediate prospect, almost the certainty, of ruin. Duchlan might perhaps be induced to forgive and forget, but not so Miss Gregor.

"And so the murder was planned. The exact nature of these plans can only be guessed at; I admit that gaps still exist in our knowledge. But the outline is clear. After the doctor's arrival on the night of the murder, Mrs. Eoghan went to her aunt's room and told her that she was much alarmed about her child. That prepared the way for Dr. McDonald's coming to the bedroom. When he came, Mrs. Eoghan went downstairs to the study. The doctor must then have struck his blow. As you know it was a blow of terrific violence which, nevertheless, was not mortal. But the old woman's heart failed. He locked the bedroom door on the inside, assured himself that she was dead, fixed his rope in a single loop over the spike and let himself down from the window, which he had closed behind him. The rope was not long enough to bring him to the ground. There was a short drop. As we saw, it only remained to climb into the smoke-room, coil up the rope, get rid of the weapon, and cover the footprints. McDonald then left the house by the front door. He knew that he would be sent for as soon as the crime was discovered. Things fell out so well, as you know, that he was actually afforded the opportunity next morning of bolting the window without being observed, thus placing a most formidable barrier between his pursuers and himself."

Barley spoke with a pride which, in the circumstances, was pardonable. His case was complete; there remained only the work of rounding it off.

"I hope," he added, "that you will criticize me without mercy."

Dr. Hailey shook his head.

"The only criticism I could make has been made already by yourself. The facts and the people seem to be ill-mated. On the other hand, so far as I can see, the people, in this case, must yield to the facts. There is no other possible explanation."

"No." Barley made the plates rattle again. "The murder of Dundas is incredible if Dr. McDonald did not commit it. Think of it; you were on guard, so to speak, at the door of his room; that young fisherman was watching the window. You're ready to swear that nobody entered by the door; he's ready to swear that nobody entered by the window. And we know that Eoghan Gregor's story is an invention."

"We presume that, at any rate."

"No, sir." Barley smiled suddenly. "You noticed perhaps that I left you on the way up to this room. I looked into Dundas's bedroom. The mattress in his bed is a hair mattress, a hard hair mattress at that. I presume that he must have asked that the feathers might be taken away. Eoghan was unaware of the change."

There was a knock at the door of the pantry. Christina entered and asked Dr. Hailey to come into the nursery for a moment.

"It's Hamish," she explained. "He looks queer again."

She led the way, but turned back to close the door of the nursery behind the doctor. He walked to the cot where the child was lying asleep and bent over him.

"What happened?" he asked.

"His face was twitching."

"I don't think there is anything to be alarmed at."

He listened to the child's breathing for a few minutes and then turned to the old woman who stood behind him plucking nervously at her apron.

"What he wants is sleep, rest."

Christina's eyes were troubled. She shook her head in a fashion that expressed melancholy and resentment.

"Where is the poor lamb to find rest in this house?" she asked in her rich tones. Suddenly she took a step forward; she raised a skinny hand.

"Will you tell me: is it true that the detective from Edinburgh will be suspecting Hamish's mother?"

"I…I don't think I can discuss that."

The old woman uttered a cry.

"Oh, it will be true then, if you will not tell me." She put her hand on his sleeve and raised her black eyes to his face. "She is not guilty," she declared in tones of deep conviction. "I know that she is not guilty."

Dr. Hailey frowned.

"How can you know that?"

"Mrs. Gregor would not hurt a fly."

He shook his head. He had no wish to argue the case

with this old woman and yet there was something in the passionate earnestness of her voice which challenged him.

"I hope you're right."

She continued to clutch his arm.

"I know what the man from Glasgow will be saying," she declared. "That it was Dr. McDonald who killed Miss Gregor, him being helped by Hamish's mother." She released him and stood back from him. "Will you please sit down? There is something that I must tell you."

He hesitated a moment and then did as she asked. She sat down opposite to him in a low chair that he guessed had been used for generations in the Duchlan nursery. Her face was dark and drawn and the muscles round her mouth were twitching.

"Did you see the scar of a wound on Miss Gregor's chest?" she asked him.

"Yes."

"I will tell you about it."

She pressed her hand to her brow and remained for a moment as if praying. Then she faced him.

"I came to Duchlan," she said, "the year that the laird was married. When Mr. Eoghan was born, his mother asked me to be his nurse. Many's the time I've sat on this chair and bathed him before the fire there. His mother used to sit where you are sitting now."

She covered her eyes again. An uneasy silence filled the room. Dr. Hailey found himself listening attentively to the soft breathing of the child.

"Well?" he asked.

"She was one of the angels; very beautiful too. The laird he was mad for her. I can hear his step on the stair now, coming up to sit beside her while I bathed Mr. Eoghan. Ah, he was a different man in those days from the man he is now, full of jokes and laughter. But Miss Gregor was the same always and he was afraid of her. Do you know she stayed in this house all the time that the laird was married?"

Again she paused. When her eyes were shut she looked like some very old bird moulting its last feathers.

"Miss Gregor had not a good word for her brother's wife. And she was clever and cunning to wound the poor lady. Every day she was making hints and finding faults. The food was not fresh; there was waste going on in the kitchen; the laird's clothes were not aired for him; Mr. Eoghan was not gaining weight. Everything. She did not complain to her sister-in-law; only to the laird. 'You must speak to her' was what she said always and he did not dare to disobey.

"The laird's wife was an Irishwoman and she had a quick temper. Because she loved her husband it was an affront to her the way Miss Gregor was carrying on. One day, after her husband had complained of her bad housekeeping, she ran to her sister-in-law and told her that she knew where these complaints were coming from. She was so angry that she did not care that I could hear her. 'Surely I am entitled to speak when I see my brother and his child neglected?' Miss Gregor said in her soft, gentle voice. 'You are not entitled to make trouble between me and my husband, nor to try to take my child away from me,' Mrs. Gregor said. I saw the blood come boiling up in her cheeks and her eyes. She cried out: 'Ever since I married, you have tried to steal my happiness from me. You are stealing my husband. Then you will try to steal my child. Other people may think you a good woman but I know what you are.' Miss Gregor smiled and said she forgave everything, as a Christian woman should. Then she went, her eyes red with crying, to her brother to tell him about his wife's temper."

Christina's toothless jaws snapped. Her eyes glowed.

"Oh, she was cunning. Have you seen a cat waiting for a mouse? The laird began to think that his wife was unjust to his sister. There were dreadful quarrels between them and Miss Gregor was waiting always to take his side. He did not come here any more when his wife was here, but he used to come with his sister. Mr. Eoghan was afraid of Miss Gregor, who was never no hand with children, but his father made him kiss her. Doctor, doctor, I knew that there was sorrow coming, and I could not do anything to help the poor young lady. Do you know I could see madness growing and growing in her face."

She bowed her head. When she spoke again her voice had fallen almost to a whisper.

"It was like that, too, with Hamish's mother, only Mr. Eoghan was away from her most of the time." She clasped her knees and began to sway backwards and forwards. "Hamish was afraid of Miss Gregor. The first time he took one of them turns was after she was here trying to give some medicine of her own. His mother she came to the room and took the poor laddie in her arms because he was screaming with fear."

She broke off suddenly and a look of anxiety came into her face.

"I mind the day Duchlan's lady did the same thing," she exclaimed. She remained silent for a few minutes and then added:

"The night Duchlan's lady was drowned, his sister was taken ill."

Chapter XXIV

By the Window

Dr. Hailey's face expressed the horror which this information caused him.

"Drowned!"

"Yes. In the burn there, at the high tide."

"What was the nature of Miss Gregor's illness?"

"I do not know. The doctor, Dr. McMillan, brought bandages with him every day when he came to see her. I saw the bandages myself in his bag."

Her voice faded away.

"What explanation did the laird give?" Dr. Hailey asked.

"He did not give any explanation. The Procurator Fiscal from Campbeltown, not Mr. McLeod, but the gentleman who was Procurator Fiscal before him, came here once or twice. When Miss Gregor was better she and the laird went away for a trip to England."

"I see." He shook his head. "Did he, the laird I mean, seem…Did you think he was distressed at his wife's death?"

Christina sighed deeply. "Maybees he was; maybees not. I could not say."

"Did he come to the nursery much?"

"No, he did not. But Miss Gregor she came every day. Mr. Eoghan was hers and she would have it that he would call her 'Mother'. When he was older Miss Gregor told him that his mother had died from a cold."

Dr. Hailey rose.

"Do you remember what kind of a dressing-gown your poor mistress used to wear?" he asked suddenly.

"Always a blue dressing-gown like the one Hamish's mother wears. They was wonderful like each other, Mr. Eoghan's mother and his wife." She rose also. "Will you tell me," she pleaded, "why they are blaming Hamish's mother now?"

He started slightly. Had she not been giving him the very information which was lacking to Barley's case? He was about to refuse her request when an impulse to reward confidence with confidence made him change his mind.

"Only Dr. McDonald can have committed these murders," he said. "He and Mrs. Gregor are friends."

"Why do you say: 'Only Dr. McDonald can have committed these murders?'"

Again he hesitated. But her distress overcame his reluctance. He gave her an outline of the case.

"I don't think that Dr. McDonald went into the bedroom," she declared.

"If you could prove that! Unhappily I saw him myself going into Mr. Dundas's room."

"They are going to arrest Hamish's mother?"

Dr. Hailey shook his head sadly.

"I suppose so."

"No, no. They must not. Hamish's mother did not do it. She did not. I am sure."

The child began to cry. Dr. Hailey watched him awaken and then descended to the ground floor. The heat wave continued and the afternoon was heavy with distant thunder. He left the castle and walked towards Darroch Mor. The woods, he thought, looked like a gipsy child he had seen once winding red leaves about her limbs. He came to an open space where was a view of the loch and the great mountains beyond Inverairy. The turf, set with thyme on which heavy bees lingered, invited to rest. He sat down and took out his snuff-box. The bees on the thyme made music for him till he fell asleep.

A woman's voice awakened him. He sat up and saw Oonagh. He jumped to his feet.

"I'm afraid I was sleeping."

She nodded.

"Yes. It was unkind of me to wake you."

She looked weary and anxious but he noticed how well dressed she was. Less observant eyes than his might have failed to recognize, in the simplicity of her frock, and in the way she wore her clothes, an attitude of mind and spirit denied to the vulgar. Most women in this crisis of fate would have relaxed their self-discipline.

"I want you to help me if you will," she said. "That I need help very badly must be my excuse for waking you. I've seen Dr. McDonald and heard about your visit to him this morning."

She broke off as if she felt that she had explained herself with enough clearness. He stooped to pick up his snuff-box, which had fallen to the ground.

"You've been so wonderfully successful in other cases, haven't you?" She caught her breath. "If murder will out, so will innocence, don't you think?"

"Yes."

"Very well, I give you my word that Dr. McDonald did not murder my aunt. Now, how can we prove that he didn't?"

Her face had become animated and her beauty, in consequence, was enhanced. In spite of himself Dr. Hailey felt the influence of that potent magic.

"I don't know how we can prove that he didn't," he said.

"At any rate it's got to be tried, hasn't it?" She came to him and put her hand on his arm: "You will help me?"

"On one condition."

"Yes?"

"That you will tell me the whole truth from the beginning, and answer any questions I may ask you."

Oonagh nodded. "Yes, I promise." She seated herself on the grass, inviting him to do the same. Tall bracken, becoming yellow, framed her face.

"Where shall I begin?"

"I want, first of all, to know about your relations with your aunt."

She frowned.

"We were rivals I suppose."

"Rivals?"

"I am Eoghan's wife and Hamish's mother. But I am not a Gregor as they are." She plucked a piece of thyme and gazed at it. "Perhaps I did not attach enough importance to that." Suddenly she raised her head and looked him in the face. "Being a Gregor, after all, was my aunt's chief interest in life. The Gregor family was her husband and children, all she had to live for."

"You would not say that, would you, if she was still alive?"

"Perhaps not. But if not, I'm sorry. I think now that there was something very sad, very lonely, in that woman's position. She was so bitterly hungry for the things I had, Eoghan's love, my child's love, perhaps even Duchlan's love. She wanted…" Oonagh broke off, her lips remained parted as if waiting the word she needed to explain her thought. "She wanted to have a hand in the future of the family. To belong to the future as women do who have children of their own. Because she couldn't bear children who would be members of her family, she wanted to steal the children other women had borne so that she could stamp her personality and ideas on their minds. Behind that too, I think, was the ordinary need of every woman for a child."

Again she broke off. Dr. Hailey nodded.

"I see."

"I feel that I'm being horribly cruel. It's like talking about a deformity."

"Deformed people, you know, have ways of their own of forgetting their afflictions."

"I suppose so."

"Family pride, I imagine, was Miss Gregor's way. I noticed that her bedroom was full of all sorts of rubbish that she had made at different times in her life."

"Yes, I often noticed that too. She was horrified once when I wanted to give an old coat of Hamish's to a child in the village. The coat disappeared and Christina told me that my aunt had burned it. Whereas she didn't mind in the least when I gave some of my own clothes to the child's mother. Duchlan's cast-off clothes were always put away in a wardrobe upstairs to be sent to a missionary in China."

"To be dedicated."

Oonagh raised her eyebrows sharply.

"Yes, that's exactly what she told me, and that was the Duchlan atmosphere."

She pulled the thyme to pieces and scattered the pieces. "After I realized what was happening I began to grow resentful. My nerves got jagged. One day I lost my temper and told my aunt that she was not to interfere with the way I was bringing up Hamish. She wept and became hysterical. Poor woman, I can hear her protesting that she had no wish to interfere in any way. But I was afraid of her. There was a look in her eyes. She told my father-in-law too that I had been cruel to her. After that the very air I breathed seemed to grudge itself. Every day things got worse. Dr. McDonald told you, didn't he, that I ran away?"

"Yes."

She shook her head. "Did he tell you why I ran away?"

"Yes."

"I suppose I ought not to have lost my temper as I did. I don't think it was for myself I was so angry; it seemed so horrible that they should suspect Dr. McDonald. I was upset too for Eoghan's sake and Hamish's sake."

She caught her breath sharply.

"Once I got out of the house I felt different. But I felt, too, that I couldn't go back again. It was like waking up out of a dreadful nightmare. In that house neither my husband nor my child belonged to me; it was only when I got away that I felt myself wife and mother again. I meant to go back to Ireland, to my people. I meant to write to Eoghan from there telling him that if he wanted me he must give me a home of my own…"

She broke off. Her voice, when she spoke again, was rather faint.

"It's not easy to be independent when you've got no money. The truth is that I was completely dependent on Miss Gregor. Eoghan hasn't enough to keep a wife and child in any kind of comfort."

"Did she make you an allowance?" Dr. Hailey asked. He watched her closely. It was just possible that Duchlan's account of the financial arrangements at the castle had been inaccurate.

"No. She had a system by which I could buy clothes at certain shops. She paid the bills. They were the kind of shops I wouldn't have gone to of my own accord. You know, good, old-fashioned places with no liking for modern ideas. It really meant that everything I got was regulated and controlled." She broke off and added:

"Very rarely Duchlan gave me a few pounds. But when he did, he always kept asking what I meant to buy with his money."

"Your husband gave you nothing?"

She raised her head sharply. Her eyes flashed.

"How could he? Eoghan really had no right to marry when he did. He wasn't in a position to keep a wife. He wasn't in a position to have a home of his own. He knew from the beginning that the girl he married would have to live with his people. To be just, though, I'm sure he had no idea what that meant. Men never understand what one woman can inflict on another woman."

"Did you talk in this way to Dr. McDonald?"

"Yes."

"What did he think?"

"He told me he felt sure that Eoghan loved me and that, in time, it would all come right."

"Did he say that on the night when you ran away from Duchlan?"

"Yes." She hesitated a moment and then added:

"Dr. McDonald begged me to return to Duchlan," she said. "He had persuaded me before Christina came."

Dr. Hailey nodded.

"How did the old people receive you when you returned to the castle?"

"Not very well. They were furious, but they tried to pretend that they were more hurt than angry. That didn't prevent them from spying on me next day."

Her cheeks flushed as she told how she had asked Dr. McDonald to meet her where they were not likely to be disturbed.

"I felt that if I was left entirely alone I might do something desperate. My nerves were in that condition. A friend with whom you can talk things over is the greatest blessing in such circumstances; besides, Dr. McDonald knows what life is like at Duchlan." She frowned and bit her lip.

"My aunt followed me from the house. When I returned, just before dinner, she came to my room and told me that she had seen us. Nothing happened then, but the next afternoon Duchlan spoke to me in her presence. My self-control broke. I told them that my mind was made up to leave Eoghan if he refused to take me away."

Her eyes more than her words revealed the extreme tension at which she had been living. She plucked at the thyme, scattering its small flowers about her.

"I didn't appear at dinner. But the evening post brought me a letter from Eoghan which changed everything. He told me plainly that he had lost a huge sum of money and was coming to Duchlan to try to borrow it from Aunt Mary. He said that, if he failed to borrow it, he would have to leave the Army in disgrace. The letter ended with an appeal to me to put my feelings on one side and help him, for the sake of Hamish." She looked up and faced the doctor: "That was why I went to Aunt Mary's room after Dr. McDonald had seen Hamish."

Dr. Hailey had been polishing his eyeglass. He put it to his eye.

"McDonald was still in the nursery when you went to Miss Gregor's room?" he asked.

"Yes. I left him there."

"When did you meet him again?"

"In the smoke-room. He had come downstairs. I told him that I had decided to make the best of things for Eoghan's sake. The window was open because of the heat. My aunt's room as you know is directly above. We heard her walk across her room to the windows and shut them."

"McDonald told me nothing of that."

Dr. Hailey's voice challenged. He saw the girl blush.

"He wouldn't, for my sake."

"Because you had been alone together in the smoke-room?"

"Yes. As a matter of fact just after we heard Aunt Mary close her windows we heard the engine of Eoghan's motor-boat. My father-in-law must have heard it too because, a minute later, we heard him coming downstairs. Dr. McDonald didn't wish to meet him. He climbed through the open window and went away round the house to his car. I put the light out and waited till my father-in-law had opened the front door…"

"What? McDonald climbed out through the window?" Dr. Hailey's eyeglass dropped.

"To avoid meeting my father-in-law. I had told him about the scene with my father-in-law before dinner. The door of the smoke-room was shut and the front door was locked. If he hadn't gone out by the window he would certainly have met my father-in-law."

"I see."

"It was really the only thing to do in the circumstances. I was glad he thought of it, because it was so important not to give my father-in-law any further cause of complaint against me."

"What did you do after that?"

"I went back to my room. Eoghan came to my room…"

She broke off. Tears she could not restrain, filled her eyes.

Chapter XXV

A Process of Elimination

"I think you must tell me," Dr. Hailey said in gentler tones, "exactly what happened between your husband and yourself."

Oonagh had recovered her self-possession but her busy fingers still plucked at the thyme.

"Eoghan told me about his loss," she said.

"Did he come straight to your bedroom?"

She gazed in front of her, at the brown sails of a pair of herring-boats which were lying becalmed far out in the loch.

"No."

"He went to Miss Gregor's room before he came to you?"

"Yes."

"He told you that he had been to her room?"

"Yes."

Her voice was scarcely audible. Dr. Hailey watched her for a moment and then asked:

"He told you that her bedroom door was locked?"

"Yes."

"And that, though he had knocked at the door, she had refused to open it?"

"He said she hadn't opened it."

"Nor answered him?"

"He said she hadn't answered him."

"Was she a light sleeper?"

"Very light."

"So he thought she hadn't answered him because she was angry with you?"

The girl drew a sharp breath.

"Yes."

"He was angry with you?"

"He was upset."

"Did you tell him that you had decided to apologize to your aunt?"

"Yes, I did."

"Well?"

"He was too upset to...to believe me. He...said I had ruined him..." She turned suddenly. "I had told Dr. McDonald about Eoghan's losses and he offered to lend me money. Eoghan was upset about that too..."

She broke off and covered her face with her hands.

"You mean that such an offer from such a quarter aroused your husband's suspicions?"

"My aunt had written to him."

"Telling him that you were in love with McDonald?"

"Hinting at it."

The doctor's eyes narrowed.

"The fact that he found Miss Gregor's door shut against him and the fact that you had received an offer of money from McDonald, taken together, convinced him that he had been correctly informed?"

"Yes, I think so."

"He accused you of being in love with McDonald?"

"Yes."

"And then?"

She raised her head; he saw that she was trembling.

"He was so dreadfully distressed."

"He didn't try to excuse himself for his gambling, then?"

"Oh, no."

Dr. Hailey hesitated.

"I kept my promise to you," he said, "about those bruises on your throat. I've mentioned them to nobody. But I think that, now, you must tell me how…"

"Please, no."

Oonagh's eyes quailed. She raised her hands suddenly, as if warding off an assailant.

"You promised complete frankness, remember."

"I can't tell you."

"That means that your husband inflicted…"

She covered her face with her hands.

"You mustn't ask me."

He frowned slightly but did not pursue the subject.

"Tell me," he asked, "didn't you think that it was strange that Miss Gregor had refused to answer your husband?"

"I thought it very strange."

"Almost incredible?"

"Yes. Aunt Mary loved Eoghan."

"Do you still think it strange?"

Oonagh started.

"What do you mean?"

"Do you still think it strange that your aunt refused to speak to your husband?"

She shook her head.

"No, not now."

"Why?"

"I think she was dead."

The words were spoken with evident distress. The doctor's face became anxious.

"If she was dead," he said, "then either Dr. McDonald or your husband had killed her?"

"Oh, no."

"Is it or is it not true that, when you heard of her death, you feared that your husband had killed her?"

She hung her head and did not reply.

"It is true?"

Suddenly she faced him.

"I can't answer directly," she said, "because my feelings weren't direct. It's as you said at Darroch Mor. If you ask me do I think Eoghan capable of murder, I say 'no'. But if you tell me murder has been committed, I become afraid. Suppose that in some terrible, unguarded moment…"

"Your husband has confessed that he murdered his aunt."

"What!"

Oonagh's eyes dilated. She put out her hands, as if to ward off some great danger. Her body began to sway as the colour ran out of her cheeks. Dr. Hailey put his arm round her shoulders.

"Let me say at once that I don't believe him," he assured her.

She tried to pull herself together and managed to regain her balance.

"Why don't you believe him?"

"Because, though it's just possible he may have got into Miss Gregor's bedroom, it's certain that he did not get out of it. The door was locked on the inside."

She gazed at him with vacant, fearful eyes.

"Somebody got out of the bedroom?"

"Yes."

She shook her head. It was obvious that, whatever her heart might suggest, her reason had pronounced judgement.

"I know," she declared in positive tones, "that Dr. McDonald did not go into my aunt's room. That idea is wrong, whatever evidence there may seem to be in favour of it." She shook her head: "And somebody did go in."

"There were other men in the house in addition to your husband remember, namely Duchlan and Angus, the piper."

"Duchlan didn't kill Aunt Mary." She put her hand on the doctor's wrist. "It's certain, isn't it, that Aunt Mary and Mr. Dundas were murdered by the same person?"

"Nearly certain."

"How can Duchlan have killed Mr. Dundas?"

Dr. Hailey shook his head. "I don't know." He added after a moment, "Your husband confessed to that murder also. But, again, there's evidence enough that he did not commit it."

"What evidence?"

"The fact that he was not in the room when I left it. He says he was hidden in the bed; he was not."

"Dr. McDonald was in the room with Mr. Dundas when you left it, wasn't he?"

"He returned to the room."

She pressed her hand to her brow.

"I know that Dr. McDonald didn't kill my aunt. So he didn't kill Mr. Dundas either."

Dr. Hailey readjusted his eyeglass. His kindly face looked troubled.

"Duchlan must have found out that Dr. McDonald left the smoke-room by the window," he stated.

"Why do you say that?"

"Because it's obvious that he thinks McDonald killed his sister—with your help."

He watched Oonagh closely as he spoke. To his surprise she accepted his suggestion.

"He saw Dr. McDonald's footprints on the earth under the window next morning. He covered them up."

"He told you that?"

"Yes."

"What conclusion did he draw from the footprints?"

"He knew that they were Dr. McDonald's, because of the difference in the two feet. One of them…"

"Yes. I know that. That's not what I mean. How did he think that McDonald had left the house?"

She hesitated. Then her expression grew resolute.

"He thought that Dr. McDonald had jumped from my aunt's window," she said in low tones.

"That means that he thought you were guilty of a share in her death?"

"Yes."

"He told you that?"

"Yes."

"And suggested that you had better anticipate the fate in store for you?"

"Yes."

"Please tell me what he said."

"He said he knew that Dr. McDonald had killed Aunt Mary to prevent her fulfilling her threat to tell Eoghan. Then he said that he had covered up the doctor's footprints to save Eoghan and Hamish from the shame of my complicity in the murder. 'There is only one thing left for you to do,' he said, 'namely, to make an end of a life that is already forfeit. That will at least spare your husband and son the horror of your death on the gallows.' He added: 'High tide is at 2 a.m.!'"

Her tones had not faltered. She seemed to be recounting events far removed from her present state.

"And you," Dr. Hailey said, "feared, if you didn't believe, that the real murderer was your husband?"

"I did fear that."

"I was right in thinking that your death would divert suspicion from him?"

Oonagh inclined her head.

"It would have done, wouldn't it?"

The doctor shook his head. "Perhaps. But it would also have fastened suspicion on Dr. McDonald."

She started.

"Oh, no. Duchlan had covered up these footprints. He would never have told what he had discovered, for Eoghan's sake."

"Forgive me; Inspector Barley discovered the footprints for himself. Your death would have hanged McDonald."

She frowned and bit her lip.

"I don't think," she said deliberately, "that Dr. McDonald could have been suspected at all if Inspector Dundas had not been murdered. Inspector Dundas did not suspect Dr. McDonald."

Dr. Hailey nodded; the point was a good one.

"I thought it all out carefully before I decided," she went on. "I'm a physical coward and I was terribly afraid. I had fearful visions of what it would be like down among the seaweed at the burn's mouth. There's a lot of ugly green weed there which I've always hated to look at. Rank, slimy-looking stuff. But I thought that, if I kept struggling, I might drift out into the loch before the end because the force of the burn carries its water out a good way from the shore. The one sure thing seemed to be that my death would put an end to all the bother for everybody. And I knew that Eoghan was terribly disappointed in me…I thought he had ceased to care for me. If I lived Hamish would see my distress and be forced to take sides between his father and me. What was there to live for?"

She shook her head sadly as she spoke.

"I talk as if all that lay in the past," she added. "But it's here now, with me. If Eoghan accuses himself, perhaps that's only because he's a brave man and belongs to a class in which, as a matter of course, the man sacrifices himself for the woman and child. With his upbringing he must think of me as a wayward and discontented child unfit to be either wife or mother. If I live, our troubles will begin all over again. He'll never understand me or forgive me and I'll never be able to make him the kind of wife he wants and needs."

"That, if I may say so, is the wrong way of looking at your trouble. I feel sure, too, that you're wholly mistaken. The truth is that whereas you tried to give up your life for your husband and child, your husband is trying at this moment to give his life for you. In other words your husband shares his father's dread that you may be guilty. That, as I said before, is presumptive evidence, that neither you nor McDonald nor your husband nor your father-in-law is guilty. By a process of exclusion, therefore, we come to Angus."

They heard steps on the carriage-way behind them. Dr. Hailey turned his head and saw Duchlan approaching.

Chapter XXVI

Once Bitten

Duchlan had aged in these last days; he walked feebly, finding his steps. But his features retained their habitual expression. He came to Dr. Hailey, who rose at his approach.

"I have been looking for you," he stated in breathless tones, "because Inspector Barley tells me that he has received a confession from my son."

His head shook as he spoke. He kept his eyes fixed on the doctor, ignoring his daughter-in-law utterly.

"Your son made a confession," Dr. Hailey said.

"It's nonsense. Eoghan never killed his aunt."

The old man's voice rose in a shrill crescendo. Fear and anger were mingled in his expression.

"I can prove his innocence," he cried. "Do you hear, I can prove it."

He continued to avoid directing even a glance at Oonagh. But that abstention did not lessen the menace with which his words evidently threatened her. Dr. Hailey readjusted his eyeglass.

"I don't think," he said, "that Inspector Barley is the least likely to treat your son's confession seriously."

"Eh? What do you say?"

The doctor repeated his statement. He was surprised to observe that it failed to reassure the anxious father.

"Don't talk nonsense," Duchlan cried. "If a man confesses to murder, a man in my son's responsible position at that, his confession is bound to be taken seriously."

"Why?"

"Why? Because the presumption must be that he has spoken advisedly." The old man's eyes flashed. "The truth is that he is shielding others whose guilt can be proved and who are wholly unworthy of the sacrifice he is making on their behalf." He turned his back on Oonagh. "I should like to talk to you alone."

Dr. Hailey shook his head.

"Much better to talk here openly. Your daughter-in-law, unless I am wrong, has just been telling me all that you propose to tell me."

"What's that?"

"About your discovery of Dr. McDonald's footprints on the earth under your sister's bedroom window."

Duchlan started. But he kept his back resolutely turned on Oonagh.

"I did find his footmarks: the one smooth, the other studded with nails. Nobody could misinterpret that sign. So you see the fellow jumped from my poor sister's window after he had committed his horrible crime. It was I, myself, who covered the footmarks lest my daughter-in-law's association with the murder should be discovered." He drew a deep breath, nodding his head all the while. "What a mistake I made. What a mistake I made. But she is the mother of my grandson, who will be Duchlan one day. Can you blame an old man because he has tried to deliver his son and his son's son from ineffaceable shame and dishonour? But God is just; murder will out. This Quixotic chivalry of my son has, perforce, unsealed my resolve to keep silence. Am I to stand by and see an innocent man, my son, led out to death while I possess knowledge that will save him? Those who have shed the blood of the innocent must bear the punishment of that dreadful crime."

His voice shook. A faint tinge of colour had mounted to his cheeks. But that common hue of living men brought with it no suggestion of human kindness. A cold, unmerciful gleam filled the black eyes. Dr. Hailey stepped back that he might see Oonagh. She remained seated; her fingers continued to pluck at the thyme. "Is your belief that Dr. McDonald murdered your sister," he asked in calm tones, "founded exclusively on your discovery of these footprints?"

"It is not indeed."

Duchlan sneered. He raised his hand and seemed to clutch at the air in front of him.

"Is it possible that my daughter-in-law's candour has not extended to her relations with McDonald?"

"On the contrary, sir."

"Why ask, then, if the footprints are the only evidence of guilt?"

"You have assumed that the relations between your daughter-in-law and Dr. McDonald are improper relations."

The old man started.

"I have drawn the conclusion which the evidence of my senses compels me to draw."

"What, because a mother whose child is showing alarming symptoms sends for the doctor…"

"No. Emphatically no. Because a wife who has flouted her husband's nearest relatives is found to be meeting a man, clandestinely, after the fall of darkness."

"You had already, before such meetings took place, made accusations which must have driven any woman to secrecy."

"We had our reasons, believe me."

"What reasons?"

Dr. Hailey's voice had grown as hard as Duchlan's. He allowed his eyeglass to fall and faced the old man.

"The doctor was summoned on the most frivolous pretexts. My dear sister was not permitted to be present during these visits…"

"I see. On that evidence, you were ready to believe that your son's wife was untrue to him?"

"Both Mary and I were jealous of Eoghan's honour."

"Because Miss Gregor was excluded from the consultations with Dr. McDonald, she, and you too, became suspicious that these consultations were not, in fact, what they appeared to be?"

"McDonald was sent for on every conceivable occasion…"

"By a mother whose child was taking convulsions."

Dr. Hailey spoke these last words slowly and with emphasis. When no reply was forthcoming he asked:

"Is it not obvious that both you and your sister were inclined to suspicion in the case of your daughter-in-law?"

"I don't understand you."

"I mean that, in her case, you were ready to suspect, perhaps even determined to suspect."

"Nonsense."

"On your own showing, you found the natural anxiety of a young mother a cause of uneasiness?"

"No."

"My dear sir, when your daughter-in-law kept sending for the doctor, both you and Miss Gregor accused her of unworthy motives."

The old man frowned, but this time offered no comment. The doctor proceeded:

"And, meanwhile, on your own showing, you were forcing her to receive your charity. You were using every means to hurt her pride and humiliate her wifehood. Men do not desire such punishments for women. I can only conclude therefore that you have acted throughout at the dictation of your sister."

"My sister, as I told Inspector Barley, possessed means of her own. I have nothing but this estate." He indicated the woods and the loch. "My sister was under no obligation whatever to give my son or his wife a penny. Eoghan married without consulting our wishes."

"Why should he consult your wishes?"

"Why should my sister give him her money?"

Dr. Hailey shook his head.

"An outsider," he said, "sees most of the game. It's obvious to me that your sister, having got your son's wife at her mercy, adopted every method she could think of to make her life intolerable. My personal view is that that was a policy undertaken with a definite object, namely, to separate husband and wife. The policy failed. Your daughter-in-law remained here, enduring everything. It began to seem probable that she would have a home of her own. A change of policy was necessary; an immediate change of policy. Your sister managed, I don't know how, to persuade you that the visits of Dr. McDonald were more than ordinary medical visits."

"I saw for myself that they were more than ordinary medical visits. Their duration…"

"My dear sir, nobody thinks anything of a prolonged doctor's visit when the case is a serious one."

Duchlan's face was pale with anger.

"I tell you," he exclaimed, "I did think something…"

"Exactly."

Dr. Hailey looked him straight in the face. He added:

"I assume, therefore, that this wholly commonplace behaviour of McDonald was distorted in your eyes by some earlier experience. Once bitten, twice shy."

The words were spoken in a low tone. But their effect could not have been greater had they been shouted. Duchlan swayed on his feet.

"No, no," he ejaculated hoarsely.

"Some earlier experience in which a young wife…"

There was no reply. The muscles of the old man's face were unloosed. His jaw fell. After a moment he moved away a few paces and leaned against a tree.

"You are speaking about the death of my wife?" he gasped.

"Yes."

"She…" A fit of coughing shook Duchlan's body. He turned and grasped one of the branches of the tree against which he was leaning. Dr. Hailey came to his side.

"I am aware of the circumstances of your wife's death," he said. "And of the events which preceded it, the wounding of your sister."

"Mary was guiltless."

"No doubt. But her accusations…"

Duchlan made a peremptory gesture.

"Her accusations were just," he declared in tones that vibrated with pain.

"At least you chose so to regard them. It comes to the same thing. What is certain is that Miss Gregor employed against your wife the methods she employed recently against your daughter-in-law, namely, a perpetual and persistent interference, a merciless criticism, and a diligent misrepresentation. These methods expressed, I believe, her jealous hatred of a rival whose presence in the castle threatened her position. She drove your wife to violence; you, doubtless, completed the work of destruction by exhibiting the callous spirit which made it possible for you the other day to suggest suicide to your daughter-in-law."

Dr. Hailey's voice thrilled with an anger which was not cooled by the spectacle of the old man's distress.

Chapter XXVII

Man to Man

Dr. Hailey returned alone to the castle. He found Barley awaiting him.

"My case is complete," the detective assured him. "I've found the axe with which the murder of Miss Gregor was committed."

He led the way to his bedroom and produced a small axe from a drawer of the dressing-table. He handed it to his companion.

"Observe, my dear Hailey," he pointed out, "that there are herring scales on the handle. The axe is nominally used to chop wood but the cook admits that she employed it the other day to break up a big bone for the stock-pot. She had been cleaning some herring just before she did this."

Dr. Hailey sat down and took snuff.

"Don't forget," he said, "that there were herring scales on Dundas's head."

"Quite. I feel sure that that blow was struck with a lead sinker. I've seen Dr. McDonald's boat. It's plentifully endowed with scales. He's a keen deep-sea fisherman and often uses herring as bait."

Barley hooked his thumbs into the arm-holes of his waistcoat and spread out his fingers.

"I confess," he declared, "that I have great sympathy—the greatest possible sympathy—with Mrs. Eoghan. Poor woman, her life has been made unbearable by her aunt, who deserved perhaps no better fate than that which has overtaken her. At the same time, let us not deceive ourselves, murder is murder. Deliberation of a most calculating kind is revealed by the use of that axe, which had to be fetched from below stairs and by the fact that a rope was kept in readiness to enable the murderer to escape. Once he had bolted the windows of Miss Gregor's bedroom, on the morning after her death, McDonald must have felt that he was secure against detection."

Dr. Hailey described his talk with Oonagh and his meeting with Duchlan and, as usual, received a careful and courteous hearing.

"More collateral proofs, in my humble judgement," Barley exclaimed. "Duchlan's discovery of the footprints seems to me of crucial import. What a feeble defence to say that a doctor left his patient's house by the window rather than face a poor, distracted old man!"

"McDonald, remember, didn't cover up his tracks. He left those footprints to tell their tale, surely an act of gross carelessness in a murderer."

Barley shrugged his shoulders and then spread out his hands.

"Yes, a point. I admit it. But how small after all! I apologize in advance for using a bad argument, an argument which, generally speaking, I deprecate; but if McDonald didn't commit this murder, who did? Again surely we are entitled to ask *Cui bono*? McDonald undoubtedly. He had access, he alone, to the murdered persons. He was able to escape, he alone, from the rooms where the murders were committed. He has left traces, unmistakable, damning, of his escape. I confess that, so far as I am concerned, not a shadow of doubt about his guilt exists."

He broke off and remained for a few minutes in silent contemplation of the carpet.

"An hour ago," he said, "I applied for warrants for the arrest of Dr. McDonald and Mrs. Eoghan Gregor. It is my purpose to effect these arrests, at the latest, to-morrow morning."

"Your case will necessarily be founded," Dr. Hailey said, "on the assumption that McDonald and Mrs. Eoghan were lovers?"

"Yes."

"Have you any real evidence to support that charge?"

"Circumstantial evidence. Besides, if Mrs. Eoghan's motives in meeting McDonald were strictly correct, the effect of the meetings remain. Both man and woman knew that Miss Gregor would report to her nephew; both had a clear idea what the effect of that report would be. The motive for murder remains therefore and is, I submit, by no means invalidated by assuming that these meetings were absolutely *en règle*."

"Innocence does not kill."

Barley frowned. He began to comb his moustache with unusual vigour.

"Exactly," he declared, "and therefore I presume that the relationship was not innocent."

"Do you believe seriously that McDonald is that type of man?"

A curious expression came upon Barley's face. He seemed, for a moment, to take off the policeman and become his ordinary, human self.

"I think, my dear doctor," he exclaimed, "that you mustn't ask me such a question. It's like…" He raised his hand. "It's like asking a surgeon if he doesn't think it cruel to wound people. I may like McDonald, I may pity him. But the one thing I can't do, the one thing I mustn't do, is to import my personal feelings into my case against him."

Dr. Hailey shook his head.

"Why not?"

"Because a detective is primarily an observer. You know very well how apt the personal equation is to obtrude on scientific observation. It's the same in this kind of work. If you begin by finding heroes and heroines and villains you won't end by finding your murderer."

"You admit that if McDonald's relationship with Mrs. Eoghan was innocent, your case is weakened considerably?"

Barley shrugged his shoulders.

"That's a debating point," he declared in brisk tones. "And I must ask to be excused the task of debating it." He rose and took the axe which the doctor had placed on a table beside him. He laid it back in its drawer. Dr. Hailey left him and went to his own bedroom. He lay down on the bed and was soon asleep. When he woke, the night was marching across the sky. He watched the changing colours of the clouds, wondering vaguely what time it was; then his critical faculty asserted itself. The fault in Barley's theory as he now recognized was its disregard of the character of Miss Gregor. That woman had been ready to sow hate and suspicion between husband and wife; but the idea that she was concerned to effect a public breach of their marriage was certainly mistaken. Such women look on divorce with lively horror, and will exert their whole strength to preserve their kin from the disgrace attending it. McDonald must have known this, and known, consequently, that he had nothing to fear. Why then commit murder? He had discovered no answer to this question when he heard light footsteps approaching his door. A moment later Oonagh burst into the room.

"Eoghan's gone off in the motor-boat," she cried.

Her face was quick with foreboding. Her eyes beseeched help. She grasped the rail of the bed and stood trying to recover her breath.

"I feel terribly anxious about him."

Dr. Hailey jumped up.

"When did he go?"

"I suppose about half an hour ago. Nobody seems to have seen him. I went to his room to talk to him. He wasn't there. I searched the house. Then I noticed that the boat had disappeared. The wind is off-shore; I imagine he let her drift from her moorings so as not to excite attention."

She gazed at the doctor as she spoke, but his face remained expressionless.

"Where can we get a motor-boat?"

"In Ardmore."

She put her hand on his arm.

"Do you think that…that he's in danger?"

"Perhaps."

She mastered herself. They went downstairs.

"I haven't told Duchlan," she said.

"Much better not."

They left the house and hurried towards the village. Once they stopped to listen; the night held only murmurings of winds. Oonagh did not speak, but the glimpses which the moon gave him of her face showed how acutely she was suffering. McDonald had not lied when he said that this woman loved her husband.

The boat hirer had ended his day's work and did not seem eager to resume it. He stood in the doorway of his cottage, from which the smell of frying herrings emerged, and expounded the many weaknesses of his motor-boat and the unwisdom of sailing in her in the dark. His round, red face grew melancholy as he emphasized this danger.

"I'm ready to run any risk, Mr. McDougall," Oonagh said.

"But surely Mr. Eoghan can be in no danger? He's a good sailor, whatever."

The tones were challenging. She shook her head.

"His engine must have broken down. We couldn't hear it; on a quiet night like this you should hear it five miles away."

"The weather is very settled. He will not come to no harm before the morning."

"I can't wait till the morning. Not another hour. Sandy Logan has a motor-boat, hasn't he?"

"Aye, he has."

The Highlander spoke stiffly. He was not concerned to enter into rivalry with anyone. Let them go where they would. He took a step back, preparatory, apparently, to shutting the door when the beat of a motor engine came faintly but distinctly to their ears. Mr. McDougall strained forward to listen.

"Yon's Mr. Eoghan's boat," he declared with assurance. "She's coming into the harbour."

He waved his hand in a gesture that absolved him from any further responsibility.

"How can you be sure?" Dr. Hailey asked.

"By the sound, sir. There's no two engines make the same sound. That one of Mr. Eoghan's is the newest and best between Rothesay and Inveraira."

The beating of the engine grew louder, more insistent.

"I think it is Eoghan's boat," Oonagh said. She pointed seaward. "I can see it."

They left the cottage and walked to the shore. The motor-boat was coming in fast and seemed to be making for the jetty under Dr. McDonald's house. Dr. Hailey touched his companion's arm.

"You realize where he's going?"

"Oh, yes." She turned to him in distress. "I feel that something terrible is going to happen."

He considered a moment.

"I think that you must leave this business to me," he said at last. "If we remain together the chances are that we'll fail."

"Oh, I can't go back to Duchlan."

"Not for your husband's sake?"

She did not reply. They could see the motor-boat clearly now in the wake of the moon. Eoghan was standing up in the stern. She grasped his arm.

"Very well." She moved away a few paces and then came back. "Promise that you'll keep him from doing anything… terrible."

"Yes."

She disappeared away among the shadows. He waited until the motor-boat had been brought to the jetty and then walked in the direction of Dr. McDonald's house. He reached the gate in time to see Eoghan ascending the steep footpath to the door. He followed, going slowly and with great caution. When he reached the top of the path he crouched down. Eoghan had been admitted to the house and was standing in the study, the windows of which were wide open. His face was very pale; even from a distance, it was obvious that he was labouring under great excitement. McDonald entered the room. The men did not shake hands. Dr. Hailey moved into the deep shadows which lay beyond the beam of light cast by the windows. He approached the house and crouched again. He heard Eoghan's clear, well-bred voice say:

"The position is this: I've done my best to persuade them that I'm the man they're looking for. I've failed. Barley has made up his mind that you and Oonagh killed my aunt between you and that you killed Dundas." He paused for an instant and then added: "Don't misunderstand me when I say that I think he's got a strong case."

"Against me, perhaps; not against your wife."

"My dear sir, his case fails unless he can associate my wife with you. He believes," Eoghan's voice hardened in spite of himself, "that you and my wife were in love with each other. My aunt thought so too; she wrote me to that effect. My father is convinced of it. So, also, I think, is Christina."

He paused. Dr. Hailey heard McDonald move across the room. Then he heard the doctor ask:

"And you?"

"No, I'm not convinced."

"Thank you."

Dr. Hailey stood erect; he took a step near to the beam of light and then retired to a point from which he could see the two men. Eoghan's expression was less friendly than he had expected.

"I don't want to sail under false colours," he told Dr. McDonald. "No man can be grateful to another for bringing suspicion on his wife. What I mean is that, although the case as others see it, is damning enough, I don't choose to be damned by it. But if I believe Oonagh against the weight of evidence, I'm not fool enough to suppose that the weight of evidence is thereby lightened. Barley has asked for warrants to arrest you and her. He means to execute them to-morrow."

His features were grim. He stood facing McDonald with clenched fists and tense muscles so that, for a moment, Dr. Hailey thought he was about to attack him.

"Your wife is innocent, Gregor," McDonald cried. "I swear it."

"I'm afraid, my dear fellow, that that isn't likely to help much; whatever you or I may swear Oonagh will be tried with you for murder. The odds, frankly, are enormous that you'll be convicted, both of you. Barley, I understand, has discovered footprints under my aunt's window. His case is that nobody but you can have committed this murder and 'pon my word, I can't see any other solution myself."

"There must be another solution."

"Can you suggest one?"

"No, but…"

"The murders are a man's doing. They've excluded me. The only other possibilities are Father and Angus." Eoghan paused and then repeated. "Father and Angus."

He stood gazing at McDonald who faced him courageously.

"Why on earth should I murder your aunt?" the doctor asked.

"I've told you. As Barley points out your professional life was at stake."

"Only if you divorced your wife." McDonald took a step forward. "I do not believe that you would ever have done that."

Eoghan did not reply for a moment. Then he said:

"I'm afraid that, from Barley's point of view, what I might or might not have done is of no consequence. I'm not here because I believe in anybody's guilt. I'm here because the evidence in the possession of the police is so strong that they're bound to succeed against you and my wife. They will ask the jury to consider what must have happened if I had got a divorce, not whether or not I was likely to petition for one. After all, no man can be sure what another man will do in such circumstances. Barley is entitled to assume that divorce was on the cards."

Eoghan's manner was very grave. He added:

"I've tried to think what my own attitude would be if I sat on the jury that will try the case. I'm afraid I should be compelled to take the view that you were in a dangerous position."

His voice challenged. He had come to make demands, the righteousness of which shone in his eyes. Dr. McDonald seemed to shrink from him.

"What do you want me to do?" he asked in the tone of a man who speaks under strong compulsion. Eoghan frowned; a moment later, however, his face cleared.

"I'm afraid," he said, "that I want you to die."

Chapter XXVIII

"Ready?"

Dr. Hailey strained forward to catch McDonald's reply. He saw the doctor square his shoulders.

"Very well."

"The position is that, if you and I are out of the way, they'll drop the case against Oonagh. You can't try a dead man and no man is guilty till he's been convicted. Lacking a conviction against you, they could scarcely hope to succeed against her."

McDonald nodded.

"Yes." He threw back his head in a gesture of defiance. "Why do you say," he demanded, "'if you and I are out of the way'? What difference can it make whether you are out of the way or not?"

"I've accused myself, remember."

"Since they don't believe you, that counts for nothing."

Eoghan shrugged his shoulders.

"Possibly not. Still, my death will give substance to my confession. In face of it, and with your death added, Oonagh should be safe."

He took his cigarette-case from his pocket and opened it. He began to tap a cigarette on the side of the case.

"I've got the motor-boat in the harbour," he added. "I propose that we go sailing."

He put the cigarette in his mouth and lit it. His coolness was admirable; but there was a quiet strength in McDonald's face that was not less striking. Dr. Hailey felt regret that Barley was not with him to see how the man he called murderer behaved in face of death.

He left his place at the window and hurried down the path to the road. The motor-boat was lying at the jetty. He reached it and stepped aboard. The bow was decked to make a fo'c'sle. He opened the door of this and entered, closing the door behind him, except for a small aperture. He struck a match. The fo'c'sle contained only a few coils of rope and a canvas bucket. It was unlikely that the two men would have occasion to enter it.

They came after the lapse of a few minutes. Dr. Hailey noticed that neither spoke a word as they cast off. The noise of the engine soon made it difficult to hear any speech. The little craft was lively and rushed out of the harbour in a few minutes. Through the small opening in the door he could see the lights of Ardmore receding behind the tops of the pine trees on Garvel point. What was Eoghan Gregor's game? Every now and then he caught a glimpse of the young man's face. The moonlight had blanched it; but it had lost nothing of its resolution. McDonald's expression was far less determined and he looked up, sometimes, at the sky in a way that was rather pitiful. After the lapse of about half an hour, Eoghan stopped the engine. The rush of water on the boat's sides and the gurgle under her stern mingled pleasantly; little by little the wide, lively silence swallowed them up.

"We must leave them guessing," Eoghan said. "This isn't

necessarily suicide, or murder; it may be just an accident. Loch Fyne is so deep out here that it holds its secrets for ever."

"Yes."

"Are you a swimmer?"

The question came sharply, like an order to fire.

"I can swim, but I tire very easily."

"So do I."

The moonbeams were reflected on a long, dull barrel. Dr. Hailey saw Eoghan raise a shot-gun, of the heavy type used for duck, to his shoulder.

"I'm going to blow the bottom out of her," he said, and then pronounced the word "Ready?"

"There's just one thing, Gregor. I'd like you to know that, though your wife has never cared for anybody but you, I cared for her." McDonald's voice broke. But a moment later he added: "She never knew, of course."

"Thanks, old man…Ready?…"

Dr. Hailey flung open the door of the fo'c'sle.

"Put that gun down, Gregor," he ordered in stern tones.

Chapter XXIX

Painful Hearing

Eoghan obeyed him so far as to lay the shot-gun across his knees.

"What the devil are you doing in my boat?" he demanded.

Dr. Hailey did not answer. He left the fo'c'sle and came aft where the two men were seated.

"This is madness," he declared. "Nothing has been proved." He addressed himself to Eoghan: "Oonagh guessed your plan. She accompanied me to Ardmore. She's waiting now for news of you."

"Barley has a warrant for her arrest." The young man's voice was cold and hard.

"What does that matter? A warrant is not a verdict."

"I believe they'll get their verdict."

"I don't."

Dr. Hailey's voice rang out with an assurance which surprised himself and which astonished his companions.

"What!" Eoghan exclaimed. "In face of those footprints on the flower-bed?"

"Which your father covered up the next morning."

"Well?"

"A murderer asking for punishment."

"It's easy to make a slip."

"Would you have made that particular kind of slip yourself?"

Eoghan considered a moment.

"Perhaps not."

"That, in McDonald's case, means certainly not."

"Why?"

"Because he has a wooden leg. People with artificial limbs are more aware of their footsteps than ordinary people and they seldom jump."

Eoghan did not answer. He bent suddenly and laid his gun on the bottom of the boat. His hands reached out to the starting-handle on the engine.

"Wait a minute," McDonald exclaimed. He turned to Dr. Hailey:

"My reason for coming here," he said, "was that Barley's case seemed to me so well buttressed by circumstantial evidence that a conviction was certain. So far as I can see you are in no position to disprove that evidence. If we go ashore with you, therefore, Mrs. Gregor and I will be arrested to-morrow, taken to Edinburgh, convicted and hanged. I prefer to drown."

He spoke with deliberation, solemnly, as a man speaks who has paid a price for his words.

"You say that, knowing that you are innocent?" Dr. Hailey asked.

"What does that signify?"

"Everything."

The Highlander moved his wooden leg to a more comfortable position.

"In actual practice innocence that cannot be substantiated," he declared, "is no better than guilt. I don't deceive myself. In Barley's place I should think and act as he has done. After all, what alternative has he got? He can prove that Gregor here didn't commit these murders; he can prove that Mrs. Gregor and I were friends; that we had reason to fear Miss Gregor; that we had access to her bedroom. If I didn't know that I hadn't killed the poor lady, I swear I would be convinced that I must have killed her."

Dr. Hailey shook his head.

"Did you fear Miss Gregor?" he asked.

"No."

"Then why do you say 'we had reason to fear Miss Gregor?'"

"I meant, that's what the jury will think."

"You know as well as I know that there was never, at any time, any question of divorce. That can be proved."

"How?"

"By reference to Captain Gregor here and to his father." Dr. Hailey turned to Eoghan:

"Did you threaten your wife with a divorce?" he asked.

"Of course not. But I'm afraid I agree with McDonald that that doesn't matter. Barley is entitled to assume that the threat of divorce existed; the jury will make the same assumption."

"I don't think the jury will do anything of the kind. Even juries have to take cognizance of human character. Is it likely that your aunt would have wished a divorce? Or your father? Divorce is still looked on by old-fashioned people as a disgrace. Any Scottish jury will understand that, I can assure you. Besides, you can go into the box and state that at no time did the idea of divorce enter your mind. You never spoke about it to your wife. You threatened nobody. What a fool McDonald must be if he committed murder in order to escape from a danger which had no existence."

"My dear sir," McDonald interposed, "the prosecution will counter that by saying that a guilty mind loses its judgement. 'The wicked flee when no man pursueth.'"

"No. My point is that this idea of divorce can be shown to have originated in Barley's mind. His whole case is founded on it. No jury, let me repeat, is going to believe that these murders were committed by a doctor who had nothing to gain by committing them and nothing to lose if they were not committed. Again, why kill Miss Gregor since Duchlan lived, since Mrs. Gregor's husband lived." Dr. Hailey found his eyeglass and put it in his eye. "That's the weak spot in Barley's case. Miss Gregor was no more dangerous to you, McDonald, than her brother, and both she and her brother were less dangerous than her nephew, who had already been informed about what was happening. Far from being a murder with a strong motive this was a wholly senseless murder if its object was to prevent a divorce. I feel sure these arguments will make a strong appeal to any jury."

Eoghan nodded; he started the engine.

"There's no doubt you're right," he declared. "We've got a fighting chance."

The boat began to move. He pulled the tiller over and set her course for Duchlan. The lights in the castle winked at them. Nearer, to the left, they saw the flares of a herring-boat which had secured a catch and was calling the buyers. Red and green lights announced the approach of the steamers of these merchants, which everywhere follow the fishing fleet. Oonagh was standing on the jetty awaiting them. She bent and caught the gunwhale, holding it till Dr. Hailey and Dr. McDonald had stepped ashore. Then she jumped into the boat. They saw her throw her arms round her husband's neck.

"I think I had better see Barley," McDonald said in hurried tones.

They found the detective in the smoking-room with Duchlan who seemed to be on good terms with him. Dr. Hailey waited till Eoghan and Oonagh came to the room and then expounded his objections to Barley's theory.

"It boils down to this," he declared. "McDonald knew that Miss Gregor had written to her nephew. The mischief was done. Murder in the circumstances was senseless."

Barley had accorded his habitual courtesy to the criticism. He bowed his head in silent acknowledgment of its weight. Then, with a gesture, he swept it aside.

"This gathering, as you know," he stated, "is not of my summoning. If what I say makes painful hearing, you cannot charge that to my account. My case does not, as you appear to think, rest primarily on motive; it rests on ascertained facts and on observations, each of which has been carefully checked." He rose and stood in front of the fireplace. "There are three separate methods of approach to this case," he declared. "The first of these is the method of observation. It can be shown that Dr. McDonald jumped on to the flower-bed under Miss Gregor's window. Again, marks which suggest the use of a rope can be shown on the iron spike above that window. You can suggest that Dr. McDonald left the house by the window of the study, which is situated under that of Miss Gregor's room. That suggestion does not explain the marks on the spike, whereas my suggestion, that these marks were made by a rope used as a means of descent from Miss Gregor's window, explains both marks and footprints. Any actuary will tell you that the odds in favour of my theory are, consequently, very long. But that is not all."

He leaned forward. The habitual good-humour of his expression had faded. He looked, Dr. Hailey thought, like an actor who has, suddenly, thrown off his mask.

"The method of deduction must also be used. Miss Gregor's death followed immediately a violent quarrel between her and Mrs. Eoghan Gregor, which quarrel was about secret meetings with Dr. McDonald. Miss Gregor had written to her nephew about his wife's behaviour; had she written about these secret meetings?"

The question was addressed to Eoghan. He flushed as he answered it in the negative.

"You see. The worst, or at any rate, what looked like the worst, had not been told. Again, the murder took place before Captain Eoghan Gregor reached home."

"How do you know that?" Dr. Hailey asked.

"I know that Captain Eoghan Gregor went to his aunt's room as soon as he landed. He was not admitted. The proof that he was not admitted is that the door was locked on the inside. The carpenter's testimony on that point is clear and final."

"Yes."

"So that the murder occurred within a few hours of the discovery and reproof of a young wife and a few minutes before the return of her husband. Who can say what secret Miss Gregor will carry with her to her grave?"

He gazed at Eoghan as he spoke. The young man's face had grown grave, but he continued to hold his wife's hand. He drew her closer to him. McDonald bent and moved his wooden leg.

"The third method is that of elimination, admittedly the least satisfactory of the three. If Dr. McDonald did not commit this murder who did? Not Captain Eoghan Gregor. Not Duchlan. Not Angus…"

Dr. Hailey interrupted: "On what grounds do you exclude Angus?"

"If, as Mrs. Gregor has told me, she and Dr. McDonald, while they were in this room, heard the windows of Miss Gregor's room being shut, then they must immediately afterwards have seen the murderer drop to the ground. Look for yourself. These windows were open then as they're open now; you can see the whole extent of the flower-bed. Do you suppose that if they had seen Angus drop from Miss Gregor's room they would not have reported the fact?"

"You're assuming that the murderer must have left the room by way of the window?"

"We know that he cannot have left by the door." He waved his hand. "You can't have it both ways. In my humble judgement if Dr. McDonald and Mrs. Gregor are speaking the truth, they must have seen the murderer making his escape. That, it appears to me, was a consideration overlooked by them when framing their story. Their story fails therefore on two separate counts: It doesn't explain the marks on the spike and it ignores completely the descent of the murderer from the window he had just closed. I reject their story, and in rejecting it, exclude Angus from the case. Somebody closed the windows; somebody descended from them. There is only one person who can have accomplished these acts. As it happens, he is also the only person who can possibly have killed Inspector Dundas, seeing that there is ample evidence that nobody entered or descended from Dundas's window."

Barley's voice had fallen to a low pitch. When he ceased to speak a chill fell on the room.

"Had Dundas not been murdered," he added, "the case against Dr. McDonald would have been overwhelmingly strong; as things are, it is irresistible."

They heard a car approaching the house, a moment later it reached the door. Everyone in the room knew what this coming portended and even Duchlan shrank in horror. He put his skinny old hand on his son's arm but Eoghan remained indifferent to him. Eoghan had his arms about his wife. A dull glare burned in his eyes. Dr. Hailey turned away; the spectacle of McDonald's distress made him avert his eyes a second time. Angus's heavy, shuffling steps crossed the hall to the front door. Then they returned, at the same pace, to the door of the room. The door opened. A policeman in uniform entered.

"Inspector Barley?" he asked.

"Yes."

The man saluted. He presented a long blue envelope.

"I'm Sergeant Jackson, sir, and these are the warrants for the arrest of Mrs. Gregor and Dr. McDonald."

Chapter XXX

The Gleam of a Knife

Oonagh rose.

"May I go upstairs to the nursery for a minute?" she asked Barley in tones which revealed an excellent courage.

"Certainly."

She hurried out of the room. Barley signed to the policeman to accompany him and followed her. They heard him talking to the man in the hall. Dr. Hailey approached Eoghan:

"I'm certain," he declared, "that a frightful mistake has been made. We must fight this case to the last."

The young man did not answer him. But his eyes were full of bitter reproach. Duchlan, who still held his son's arm, muttered something about resignation to the will of Providence. Duchlan's face wore a look of melancholy, but the doctor saw that his eyes were bright. All he cared about was his own blood. Barley returned to the room. He wore his black-and-white dust-coat and looked a garish, incongruous figure. He walked to McDonald and handed him a large sheet of blue paper.

"It is my painful duty," he said in hurried, formal tones, "to arrest you on the charge of having wilfully murdered Miss Mary Gregor and Inspector Dundas. I warn you that anything which you say from now onwards will be used in evidence against you."

He turned away and immediately left the room again. They heard him go out to the front door and speak to someone in the waiting car, the engine of which had been kept running. Was he about to arrest Oonagh? Eoghan jumped up and would have opened the door had not Dr. Hailey reached it before him.

"For your wife's sake, Gregor."

"I wish to go to my wife."

"Don't put a further strain on her courage at this moment."

The young man stretched out his hands like a blind man, groping.

"You don't understand."

The glare was still in his eyes. Dr. Hailey stood his ground, urging in conciliatory tones that Oonagh should be left free to stay away or return as she chose.

"My dear doctor, she asked me to follow her. Our child's upstairs, remember."

He opened the door as he spoke. He was about to leave the room when a young woman in a police uniform appeared in the doorway. She was gasping and her cheeks were bloodless.

"Oh, quick," she cried, "Inspector Barley has been murdered."

She caught at the jamb of the door and leaned against it. Dr. Hailey supported her.

"Where is he?"

"Outside, on the grass."

Her voice failed. He brought her to a chair beside Duchlan. McDonald had already left the room with Eoghan. He followed them and found them bending over Barley, who lay stretched out on the bank above the burn. The headlights of the car shone on the man's face. It was streaked with blood; but the blood flowed no longer. McDonald knelt and put his ear to the chest.

"Well?"

"I can hear nothing. There's no pulse."

Dr. Hailey lit his electric lamp and turned the beam on to the detective's head. An exclamation broke from his lips. Barley had been killed as Dundas had been killed.

"He's dead, McDonald."

"Yes."

"Since you were with us in the study his death disproves his theory."

The wardress who had called them, joined them. She had recovered enough to give an account of what she had seen.

"I accompanied Sergeant Jackson from Campbeltown," she explained, "because of the female prisoner. Sergeant Jackson told me to stay in the saloon till I was wanted. He left the engine running and the side-lights on. After a few minutes he came back and told me Inspector Barley had ordered him to watch the female prisoner, who had gone upstairs to say good-bye to her child. After the sergeant went away, Inspector Barley came out. I knew him because I had seen a photograph of him in that queer coat. He walked along here and stood looking up at the house. I thought he was going to try to open that window—" (She pointed to the french-window of the writing-room) "because he seemed to put his hands on it. Just as he did that he cried out and turned round. I saw his face in the moonlight. Then he seemed to stumble. He sank down. I turned up the headlights of the car as soon as I could find the switch, but by that time the man that stabbed him had escaped."

"Why do you say 'the man that stabbed him?'" Dr. Hailey demanded in hoarse tones.

"Because I saw the gleam of a knife just before he fell."

Chapter XXXI

The Invisible Slayer

Dr. Hailey turned to Eoghan.

"Might I ask you to send Sergeant Jackson here?" he asked. "I fancy he's standing guard over your wife."

The young man walked away to the house. The doctor put his hand on McDonald's arm.

"What is it?"

"Who knows?"

The words were spoken in tones that carried a burden of fear.

"Dundas was killed in exactly the same way."

"Yes."

The wardress asked if she might return to the car. Dr. Hailey accompanied her, giving her his arm.

"You saw nothing beyond the flash of the knife?" he asked.

"Nothing."

"But it was dark, was it not? Sidelights are feeble."

She agreed: "Still, I saw Inspector Barley clearly enough. I'm sure I should have seen anybody else."

"If there was a knife there must have been a man to use it. Did you hear anything?"

"The engine was running, sir."

They reached the car. The doctor switched off the head-lights, leaving the sidelights burning. McDonald's figure stood out clearly enough and even Barley's body was visible.

"You see," the girl remarked, "it isn't so dark…"

"There are heavy shadows close to the window."

"Yes. I thought the man had come out through the window."

Dr. Hailey walked back to McDonald and then examined the french-window. It was open.

"He must have come this way?"

McDonald did not reply. They saw Sergeant Jackson approaching. Dr. Hailey went to meet him and told him what had happened. He illuminated Barley's face that the policeman might see the nature of the injury.

"Dr. McDonald," he stated, "was with me in the smoking-room. I take it you can answer for Mrs. Gregor. This is exactly the same type of blow as that which killed Inspector Dundas." An exclamation broke from his lips. "Look. The herring scale."

He bent down and pointed to a shining scale which adhered to the scalp over the seat of injury.

"Oh, dear!"

"You know, of course, that herring scales were found on Miss Gregor's and Inspector Dundas's bodies?"

"Yes, sir."

"These three people have died by the same hand, Sergeant."

The policeman glanced about him uneasily.

"I went upstairs with Mrs. Gregor as directed by Inspector Barley," he stated in the manner of the police court. "She entered the nursery and I heard her and the nurse crying.

Not wishing to intrude further than was necessary on their trouble I came downstairs to the first landing. Nobody passed me on the stairs going up or going down."

"Where was Angus, the piper?"

"The old man that opened the door?"

"Yes."

"I think he was in the hall. Leastways, he was there when I went upstairs."

They returned to the house and went to the little writing-room at the window of which Barley had been struck.

"It's possible that the murderer was waiting here," Dr. Hailey said. "If that is so he must have escaped back into the house. We know exactly where everybody in the house was at the moment of the Inspector's death—with the single exception of the piper."

"Ah."

"No, I confess I feel no confidence in that theory." He passed his hand across his brow. "Let me see, the front door was open and the wardress was in the car. She must have had a good view of the hall all the time. Ask her to come here, will you?"

Sergeant Jackson went away. The doctor walked back into the hall where McDonald was awaiting him. A moment later the wardress entered the house. He asked her if she had seen anybody in the hall at the time of the murder.

"Only the butler."

"You saw the butler?"

"Yes, sir. He was standing where you are standing now. When I saw Inspector Barley fall I called to him, but he didn't hear me. As you know I ran into the house."

"Where was the butler then?"

She pointed to the foot of the stairs.

"He was standing over there. I didn't notice much."

"You are quite sure," the doctor asked in deliberate tones, "that you saw him standing here a moment after Inspector Barley fell?"

"Quite sure. And a moment before he fell too."

"What I am really asking you is whether or not it is possible that the butler could have reached the french-window from the inside of the house, and got back to the hall again in the few minutes during which you were watching Inspector Barley."

The girl shook her head.

"Oh, no."

"It doesn't take long to go from here to that writing-room."

"I'm sure he couldn't have gone anywhere in the time."

Dr. Hailey turned to McDonald.

"Where is Gregor?"

"He's gone upstairs to his wife."

"And Duchlan?"

"He went upstairs a few minutes ago. Angus was with him."

They entered the study with Sergeant Jackson. The doctor closed the door.

"I fancy," he said, "that we can exclude Angus. It is incredible that he had any part either in the murder of Miss Gregor or in that of Inspector Dundas. This third murder is more mysterious, if that is possible, than its predecessors. I confess that I haven't the slightest idea how it was committed."

He gave the policeman a careful and detailed account of Barley's work adding:

"His own death, as you see, disproves his case. But it leaves us under the necessity of explaining how this murderer entered and left a locked room, how he entered and left a room the door and windows of which were under constant observation, finally how he killed in the open, in the presence of a witness, without betraying himself further than by a gleam of his weapon. We must explain, too, why that weapon, on each occasion, carried herring scales into the wounds inflicted by it."

Sergeant Jackson had nothing to say except that he must report immediately to headquarters, so that another detective officer might be sent. When he had gone, Dr. Hailey helped himself liberally to snuff, an indulgence which appeared greatly to soothe him.

"Three murders," he said at last, "and not a shred of evidence, not a breath of suspicion against anybody. This case, my dear McDonald, must be unique in the history of crime."

"Yes."

"I've experienced nothing like it. Think of it: that girl actually saw the weapon that killed Barley; you reached Dundas within thirty seconds of his death; Miss Gregor was shut off from the world by locks and bolts!" His eyes narrowed: "Barley was reasoning soundly enough when he said that you ought to have seen Miss Gregor's murderer drop from the window, eh?"

"Yes. But we didn't see him."

Dr. Hailey shook his head. "The wardress ought to have seen Barley's murderer, and she didn't," he said. "You ought to have seen Dundas's murderer. You didn't." He glanced about him. "This assassin kills but remains invisible."

"And moves about," McDonald added, "without leaving any trace of his movements. Presumably he descended on the flower-bed out there. But only my footmarks are found on the bed." He remained silent for a few minutes. Then he asked:

"Do you wonder, in face of all this, that stories such as that about the fishlike swimmers who come out of the deepest parts of the loch get widely believed?"

"No." The doctor started. "That's a clue that we've neglected," he declared. "I had meant to follow it up but Barley's theory made that impossible."

McDonald sighed. He had aged in these last, terrible moments and his features were haggard. He pressed his hand to his brow.

"What an immense difference there is," he remarked inconsequently, "between thinking about a thing and actually experiencing it. No wonder novelists write about what they know." He seemed to shake himself out of a lethargy. "Poor Barley," he exclaimed. "How upset he would be if he was still alive!"

"Yes."

"He was very able, I thought."

"Yes."

Again McDonald sighed. "It's queer that the detectives should have been chosen as victims. After all, too, Dundas had failed. He wasn't killed because anybody had cause to fear him."

Dr. Hailey nodded.

"I was just thinking that. Barley tried to make out that Dundas was bluffing when he said that he had failed."

"He was not. You saw him yourself. The man was at his wit's end. He told me again and again that this case was likely to ruin him with his superiors. The papers were saying nasty things at the time."

"That was my impression."

"It was everybody's impression. Even the servants here knew that no progress had been made. The fishermen, as I told you, jumped at once to the conclusion that no murderer would ever be found. They drove poor Dundas to distraction with their superstitious ideas. He wouldn't listen to them and yet he had nothing to advance against them. In this atmosphere of credulity, Dundas represented reason at bay. Why anybody should have wanted to kill him I cannot imagine."

The room was silent and the whole house seemed to have become partner in its silence. Dr. McDonald, who was standing at the fireplace, with his elbow on the mantelpiece, looked uneasy.

"Things which happen in houses frighten me more than things which happen in the open," he said. "I can say honestly that I wasn't afraid in the motor-boat."

"You're afraid now?"

The Highlander turned sharply to the window and then faced his companion again.

"Yes."

He smiled as he spoke. Dr. Hailey nodded.

"So am I."

Chapter XXXII

Mother and Son

Dr. Hailey had reached the age when a man knows, and is inwardly convinced of his knowledge, that life is short. That is a time when imagination loses something of its power. The vigour of his apprehensiveness in face of these murders, consequently, surprised him. He was punished, it seemed, for his discounting of Highland superstition. He took more snuff and rallied his thoughts.

"I abandon the search for the method of these crimes," he told his companion. "And I shall not concern myself any more with their occasions. There is left only the strictly human business of motive. After all, it takes two to make a murder."

McDonald nodded: "One can perhaps understand the murder of Miss Gregor," he said. "But the murderer can scarcely have had any personal feeling against Dundas and Barley."

"No. Especially as Dundas had failed to discover any-thing and Barley had built up a strong case against innocent people. But it seems to me quite useless to trouble about that aspect of the case. I mean to concentrate on Miss Gregor. I believe I know enough now about her character to warrant certain broad conclusions." He leaned forward in his chair. "Don't forget for a single instant that Miss Gregor narrowly escaped being murdered long ago. The healed wound on her chest was inflicted by Duchlan's wife. Here is a woman who knew how to drive her sister-in-law to madness, to death, without losing her brother's regard. Duchlan isn't a fool. We may very well ask by what alchemy of persuasion he was held during all these years."

McDonald agreed fervently. "As I told you," he said. "My own impression of Miss Gregor was one of inhuman perseverance. She had a way of restating the most cruel slanders in the kindest terms, assuring you that she had forgiven faults which existed only in her own invention and pleading with you to be equally generous. When she spoke about Mrs. Eoghan in that way I wanted to tear her to pieces. She knew; she understood; and she persisted."

Eoghan entered the room. His face expressed profound relief, but he looked, nevertheless, very grave.

"Has the policeman gone?" he asked Dr. Hailey.

"Yes. He said that he must report at once."

"I've been with Oonagh in the nursery. What courage that girl has shown." Suddenly he held out his hand to Dr. Hailey. "I want to thank you for what you did to-night in the boat."

He sat down and covered his face with his hands. He exclaimed:

"Shall we ever come to the end of this horror? It's worse than death." He raised his head. "I'm a coward, I know, but I've never been so frightened before. I was frightened to come downstairs just now. I swear I looked for a murderer at every step."

He pronounced the word murderer like a personal name, a manner which neither of his companions found odd.

"That's exactly how I feel," McDonald confessed. He stretched out his arm in a vague, uncomfortable gesture. "Murder is here."

Dr. Hailey put his eyeglass in his eye.

"We had better stop this kind of thing," he declared firmly, "and get to work, to business. If murder is here, let us try to find and end it." He turned to Eoghan. "I want you to tell me," he asked in earnest tones, "exactly what your feelings were towards your aunt."

His voice recalled the young man sharply.

"She brought me up."

"That isn't what I want information about. What did you feel towards her?"

The question wrought a silence which became uncomfortable.

"One hates to speak about such things," Eoghan said at last.

"I beg that you will speak."

"I suppose I didn't feel as grateful as I ought to have felt."

"You disliked her?"

"In a way. Yes."

"Why?"

Eoghan shook his head.

"I don't know. She was very, very kind to me."

"Did you quarrel with her?"

"Yes, I did. Very often."

"About your mother?"

The young man started.

"Yes."

"Although you had never known your mother?"

"I don't remember anything about my mother."

"So that what upset you was the picture of your mother which your aunt gave you?"

Eoghan started again.

"I suppose it was."

"Children are always conventional. Other boys had mothers whom they liked; you naturally wished to believe that your mother had been as good and lovable as theirs. It seems that such an idea was not welcome in this house."

Dr. Hailey's earnestness was such as to disarm resentment.

"A child," he added, "usually goes straight to the heart of things. I take it you told your aunt that she hated your mother?"

"Yes."

"She denied that?"

"Yes."

"Did you ask your father about your mother?"

"No. I was afraid of my father." Eoghan took out his pipe and tried to fill it. "As a matter of fact I was a solitary sort of kid. I was happiest when they left me to myself in the nursery. I used to pretend that my mother came and played with me there and that we were both frightened of Aunt Mary and father. I don't know where I got the idea but I always thought of my mother and myself as the Babes in the Wood."

"Your aunt was the oppressor?"

He nodded. "My head was full of fairy tales. My mother was Red Riding Hood and Goldilocks and Cinderella in turn."

"And your aunt the wolf and the bear and the ugly sister?"

"Perhaps, yes. It was vague, you know."

"Your mother was Irish?"

"Yes."

Dr. Hailey allowed his eyeglass to drop.

"Do you possess a picture of your mother?" he asked.

"Only a small photograph." He flushed as he said this.

The doctor held out his hand.

"May I look at it?"

There was a moment of silence. Eoghan had stiffened in his chair, resentful apparently of the fact that it should have been guessed that he carried his mother's photograph about with him. But his resentment was soon lost in confusion. He took a small leather case from his pocket and handed it to the doctor.

"My mother gave the photograph to Christina," he said in hurried tones which revealed how deep was his hurt that his only relic of his mother had come to him thus, at second hand.

There were two photographs in the case. One faded, inscribed to "my dear Christina", the other new, of Oonagh. Oonagh bore a likeness to Eoghan's mother that was unmistakable. Dr. Hailey handed the case back without comment.

"You're a poor man?" he asked gently.

"I am."

"Was that why you left your wife and child here, in this house?"

The question seemed to cause the young man acute distress.

"I don't think that was the only reason," he said in hesitating tones.

"May I ask your other reason?"

"I didn't realize that Oonagh would be so unhappy here. I felt that I would like her to be here, where I had lived so long."

"I see." Dr. Hailey nodded several times. "Just as you would have liked your mother to be here?"

"Perhaps that is part of the reason, although I didn't think of it at the time. I wanted Hamish to have Christina as his nurse and I knew she would never consent to leave my aunt even if my aunt consented to part with her."

"Were you gambling to make money?"

The question came abruptly. But it produced very little reaction.

"Yes."

"To have enough to set up a home of your own?"

"Yes."

"So you realized that your wife's position was hopeless in this house?"

"Yes."

"Your aunt knew that you meant to have a home of your own?"

"She may have known."

"What do you mean by that?"

"I had told her that I thought a married woman ought to have her own home." Eoghan hesitated again. "I suppose I knew that she was opposed to the idea, because I didn't develop it."

"You were afraid of her?"

"I think everybody was a little afraid of her. My aunt had a way of making people who disagreed with her feel guilty. I can't tell you how she did it, but I often noticed the effect. I think her secret lay in her absolute conviction that whatever she thought or felt must be right. She was a deeply religious woman in rather a superstitious way. Perhaps it's necessary to be a Highlander to understand exactly what that means."

The doctor nodded again.

"Without being a Highlander," he said, "I had guessed that."

"She was kind in making me an allowance. I couldn't have married Oonagh when I did but for that allowance."

"It was paid to you?"

"Oh, no. It was paid chiefly in kind. My aunt dressed Oonagh and Hamish. She contributed to their board because my father is very poor. In addition she was constantly giving little presents."

Eoghan broke off. Dr. Hailey gazed at him in silence for a few minutes.

"I want you to tell me quite frankly whether or not your wife's responses to those gifts seemed to you ungrateful," he said.

"Sometimes they did seem to me a little ungrateful."

"You told your wife that?"

"I tried to explain to her that my aunt's up-bringing and her up-bringing had been entirely different. Oonagh's people live a care-free sort of life. They have no money but they hunt and go about a great deal. Oonagh never knew what it was to be restrained till she was married. And she never knew what it was to lack money because she possessed everything she wanted. Coming here was like coming to prison. I tried to make her realize that Aunt Mary couldn't be expected to understand this and that, consequently, it wasn't fair to judge her as one might have judged a younger woman."

He passed his hand across his brow. He, too, looked haggard and weary.

"Your wife wasn't persuaded?"

"No, she wasn't. She said she would prefer one room of her own anywhere. I had made up my mind to take her away from here no matter what it cost."

"You mean, no matter whether or not your aunt refused to help you if you did?"

"Yes. Unfortunately I made a bad break in trying to get money quickly. I had to fall back on Aunt Mary."

Dr. Hailey frowned.

"Surely that was an extraordinarily foolish thing to do?" he said.

"Yes, it was. But I was getting desperate." Eoghan glanced at McDonald and then braced himself to tell the truth. "The truth is I felt I was losing Oonagh. Aunt Mary hinted that I had lost her. When she wrote me about Oonagh's flight from this house, I nearly went mad. If I could have got leave I would have rushed back here. Then I thought of blowing out my brains, so that she could be free. That moment of madness passed. I told myself it was a punishment for my not having got Oonagh a home of her own. I determined to try my luck there and then, because I felt somehow that a miracle would save me. I felt that it was impossible that Oonagh could be taken away from me. I could scarcely think. I hadn't slept for nights. All my thoughts were whirling in my brain like peas in a drum. I plunged and plunged till my friends were aghast. And I lost…"

He broke off. A bitter smile curved his lips.

"Lost. So that I hadn't a bean left in the world. I went back to my quarters and took my pistol out. There was nothing for it now but a quick ending. I think I would have shot myself if my best friend hadn't found me. He sat with me all night, listening while I talked. And I talked till dawn. Talked and talked. I told him everything, about my mother and my aunt and Oonagh. About you, McDonald. At the end he swore that Oonagh was in love with me. 'Go back to her,' he begged, 'and raise the money you owe somehow, anyhow. It'll come right in the end.'

"I was calmer and I saw what a fool and coward I had been. I asked for leave and got it."

"You meant to borrow from your aunt?"

"Yes. I had a tale ready that my friend concocted for me—about losses on shares. Aunt Mary had no objection to gambling on the Stock Exchange."

"That was business?"

"That was business."

Dr. Hailey shook his head. His eyes expressed the wonder which so many human prejudices and misunderstandings caused him.

"You had written to your wife?" he asked.

"Yes. I had to appeal to her to keep on good terms with my aunt. I know now that it was that letter which sent her to Aunt Mary's room. When I arrived here I went straight to my aunt's room. My madness had returned on the long, lonely journey across the Firth. I was terribly worked up and felt I must get an answer immediately. Her locked door and her silence convinced me that she had made up her mind to have nothing more to do with me. Naturally, murder never entered my head. I rushed off to Oonagh's bedroom."

He paused again. He shook his head sadly.

"I don't want to excuse myself in any way. But you had better know the facts. I suppose I was half-crazy with anxiety and worry and loss of sleep. I accused Oonagh of ruining me—not perhaps in those words, but she knew very well what I meant. I said I would have to leave the Army and go abroad. There was no hope now because Aunt Mary was against me. 'There was only her money,' I cried, 'between me and ruin. That's gone. I must go too.' I saw a terrible fear in Oonagh's eyes. She jumped up and tried to put her arms round my neck. She told me that you, McDonald, had offered to lend me money…"

He drew a sharp breath.

"That was like a wound in my heart. 'Do you know,' I said very quietly, 'that I would rather rob my aunt, cheat her, murder her if need be, than touch a penny of that swine's money.' Suddenly everything seemed to go red in front of my eyes. I sprang at Oonagh. I seized her by the throat. 'Tell me,' I shouted, 'exactly what has happened between you and that man.' I believe that, for one awful moment, I was prepared to strangle her."

He covered his face with his hands. The room grew so still that the voice of the burn reached them, gurgling in its immemorial delight. Dr. Hailey saw that McDonald's face had grown stiff, like a mask.

"Yes?" the doctor asked.

"Oonagh swore that nothing had happened. She swore that her love for me had not wavered. I had the feeling that she was pleading for her life. I wasn't convinced. But the first gust of my rage had passed. I began to tremble. The tension of my nerves gave way suddenly and I broke down. She told me that she didn't care whether we were rich or poor. She said she was able to work and ready to work and that between us we would make enough to keep Hamish. I don't know why, but when she spoke in that way my troubles seemed to get less. I began to believe her."

His voice faded away. Dr. Hailey waited for a few moments and then said:

"It was your statement that you would rob or kill your aunt sooner than borrow from McDonald which made your wife fear that you had murdered her?"

"I suppose so. That, and my attack on herself. I believe I was mad for a few minutes."

"She was ready to die for you?"

Dr. Hailey's voice was low but his tones thrilled with admiration. Eoghan raised his head sharply.

"God knows," he cried, "I never was worthy of Oonagh. I never will be worthy of her."

Eoghan drove McDonald home. When they left the house Dr. Hailey went out to the place where Barley had been killed. The fear, which had oppressed him indoors, lost its power as soon as he crossed the threshold. He stood listening to the voices of night, softly-moving winds, the gurgle of the burn and, louder than these, the fall of waves on the shingle. He walked to the spot where Barley had fallen. His lamp revealed nothing. The tide was ebbing but remained high, so that the mouth of the burn resembled a tiny harbour. He descended the steep slope to the water's edge, and stood there for a few minutes. Then he climbed the bank again. It was obvious that, at the moment of his death, Barley had been concerned about the murder of Dundas, whose bedroom was immediately above the spot where he had been standing. The doctor wondered what doubt or question had sent the poor man on this fatal errand. If Barley really believed that McDonald had killed Dundas, why should he trouble about the ground under Dundas's window?

He returned to the house and went upstairs to his bedroom. The more he thought about it, the stranger this last act of Barley's seemed. The only possible explanation seemed to be that the detective had begun to doubt his theory that McDonald had killed Dundas; but if so, why had he arrested McDonald? Barley was an honest man and as such would certainly have delayed making an arrest so long as any substantial doubt remained in his mind. But he was a practical man who would not have gone out of his way except for a reason. It seemed certain therefore that a reason why he should examine the ground under Dundas's window must have occurred to his mind or been forced upon his mind after he had effected the arrest of McDonald. The doctor frowned. How could any such reason have arisen at the time? He mastered his fears and walked along the corridor to Dundas's bedroom. Barley's body lay on the bed, under a sheet. He removed this and searched the dead man's pockets. He found nothing except a diary, in which notes of the progress of the case had been made from time to time. The last of these notes consisted of a summing-up of the evidence against McDonald and Mrs. Gregor. He replaced the book and went downstairs. Eoghan had just returned and was in the smoke-room pouring out a whisky-and-soda. The young man looked relieved when he saw the doctor.

"I heard you coming downstairs," he exclaimed, in tones which betrayed the anxiety that sound had occasioned him. He added: "When I was outside I felt all right. This house seems to have become different."

He offered Dr. Hailey a drink and poured it out.

"People can say what they like about whisky," he declared, "but there are times when it's the most sobering drink in the world."

He lit his pipe and carried his glass to an arm-chair. He sat down and put the glass on the floor beside him. The doctor told him about his difficulty in accounting for Barley's last excursion.

"Can you think of any reason," he asked, "why he should suddenly have developed a fresh interest in Dundas's murder?"

"No."

"You saw him arrest McDonald. Did it strike you that he had any doubts about the justice of what he was doing?"

"What, after the lecture he had given us? 'Pon my soul, doctor, he made out a strong case, a terrible case."

"Exactly. And then, apparently, hurried off to test its merits. It seems absurd on the face of it."

"Possibly he had some other reason for going…"

"Yes, but what other reason? Barley was a man who knew how to economize his efforts. I feel absolutely certain that it was no trivial cause that sent him along that steep bank at that moment."

Eoghan shook his head. Among so many mysteries, this one, he seemed to think, was too small to deserve notice.

"I'm sorry for Barley," he declared, "but the big fact about his death, so far as I'm concerned, is its effect on Oonagh. When I heard that last summing-up I thought…" His voice broke; he gulped the remains of his whisky. "They'd have been convicted," he concluded in hurried tones.

Dr. Hailey started slightly. He leaned forward.

"So the reason which sent Barley to Dundas's window was an essential element in their salvation?"

"As it happened, yes."

"My dear sir, it did happen. How can we say that in this case cause and effect are unrelated?"

Eoghan frowned: "You don't suggest, do you," he asked, "that McDonald or Oonagh supplied a reason for Barley's going to that place?"

"Of course not. But somebody else, who was interested in them, may have supplied that reason."

"Who? My father was here, so was I."

"The murderer perhaps."

"The murderer?"

"Angus was in the hall when Barley left this room."

Eoghan drew a sharp breath.

"What! My dear doctor, if I may say so, that's the most absurd suggestion I've ever heard in my life. If you knew Angus you would realize just how absurd it is."

"Possibly."

"If Angus murdered Barley, he murdered Dundas and my aunt also. Can you imagine him dropping from my aunt's window, or Dundas's window? How did he get into my aunt's bedroom? How did he get into Dundas's bedroom? How did he kill Barley, seeing that he remained in the hall?"

The questions came sharply, like the rattle of machine-gun fire. Dr. Hailey shook his head.

"No. I can imagine none of these things," he confessed. "But in a case like this one is driven to ask every possible and impossible question." He pressed his hand to his brow. "Surely no theory can be dismissed as ridiculous in respect of a series of events each of which is itself ridiculous to the point of utter impossibility." He helped himself to a pinch of snuff. "And so I return to Angus. He is the only person who can have spoken to Barley after Barley left this room. He is consequently the only person who can have supplied a motive for that sudden, and in the circumstances, amazing visit to the bank under Dundas's window..."

Dr. Hailey broke off. Footsteps were approaching the door.

Chapter XXXIII

The Swimmer

There was a knock at the door; Eoghan jumped up and opened it. Dr. Hailey saw Angus standing with a lighted candle in his hand which shook so that the flame danced. The man's face had a sickly green complexion. Behind him, half-hidden among shadows, were two women in hats and coats.

"You'll forgive us, sir," Angus said in a shaky voice, "but we cannot sleep in this house."

He came a little way into the room as he spoke and the women also advanced. The women's faces were tear-stained and one of them, the younger, was whimpering.

"Why not?"

"Because, sir, we cannot."

"That's no reason, Angus."

The old man glanced behind him suddenly as if he expected to be stabbed in the back. His mouth opened.

"It's down in the burn, sir," he ejaculated wildly.

"What?"

"It's down in the burn, sir."

"Down in the burn? What's down in the burn?"

Again the piper glanced behind him. He tried to speak but his voice failed.

Eoghan drew himself up.

"Pull yourself together man and don't talk nonsense," he ordered.

Fear gave the old man courage of a sort. He faced his master.

"I heard It myself, sir, splashing in the burn this night before Mr. Barley was killed," he declared. "And Mary, she heard It too. And she heard It when Mr. Dundas was killed…"

"Rubbish."

"It is not rubbish, sir. To-night, after Mr. Barley was killed, Mary saw It swimming away from the mouth of the burn to the loch. And she called Flora and Flora saw It too, a black head It had, like the head of a seal, and It was swimming slowly…"

Angus began to shake. The candle he was holding swayed in its socket and fell to the floor. Eoghan snatched the candlestick out of his hand and made him sit down. He gave him a stiff glass of whisky. Then he turned to the women, who seemed to find his energy reassuring:

"What is he talking about, Mary?"

"It's the truth, sir, he's been telling you," the elder of the two girls declared. "I saw It with my own eyes, swimming out of the burn's mouth and I heard the splashing It made when It came up out of the water and went back to it…I called to Flora 'Oh, look, look,' I cried to her, and she jumped out of her bed and came to the window and there It was swimming away."

"What was?" Eoghan cried irritably.

"The thing that is covered with fish's scales…"

"Good gracious, girl, are you crazy?"

"I saw It, sir, and Flora saw It. It was black, like a seal, till It came to the place where the moon was shining on the water. And then we saw the scales on Its head shining like the body of a fish." Her voice fell. "You know, sir, that there was fish's scales…"

She broke off, overwhelmed by fresh fears. Eoghan turned to her sister.

"Well?" he asked.

"Yes, it's true, sir. I saw It as Angus and Mary has told you. Its head was shining like the body of a fish…"

"Are you trying to tell me that a fish climbed up to my aunt's bedroom?" Eoghan exclaimed in mocking tones.

"Oh, no, sir."

"That's what you're saying."

"Oh, no, sir."

"What are you saying, then?"

The girl gathered her courage. "The Evil One," she declared in shaking tones, "can take any form he wishes to take."

"Oh, so it was the Devil you saw?"

There was no answer. The young man glanced at Angus:

"What do you mean by saying that you can't stay in this house?" he demanded sternly.

"There is something wrong with this house, sir."

Fear and whisky had combined to excite the old Highlander. He rose to his feet; his eyes, lately so dim, began to flash.

"God is my witness," he cried in solemn tones. "It was into that very water that your mother threw herself."

He stopped, suddenly afraid. Dr. Hailey saw the blood rush into Eoghan's cheeks and then ebb out of them again suddenly.

"Angus, what are you saying?"

There was no answer. Both the women drew back.

"What are you saying, Angus?"

Eoghan's pale face expressed a degree of emotional tension which brought Dr. Hailey to his side.

"I shouldn't trouble..."

The young man interrupted with a quick, peremptory gesture. He took a step towards his father's servant.

"You said my mother threw herself into the burn?" he cried. "Is that true?"

Angus had recovered from the first shock of his boldness; he was still in close enough touch with the emotions which had driven him to the room and enough under the influence of the whisky he had drunk to be unwilling to recede.

"It's the truth, Mister Eoghan," he declared. He thrust out his hands. "It was these hands which helped to carry her back to this house."

"You are saying that my mother drowned herself?"

The piper bowed his head.

"Well?"

"Yes, Mister Eoghan."

A queer, wild light shone in the young man's eyes. But his features remained stiffened in immobility.

"And now you think that this...this thing which splashes and kills...is come to avenge her?"

Angus's excitement was abating. He stood gazing at his master with sorrowful eyes, already remorseful because of the pain he had inflicted. Eoghan turned to the doctor.

"Do you know anything of this?" he asked.

"Yes."

"You too. Everybody except me." He addressed the servants. "Go where you like," he cried. "I've no wish to keep you here. In this house. I've no wish to keep you in this house." He waved his hand, dismissing them. "Why should you suffer in this house for other men's crimes?"

He sank into a chair. Dr. Hailey approached him.

"May I take them into another room and ask them some questions?"

"No. Ask your questions here. Let me, as well as everybody else, be informed this time."

Eoghan's tones rang out full of bitterness and derision. He gripped the arms of his chair with fingers the joints of which blanched. His lips moved up and down on his strong teeth. Dr. Hailey signed to the servants to sit down and sat down himself. He turned to the girl Mary.

"You say you heard a splash on the night when Inspector Dundas was murdered?" he asked.

"Yes, sir. But I didn't think at the time what it might be. There were fishing-smacks lying off the burn that night, sir."

The doctor nodded.

"I know. And your brother was on one of these smacks?"

"Yes, sir."

"Your brother came here to report what he had seen that night. He didn't mention hearing any splash."

"No, sir. Please, sir, it wasn't till to-night that I thought anything about the splash." She fumbled with the buttons on her coat. "There's often splashes when the fishing is going on," she added. "If my brother heard the splash, he would think it was made by somebody on one of the other boats throwing something overboard."

"I see."

"It was not a very loud splash."

"Where were you when you heard it?"

"I was going to bed, the same as I was when I heard the first splash to-night. Flora was sleeping."

Dr. Hailey leaned forward eagerly:

"You heard two splashes to-night?" he asked.

"Yes, sir."

"Loud splashes?"

"They were not very loud, sir."

He adjusted his eyeglass.

"Why should you have troubled about them to-night when you didn't trouble before?"

"Because there were no smacks fishing to-night. I thought it was very strange that I should be hearing a splash when there was nobody to make it."

She glanced over her shoulder as she spoke.

"Did you hear anything between the splashes?"

"No, sir."

"Did you see anything?"

"No, sir."

He leaned forward again:

"Tell me exactly what you saw after the second splash."

"I have told you sir. There was something swimming out of the mouth of the burn. It had a head like a seal, that looked black till the moon shone on it. Then I saw that it was shining like the body of a fish."

She repeated the words mechanically but her voice shook.

"It was then you called your sister?"

"Yes, sir. 'What is it?' she said to me. 'I don't know what it is, Flora,' I said, 'but it's what I heard splashing in the water and maybe it's what I heard splashing when Mr. Dundas was murdered.' When I was speaking we heard voices below the window and somebody said 'He's dead' and Flora caught hold of my arm and began to cry. We went down to the kitchen and there was Angus sitting in a chair as white as death. I told him what we had heard and he said, 'Mr. Barley's been murdered, too, I heard the splashes when I was standing in the hall!'"

The girl shook her head when she finished speaking, and then again glanced behind her. She added:

"Angus was crying and saying…"

"Never mind that." Dr. Hailey's voice was stern. "How long did you watch the thing you saw swimming?"

"Until we heard the voices."

"So you didn't see where it went to?"

"No, sir, we did not."

The doctor turned to Angus.

"You were standing in the hall when you heard the first splash?" he asked in sharp tones.

"Yes, sir. I was waiting in case Duchlan might require me."

"Where was Inspector Barley at that moment?"

"He had just gone out of the house. He was standing at the front door, near to the motor-car."

"Do you think he heard it too?"

"Yes, sir, I think he did, because he walked towards the burn."

"You saw that?"

"Yes, sir."

"Did you hear anything after that, before you heard the second splash?"

Angus's face stiffened with new fear. He bent forward in his chair.

"I heard a sound, sir," he whispered, "that I know was the rattle of death."

Chapter XXXIV

"Something Wrong"

The sweat gleamed on the old man's brow. He wiped it away with his hand. Eoghan rose and gave him more whisky.

"You were standing near the door of the small writing-room, were you not?" Dr. Hailey asked him.

"Yes, I was."

"And the window of the writing-room was open?"

"Yes, it was open."

"So that you were bound to hear everything that passed between Inspector Barley and his murderer?"

"I did not hear anything except the sound I have told you about."

"What you call the death-rattle?"

"It was that, sir; I have heard it before."

"The second splash followed?"

"Yes, sir. And when I heard it I knew that..."

"I don't want to hear what you knew, only what you heard and did. What did you do?"

"A young woman who was dressed like a policeman came running into the house."

"I know that. Please answer my question: What did you do yourself?"

The piper shook his head.

"I went back into the kitchen."

"Because you felt afraid?"

"Because I knew that the day…"

Again the doctor interrupted sharply. He rose and announced that he had no more questions to ask. He glanced at his watch.

"You had better go back to the kitchen. You can keep two or three candles burning till dawn," he said.

He waited until they had gone. Then he turned to Eoghan.

"At least we know now why Barley went to the place where he was killed," he said in eager tones. "The next step, clearly, is to discover the truth about this swimmer."

"I suppose so."

The young man rose and walked to the fireplace. He stood leaning with one elbow on the mantelpiece, a dejected figure.

"I understand your questions about my childhood now," he said in low tones. "I understand everything now."

"Your father was very much under your aunt's influence," Dr. Hailey said in the accents of a man who feels it incumbent on him to be special pleader.

"Yes."

"From what I could gather it was such another case as that of your wife and McDonald. The atmosphere of this place broke down your mother's nervous strength."

"You mean it broke her heart?"

The words came with extraordinary vehemence.

"No, I don't mean that. I feel sure that your father loved your mother in his own, strange way. But he was held in a kind of bondage by your aunt. He could not prevent himself from seeing and feeling what his sister willed that he should see and feel…"

Eoghan started and took a step towards his companion. His face had flushed suddenly:

"Dundas told me," he exclaimed, "that my aunt had a healed wound on her chest. A wound that must have been inflicted long ago by someone…"

His voice broke. He covered his face with his hands. But a moment later he recovered his self-control.

"You know that it was my mother who inflicted that wound?" he asked in level tones.

Dr. Hailey drew his hand across his brow. "My dear fellow," he said gently, "your mother was no longer in her right mind."

"They had driven her mad!"

"Perhaps not intentionally."

He clutched at his brow with both hands.

"Horrible, horrible," he cried. "And to think that I was taught to call my aunt 'Mother'…that I called her 'Mother'."

A strong tremor passed over his body.

"That was why my father thought that Oonagh had killed her," he added. "Because Oonagh is like my mother."

Suddenly a cry broke from his lips. He seized Dr. Hailey's arm.

"Did he, did my father make the same suggestion to Oonagh as he made to my mother? That she should drown herself?"

"He believed her to be guilty, remember."

"Oh, I might have guessed it."

"My dear fellow, as you know the evidence was very strong."

The rebuke was spoken gently but exerted its effect. Eoghan's eyes fell. He shook his head.

"Angus was right," he said, "there's something wrong with this house."

Chapter XXXV

The Chill of Death

A moment later both men started and remained tense, listening. Shuffling feet were approaching the open window of the room. Dr. Hailey walked to the window and reached it just as a tall figure in a black dressing-gown emerged from the darkness. It was Duchlan.

"Is Eoghan with you?" the old man asked.

"Yes."

"I desire to speak to him. I'll come round by the writing-room."

He gathered his gown about him and disappeared. Then they heard him crossing the hall. As he stood in the doorway the colour of his dressing-gown made painful contrast with the faded whiteness of his cheeks. His features were haggard and his long eyelids had fallen over his eyes, as if he might no longer face a world that had overthrown him. His son rose at his coming.

"Sit down, Eoghan."

The withered hand made a gesture that was a plea rather than a command. Duchlan sat down himself and leaned his head on the back of the chair exposing his stringy, vulture-like throat.

"Sleep has gone from me," he said. "To-night I cannot rest."

The slight affectation of his tone and language did not hide his agitation. Dr. Hailey glanced at Eoghan and saw that the son shared fully the distress of the father.

"You have no idea, I suppose," Duchlan asked the doctor, "how this man Barley met his death?"

"None."

"These murders are inexplicable, is it not so?"

"We have not yet discovered the explanation of them."

The long eyelids closed.

"You will not discover any explanation. And if you go on seeking, sorrow will be added to sorrow."

Duchlan's fingers began to beat on the arms of his chair. The muscles round his mouth were twitching.

"God is just," he declared in tones of awe. He turned to his son. "I feel that my end is approaching; before it comes there is something that I must tell you."

He raised himself in his chair as he spoke. Eoghan recoiled.

"I know it already," he said.

"That's impossible."

"Why and how my mother met her death."

Silence filled the room. The song of the burn, now in the ebb became a deep crooning like a mother's song to her babe, came up to them.

"Your mother," Duchlan said at last, "died of diphtheria."

"You know, sir, that my mother drowned herself in the burn?"

The old man did not flinch.

"That is the other part of the truth."

"What do you mean?"

"There was an epidemic of diphtheria, during which many children died, Christina's son among them. Your mother insisted on helping with the nursing and contracted the disease herself. As you know, diphtheria sometimes attacks the brain…" Duchlan sighed deeply. "What followed, therefore, was due to the promptings of a disordered mind."

He paused. His breathing had become laboured. Eoghan remained in a posture of tense expectancy.

"But that is not all. Far be it from me at such an hour as this to hide from you any longer the burden of guilt which lies upon my heart. If it was disease which finally wrought your mother's death, there were other causes, operating through weeks and months of sorrow, which led up to that tragedy. I am here to confess that my own weakness was the chief of these causes."

"Please don't go on, father."

Duchlan raised his hand.

"I beg of you to hear me." He tugged at the neck of his gown, opening it wider. "From my childhood, I suffered a weakness of character which I found it impossible to overcome. I was timid when I would have been brave, fearful when resolution was required of me. It was my calamity that the qualities I lacked were possessed in fullest measure by my sister, your Aunt Mary. In consequence, she acquired, from the beginning, a dominion over me which I was unable to resist. She is dead; that dominion lives so that now I feel powerless to conduct my life without her. Your mother possessed an excellent strength of mind, but her strength was inferior to that of my sister; our marriage consequently was doomed."

He paused. His fingers continued their ceaseless drumming.

"When she was eighteen your aunt became engaged to be married to an Englishman and I felt myself suddenly and terribly alone. I went to stay with an old friend in Dublin and there I met your mother."

The old man sighed deeply.

"She was a lovely girl, as lovely as Oonagh. Her people had a small place in the west, by the sea. A lonely, desolate place where the bogs stretched for miles like a desert under the wild skies. She had been brought up there and had lived free of all restraint with her dogs and horses. The sea was in her eyes, and the love of the sea was in her heart. I felt as I looked at her that she had discovered the secret which, all my life, I had been seeking, namely, release from spiritual bondage. If I could only capture this wild, wonderful creature, she would teach me the way of her strength and courage and deliver me from my fear. I tried to tell her what was in my heart and I saw that she pitied me. It seemed so easy, in that land of hers, to possess one's own soul and live out one's dream. We fell in love with each other…"

He broke off. They saw a shiver pass over his body.

"She called me her 'dour Scotsman' and promised to make a wild Irishman of me. I stayed on at her home, week after week, forgetting everything but my love of her. This place and its associations became a dim memory, like the evening memory of a distressful dream. We needn't, I thought, spend very much of our time at Duchlan. I can let the place and we can come and live in Ireland."

His voice had developed a rhythmic quality. As he bent and swayed in his chair he looked, Dr. Hailey thought, like some old bard singing of times long buried in the earth's womb. Tears had gathered in his eyes; they crept down his cheeks, going from wrinkle to wrinkle.

"That was treason; because my father had vowed that no stranger should ever dwell in Duchlan. But even my father had lost his power over me in that wilderness. I had fallen under the spell of your mother's folk, who cared nothing for the ideas which live in this place. Your grandfather and your grandmother, your uncles and aunts were all of the same way of thinking. They belonged to life, to the present, to the Nature which surrounded and nourished them, and to each other. They were as generous as they were brave and their hospitality had no end. It never occurred to one of them to ask questions and whatever I said about myself was accepted as the whole truth. I ceased to feel lonely. I began to be thankful that my sister had got engaged. In other words, I surrendered myself completely to your mother's influence.

"We were married a few months later. When we returned from our honeymoon your aunt's engagement had been broken off. She begged that she might be allowed to remain here for a few months until she was able to find a home elsewhere. I will not hide from you that, when I yielded to that request, I knew that I was making a sacrifice of your mother."

He sighed again. "And so it proved. My sister had broken off her engagement, as she confessed to me, because she could neither endure to leave this place nor to enter another family. Naturally, your mother resented her intrusion on our married life and wished to be quit of her. A duel began between them, of which I was the helpless and unwilling spectator. Both appealed to me daily. Soon, very soon, the strongest character asserted itself.

"Your mother had a quick temper but with it a fatal generosity. Mary possessed neither the one nor the other. I used to marvel at the way in which she achieved her ends. She was as sleepless as a spider and as calculating. Everywhere, webs, webs, webs, until her victims were bound with gossamer that was stronger than steel. Violence could gain nothing against that subtlety."

He leaned forward. His voice grew louder.

"For I was violent too; it is the way of the weak. I loved your mother and sometimes I dared to rebel. Sometimes I stormed and raged against the tyranny which threatened us; it was like the rage of a young child against the nurse who takes away its playthings. Then you were born."

Duchlan's eyes closed again. He remained silent for a few minutes, motionless, like a figure carved out of old ivory. Then his fingers began to drum once more on the carved wood.

"Your birth," he continued, "made everything much worse because you are the heir. Your mother felt that you belonged to her; your aunt that you belonged to the Gregors. Your aunt was determined to take you away from your mother and in addition she wanted you because she had no child of her own. Thus all the furies which dwell in the hearts of women were unleashed." He made a despairing gesture. "The tide of hatred flowed and submerged me. I felt that my marriage was drifting to utter catastrophe and yet I possessed no power to save it. Your mother grew to hate and then to despise me. Her natural goodness was turned to a scorn that stung without stimulating. One day she threatened to leave me unless I ordered your aunt out of my house. Her anger and bitterness were terrible and for the moment they prevailed. I told my sister that a new arrangement was imperatively necessary. She took to her bed and became ill so that the doctor had to be summoned. He told me that she was very ill and that, if I persisted in my plan to make her leave her home, he would not be responsible for the consequences. By that time your mother's anger had cooled and her generosity had asserted itself. Your aunt stayed; our marriage was wrecked."

He held up his hand, forbidding interruption.

"At the moment when my wife's body was carried into this room a chill of death struck my heart. I had heard the splash of her fall into the water. They laid her body on that couch." He pointed to the piece of furniture and continued to keep his finger stretched towards it. "There were little pools of water on the floor and they grew bigger and became joined to each other. Water was running in thin streams from her hair and from her elbows, because they had crossed her arms on her breast. Angus and the men who had helped him to carry her up from the burn went away and left me here, alone with her. But I felt nothing…nothing but curiosity to watch the little streams and pools of water. I counted them; there were eleven streams and seven pools. Eleven and seven. Then I thought about the last moments we had spent together the night before, after the wounding of your aunt, and I repeated aloud what I had said to her: 'You have killed my sister, you have ruined my life and my son's life. There is only one thing left for you to do. It will be high tide at…' Well, she had done it. But it seemed unreal and far away like something one has read about long ago and forgotten and remembered again. So I called to her to open her eyes…"

His head shook, nodding assent, perhaps, to some remote voice of his spirit.

"I thought: is she dead? And I kept repeating that word, 'Dead', over and over again so as to recall the meaning of it. But it had no meaning. Then it occurred to me, suddenly, that all the difficulties and troubles of my life were ended. If Mary got well, and the doctor expected her to get well, because the knife had missed her heart, we should have the house to ourselves again, as in the old days. You see, I had given my mind and my will wholly to my sister. It was with her eyes that I was looking at my wife's dead face." He plucked again at the neck of his gown. "Now I have no eyes but hers, for you, for this house, for our family. When I thought that Oonagh was a partner in Mary's death I spoke the same words to her as I had spoken to your mother: 'You have killed my sister…It will be high tide…'"

"Stop, father!"

Eoghan had jumped to his feet. He stood with quivering features and clenched fists. The old man bowed his head.

"I ask your forgiveness."

"Why should you tell me this? Why should you tell me this?"

Dr. Hailey saw a shudder pass over Duchlan's body. The old man faced his son.

"To give you back to your mother," he said simply. "That is all that is left to me now; to give you back to your mother."

Duchlan rose as he spoke. Again he pointed to the couch.

"I killed your mother; I would have killed your wife. What are these other crimes compared to my crime?"

He walked to the couch and stood gazing down at it as if he saw his wife once more as he had seen her with the water dripping from her hair and her elbows. But his face expressed nothing. He had spoken the truth when he said that the chill of death was entered into his spirit. Eoghan followed him with horrified eyes until he left the room.

Chapter XXXVI

The Mask

Dr. Hailey put his hand on Eoghan's shoulder.

"Have pity," he said gently.

"Pity?"

The young man spoke the word mechanically as if its meaning had escaped him. He continued to gaze at the door through which his father had just passed.

"For a mind in torment."

Eoghan turned suddenly and faced the doctor.

"You call that a mind in torment?" he asked bitterly. He strode to the fireplace and stood looking down into the empty grate. Dr. Hailey followed him.

"Men whose faces have been dreadfully disfigured," he said, "are condemned to hide them behind a mask. It is the same when the disfigurement is spiritual."

"What do you mean?"

"When your father yielded his will to your aunt, he condemned himself to a punishment that is exacted in shame and despair. The only refuge of the weak is another's strength. To escape from the hell of his own thoughts and feelings it was necessary that he should adopt completely and blindly those of your aunt. Moral cowardice has used that mask from the beginning. But the face behind the mask still lives."

"I see."

"Your mother found something to love in that weakness, remember. She allowed your aunt to stay here. She was even ready, perhaps, to endure the bitterness of that arrangement when illness deprived her, momentarily, of her reason. I feel sure she would have wished that you should not be less generous and forgiving. Your father is stricken because you had nothing to say to him. As you heard, he looks on these murders as supernatural occurrences, the expression of Heaven's anger against himself. The man is utterly forsaken."

Dr. Hailey spoke in very gentle tones which were free of any suggestion of reproof. He added:

"At least he didn't spare himself."

Eoghan stood erect.

"Thank you," he said. "I'll go to him."

He strode out of the room. When he had gone, Dr. Hailey sat down and helped himself to snuff. He remained for some minutes with his eyes closed and then rose to his feet. He left the room and ascended the stairs, going as quietly as possible. When he reached the first landing he stood, listening. The house was silent. He began the second ascent, pausing every few steps. As he neared the top of the stairs he crouched down suddenly. A faint sound of voices had reached his ears.

He waited for a few minutes and then completed his ascent. He could hear the voices distinctly now. They came from the nursery and he recognized Oonagh's clear, well-bred accents. He hesitated for a moment and then decided to continue the enterprise which had brought him upstairs. He crossed the narrow landing and put his hand on the door of the pantry from the window of which he and Barley had examined the spike in the wall above Miss Gregor's bedroom. He turned the handle and opened the door. At the same moment the nursery door was thrown open by Oonagh. She uttered a little cry of dismay and drew back a step. Then she recognized him.

"Dr. Hailey! I…I thought it was…"

She broke off and came towards him. He saw that she looked pale and strained but there was a new light of happiness in her eyes.

"Hamish has been rather restless," she said. "Christina and I have been trying to get him to sleep."

She led him into the nursery as she spoke. In spite of the heat of the weather there was a peep of fire burning in the grate and on this a kettle simmered. The room possessed an air of repose which affected him the more graciously in that it contrasted in so sharp a manner with the unease of the room he had just quitted. He walked to the cot and stood for a moment looking down at the sleeping child. Its small face had that flower-like quality which is childhood's exclusive possession; its features expressed an exquisite gentleness. Christina joined him at the cot. She pointed to a number of small red spots on the child's brow.

"I think he's had a little touch of the nettle rash," she said in her soft accents.

"Yes. That's the real origin of his trouble."

Oonagh was standing at the fire.

"You can't think," she exclaimed, "what a relief to me your view of his case has been. That was the one bright spot in all our troubles."

She crossed the room as she spoke.

"Is there any light on the death of that poor man?"

"None." Dr. Hailey polished his eyeglass between his finger and thumb. "Were you here when his death occurred?" he asked in earnest tones.

"Yes."

"The window was open?"

She started and then nodded assent.

"Did you hear anything?"

There was a moment of silence.

"It's strange but I thought I heard a splash…two splashes." She spoke with hesitation as if the sounds had troubled her.

"Did you look out of the window?"

Again he saw her start.

"Yes, I did, after I heard the second splash." A note of fear crept into her voice. "The moon was shining on the water where the burn flows into the loch. I saw a black thing, like a seal's head, swimming down the burn, but when the moon struck it it flashed and glimmered."

"Like a fish's body?"

"Exactly like that."

The doctor put his eyeglass into his eye.

"Other people saw the same object," he stated in deliberate tones. "And put their own interpretations on it. What did you think it was?"

"I couldn't think what it was."

Dr. Hailey turned to the nurse.

"Did you see it?"

"No, sir, I was getting the baby's milk at the time. But Mrs. Gregor told me about it."

"Has anything of the sort ever been seen here before?"

"Not that I've ever heard, sir."

Christina's hands were locked together. She kept wringing them. A lively fear had come into her eyes.

"The fishermen do say," she exclaimed in awe-struck tones, "that sometimes there be them that splashes round their boats at night."

"Yes?"

"They will be afraid when they hear the splashing…"

Dr. Hailey shrugged his shoulders.

"Loch Fyne is full of porpoises, you know," he said. "A school of porpoises can make a lot of noise."

The old woman did not answer. She continued to wring her hands and shake her head. He stood looking at her for a moment. His eyeglass fell.

"One of the maids says that she heard a splash on the night when Inspector Dundas was killed. Did you hear anything that night?"

"No, sir."

"The windows were open on that night also?"

Christina assented. "I've kept them open," she said, "ever since this spell of heat began."

Dr. Hailey walked to the window and stood looking out. The moon had travelled far since the time of Barley's death but its light still fell on the water in intermittent gleams as clouds, newly come from the west, moved across its face.

"One ought to hear a splash from any of these windows," he commented in tones which seemed to carry a rebuke. He turned back to face the occupants of the room. "The weather seems to be breaking. I thought this heat could not last much longer."

Again he surveyed the water. His face was troubled as if some important decision was toward in his mind. It seemed that he was in doubt how to explain himself because he frowned several times. At last he left the window and returned to Oonagh.

"That splash may be more important than you suppose," he said in guarded tones. "I feel that we ought to know everything about it that can possibly be known."

He paused. The girl's clear eyes looked into his. She shook her head.

"I felt dreadfully afraid," she confessed, "when I heard the splashes. It was a strange, eerie sound at that hour of the night. But perhaps my nerves were overwrought because of what was happening."

She made a little gesture of apology for herself, adding: "When one knows there is a policeman waiting at the foot of the stairs."

"The other people who heard the splashes were terrified so that they wanted to leave the house."

She shook her head again. "I think I would have felt the same wish myself in other circumstances." He saw her glance at the cot as she spoke. Her eyes filled with tears and she turned away.

"You can help me," he told her gently, "by listening again during the next few minutes. I'm going downstairs to carry out an experiment, the results of which may or may not clear up this horrible business." He paused and considered for a few moments. "The points I wish to determine," he resumed, "are these: can you hear doors and windows being opened; can you hear every splash at the mouth of the burn; are small objects on the surface of the water clearly visible from these windows? I won't explain myself further because I want your judgement to be unbiased, but I will tell you that I mean to go out of the house by the french-windows in the little writing-room. I shall cough rather loudly just before I come out of the room and I wish specially that you will listen for this cough. A splash will follow, perhaps several splashes."

He watched Oonagh closely as he outlined this programme. She showed no sign of any deeper interest in it than the facts warranted.

"There is one other point. I want these observations made in this room. Can I therefore ask you to remain in this room until I come back?"

He had emphasized the words "in this room" each time that he spoke them. He saw a look of surprise in her face but she offered no comment.

"I shall not leave this room," she said, "until you come back. Do you wish me to stand here or beside the window?"

"Here at first. If you hear a splash go to the window at once and watch the mouth of the burn."

He walked to the door, treading softly so as not to disturb the child. At the door he turned again.

"Remember," he said in a loud whisper. "You will hear a cough just before I come out of the french-window. I will leave this door ajar. So you may hear the cough either through the door, that is through the inside of the house, or through the window, that is from the outside. Try to discriminate between these two ways."

He descended the stairs to the ground floor. The only illumination of the hall came from the study which remained empty. He listened and heard voices in the gun-room behind the writing-room. He knocked on the door of this room and was invited by Duchlan's shrill voice to enter.

Duchlan, still in his dressing-gown, was seated in an arm-chair, the only chair in the room. His son stood beside him and the old man had his hand on Eoghan's arm. There was a look of such happiness on Duchlan's face as caused the doctor to regret that he had intruded. But the old man showed no resentment at his coming.

"Forgive me," Dr. Hailey said, "but at last there is a gleam of light. I am anxious to act quickly in case it should be extinguished and I need help."

Both men stiffened to hear him; he saw anxiety in both their faces.

"A gleam of light." Duchlan repeated in the tones of a prisoner who has abandoned hope and now hears that hope remains.

"That, or an illusion, perhaps. I won't raise false hopes by entering into any details, and besides, time is short." He glanced at the window as he spoke. The deep, transparent blue of the night sky was unchanged in colour but the outlines of the clouds had become sharper. He turned to Eoghan. "Will you come with me?"

"Of course."

"What about me?" Duchlan asked.

"We will report to you at the earliest moment."

They left the old man with his happiness and crossed the hall to the study. Dr. Hailey shut the door.

"I am about to keep an appointment," he stated. "May I ask that, if you agree to accompany me, you will obey implicitly any directions I may give you, and not ask any questions?"

"With whom is the appointment?"

The doctor hesitated. Then a slight frown gathered on his brow.

"With murder," he declared in laconic tones.

Chapter XXXVII

The Swimmer Returns

"I want you to obtain a reel of black cotton and some pins." Dr. Hailey spoke sharply. "You must find them downstairs, possibly in the servants' quarters. On no account are you to set foot on the stairs."

Eoghan did not try to hide his surprise, but his Army training instantly discounted it.

"Very well."

He left the room. The doctor followed him and went to the little apartment opening off the hall, where hats and coats were hung. He took his own hat from its peg and carried it into the study. He glanced out anxiously at the night and then looked at his watch. The outlines of the trees below the window were dimly visible. After about five minutes Eoghan returned with the thread and pins. He handed them to his companion without comment.

"Wait here," Dr. Hailey told him. He left the room, closing the door gently behind him. When he returned he was wearing an overcoat and carried a second overcoat over his arm.

"Put this on, please," he ordered Eoghan, "and turn up the collar, then follow me."

He extinguished the lamp and climbed out of the window on to the bed of earth on which McDonald's footprint had been discovered. He glanced up as he did so at the window of Miss Gregor's room, shut now, and lighted by the moon. The gravel crunched under his feet and he stood still, in sudden hesitation. When Eoghan joined him he urged that the utmost care was necessary to avoid noise.

"The slightest sound may betray us. Ears are strained at this moment to catch the slightest sound."

They crossed the gravel path, passing the front door. When they reached the grass bank the doctor told his companion to lie down and remain without moving. He threw himself on the grass as he spoke and crept forward towards the window of the writing-room. Eoghan lost sight of him among the shadows and then fancied that he could see him again near the window; but a moment later he gave up this idea. The air was still heavy with heat and felt oppressive and damp. He thought that it was true that the darkest hour comes before the dawn, perhaps the eeriest hour also, since the clear lines of night are blurred by mists and shadows. What had happened to the doctor and what was he doing?

A cough, short and dry, came from the darkness. Then Dr. Hailey's voice rang out in accents that vibrated with fear and distress:

"Don't come out!"

There was a gleam, as of steel, Eoghan thought he heard a thudding sound. Then something that went heavily came galloping down the bank towards the place where he lay. He wiped his brow with his hand as it passed. There was a splash in the water below. He turned and looked down at the water.

A black object, like a seal, was swimming quickly out to sea. He felt sure that it was a seal.

The moonlight touched it. It gleamed.

Eoghan wiped his brow again. He could hear his heart thumping against his ribs.

A groan, low and piteous, came to him from the direction of the french-windows. He heard his name pronounced in feeble tones.

Chapter XXXVIII

The Face in the Water

Eoghan rose and ran to the window. As he approached it he saw the large form of Dr. Hailey bending over someone who lay on the ground on the spot where Inspector Barley had fallen. The doctor lit an electric lamp and illuminated the face of the man. A cry broke from Eoghan's lips. It was his father.

The old man spoke his name again. He threw himself on his knees beside him.

"Here I am, father—Eoghan."

The long withered eyelids opened wide. A smile of wonderful contentment appeared on the thin lips.

"Give me your hand…"

Eoghan took his father's hands in his own. He bent and kissed the old man on the brow.

"I'm killed, boy…" A fresh groan broke from Duchlan's lips and his features became convulsed. But the spasm of pain passed. "He struck me on the head…as he struck the policeman." He broke off, gasping for breath. Dr. Hailey bent forward.

"Please don't try to talk, sir, it's only wasting your strength."

Duchlan shook his head. His grip of his son's hands tightened.

"It was my fault," he whispered, "from the beginning. But you've forgiven me. Tell me again, Eoghan, boy, that you've forgiven me?"

"Yes, father."

He smiled again. His face, Dr. Hailey thought, looked younger. But suddenly they saw the light in his eyes grow dim. A cold rigidity spread over his features, fixing them in an expressionless stare. He moved convulsively, like a man who tries to break strong bonds; he managed to raise himself on his elbow.

"This must be death…"

Suddenly his voice rang out clear and full of passion. He pronounced the name "Kathleen". A moment later he was dead in Eoghan's arms. Dr. Hailey opened his dressing-gown and put his ear to his chest.

"He's dead."

"What happened, doctor? What is this frightful thing?" Eoghan's voice was hoarse with emotion.

"Your father came out through the window. I wasn't able to warn him in time. He came on in spite of my shout."

The young man's breath had become laboured. He bent his head.

"It passed close to me going down to the burn. If I hadn't promised you to obey orders I could have prevented It. I saw It swimming away."

His voice faded in horror.

"We must carry him into the house," the doctor said. "Unhappily there's something that remains to do. You must prepare your courage."

"What do you mean?"

"Come—"

As he spoke Dr. Hailey passed his hands under the old man's body and after a moment of hesitation Eoghan followed his example. They lifted the body and began to walk slowly towards the french-window.

"We had better take him to the study."

They moved very slowly in the darkness and several minutes elapsed before they found the couch. As they laid Duchlan on this bed, on which his wife had been laid, a sob broke from Eoghan's lips. Dr. Hailey struck a match to light the lamp. He saw the young man kneeling beside the couch, with his arms outstretched over his father's body.

The sound of a thud, dull, sickening, came to them through the open door.

Eoghan jumped to his feet.

"What was that?"

He strode out into the hall and stood listening. Dr. Hailey joined him. The sound of heavy breathing came to them through the open window of the writing-room. The doctor lit his torch. Suddenly a shrill cry rang out. It was followed by a splash. Eoghan gripped his companion's arm so that the beam of the torch was turned on to his face. His face was bloodless and his brow shone with sweat.

"There it is again."

They rushed to the french-window. The first breathing of dawn showed them the mouth of the burn, black as old pewter. The surface of the water was troubled though no wind blew.

They ran down the bank to the water's edge. The troubling had ceased and the surface of the little estuary lay, mirror-like, under the lightening sky. Dr. Hailey plunged into the water, which reached above his waist, and then bent down. Eoghan saw a white object, which he recognized suddenly as a human face, emerge from the water.

Chapter XXXIX

Dr. Hailey Explains

An hour later Dr. McDonald came limping into the study where Oonagh, Eoghan, and Dr. Hailey awaited him. He sat down and arranged his wooden leg.

"Well?" Dr. Hailey asked.

"I agree with you. Duchlan was murdered exactly as Dundas and Barley were murdered. Christina died from drowning but her arm had been broken. There are herring scales on Duchlan's wound and on one of Christina's hands." McDonald's face expressed a lively horror. He added: "And still we remain without an explanation."

"I don't think so. I know the explanation." Dr. Hailey put his eyeglass in his eye as he spoke. He turned to Eoghan: "The first gleam of light," he said, "came when your father told me that during the epidemic of diphtheria here your mother nursed Christina's son through his last illness and so gave her life for the boy. I know the Highland character. Gratitude is one of its strongest elements."

He rose and stood in front of the fire.

"Christina from that hour, I feel sure, gave you all the mother-love which had belonged to her son and, in addition, all the kindness which your mother's sacrifice had awakened in her warm heart."

"She did," Eoghan exclaimed. "She was my real mother."

There were tears in his eyes. He brushed them hastily aside.

"For which reason her feelings towards your aunt cannot have been other than bitterly hostile. In fact she admitted to me that they were hostile. She knew to what distresses your aunt had subjected your father's bride, she knew that your mother's happiness had been ruined by a process of exhaustion against which no happiness could be proof and she knew that, in a sense, at any rate, Miss Gregor was directly responsible for your mother's death." The doctor leaned forward. "But she was a Highland woman, a member of this household, in whose faithful eyes duty to your father, her master and chief, overshadowed every other duty. Since your aunt was Duchlan's sister, she must continue to serve her.

"That attitude endured right through your childhood, till your marriage. Christina's behaviour towards your aunt was respectful and solicitous until the illness of your little son began. But Hamish's illness effected a great change…"

The doctor broke off. He readjusted his eyeglass.

"That illness was undoubtedly most alarming both to nurse and mother. To a superstitious mind, and Christina shared the mental outlook of her race, fits, even the mildest and least serious fits, always seem to partake of the supernatural. It is for that reason that epileptic children are called 'fey' in so many country villages all the world over. Christina undoubtedly felt that some evil influence was at work. She did not need to look far in order to discover it. Your aunt was already behaving towards your wife as she had behaved towards your mother. The tragedy of your father's marriage was being re-enacted before the eyes of the woman who loved you as only a mother can love. To the strong emotions of motherhood was added, therefore, that fear which haunts superstitious minds and, sooner or later, compels them to action. Your aunt, in Christina's eyes, was become the deadly enemy of the Duchlan family in that she was secretly, by evil influences, destroying the health of its youngest heir, possibly even threatening his life. Thus the reason which had existed for serving your aunt faithfully was changed into a reason for opposing her by every means. Motherhood and loyalty to this family were joined against the enemy of both."

Dr. Hailey allowed his eyeglass to drop. It touched one of the buttons of his waistcoat and the sound struck sharply on the silence which filled the room.

"Christina told me," Oonagh said, "that she was sure some evil influence was at work against Hamish's health. She said the child would not recover until that influence was destroyed."

"Exactly."

"She repeated it again and again."

Dr. Hailey readjusted his eyeglass.

"Bearing this in mind, let us come to the night of Miss Gregor's death. That event had been preceded by two important happenings, namely, your flight from this house, Mrs. Gregor, and the discovery of your meetings with Dr. McDonald on the shore. In the first instance Christina was sent as an ambassador to bring you home and from what you, McDonald, told me I conclude that, though Christina exonerated her young mistress from all blame, she was less ready to pardon you. You told me that she quoted the words: 'Whom God hath joined together…'"

"She did, yes, as she was leaving the house."

"Note how jealous she was of the Duchlan honour. That jealousy was certainly re-awakened when she learned about the meetings on the shore. Hers was not a mind, I think, able to understand the need of asking advice in a difficulty. Her own feelings compelled her so powerfully that she could not imagine the state of mind in which such compulsion is absent." He turned to Eoghan. "Consequently she foresaw the immediate disruption of your marriage if news of what was afoot reached you. Here again the danger was your aunt." Oonagh had flushed hotly. She put her hand on her husband's hand.

"Christina told me," she stated, "that she was very much afraid of Eoghan's return, because his aunt was going to poison his mind."

"Did she urge you to see as little as possible of Dr. McDonald?"

"Yes. I told her Eoghan was incapable of misunderstanding."

"Which she did not believe?"

"Which she did not believe."

Dr. Hailey nodded. "Very well, now we come down to the night of the murder. The important fact to grasp is that, on that night, you, Mrs. Gregor, had gone early to bed after a severe quarrel with your aunt. But you were roused because Hamish was ill again. You put on a blue dressing-gown to go to the nursery. Incidentally you received a letter from your husband in which he told you of his financial loss and begged you to keep on good terms with Miss Gregor. This letter was the cause of your going downstairs, while Dr. McDonald was busy with Hamish, to report to Miss Gregor on the boy's condition. Christina was coming out of Miss Gregor's bedroom candle in hand. As soon as she saw you your aunt showed the liveliest terror and drove you from the room, locking the door behind you."

He glanced at Oonagh for confirmation. She nodded. "Yes."

"Why should Miss Gregor have reacted in that extraordinary way? I believe the answer is that, standing in the dim candlelight, in your blue gown, you looked exactly like Eoghan's mother. So, years before, Eoghan's mother had come into that room, knife in hand, and with the light of a feverish insanity in her eyes."

Dr. Hailey's voice fell to a whisper.

"That insanity, the result of a fatal attack of diphtheria, had momentarily deprived its victim of her self-control, Miss Gregor was stabbed over the heart and severely wounded. The memory of that hour remained, quick and terrible, in her spirit. Panic seized her. In her panic she locked herself in, closing the windows as well as the door." He turned to McDonald: "You heard the windows being shut?"

"I did."

"She was therefore shut up in her bedroom. There is no question that the door was locked. Now consider the case of Inspector Dundas. That poor man made one important discovery, namely, that you, Captain Gregor, had just suffered a heavy loss at cards and must, if possible, obtain money from your aunt. I take it that you told your wife that Dundas had learned of this necessity?"

"Yes, I did."

"Where did you tell her?"

Eoghan looked surprised. He frowned and then his brow cleared.

"I remember. I told her one night while we were sitting in the nursery."

"Was Christina present in the room?"

"Yes, she was. I remember it all quite distinctly now. Christina said she didn't trust Dundas who, she was sure, would give us great trouble. She had suffered cross-examination at his hands, and in addition he had dared to order her about like a servant."

"I see. Dundas threatened your safety. There could be no greater crime in Christina's eyes. Barley's case resembled that of Dundas except that the threat in this instance was to your wife." Dr. Hailey turned to Oonagh. "Was Christina in the nursery when you heard the splashes and saw the black, shining object swimming down the burn?"

"No, she wasn't. She'd gone into the pantry..."

"Was she in the nursery when Dundas was killed? You were there then, if you remember, awaiting my coming to see Hamish?"

Oonagh started; fear dawned in her eyes.

"She was going back and forwards to the pantry that night too," she said.

The eyeglass fell. Dr. Hailey sat down and took out his snuff-box.

"In each of these wounds, as you know, one or more herring scales have been found. Throughout this investigation, therefore, efforts have been made to find a weapon likely to bear such scales. They have been unsuccessful. No weapon was found in Miss Gregor's room; none in Dundas's room; none near Barley's body, though the wardress in the car says she saw the gleam of steel." He addressed Eoghan. "You say you saw the gleam of steel when your father was struck down?"

"I'm certain I saw it."

"Yet there was no weapon in that case either?"

The young man shook his head.

"No."

"Your aunt's wound was of a terribly severe nature but it was not mortal. In these circumstances one would have expected very severe bleeding. In fact there was very little bleeding. Only two explanations are possible; either she died of shock the moment she was wounded or the weapon remained impacted in the wound. She did not die the moment she was wounded because there is a trail of blood from the window to the bed. Nobody escaped from her room. That is certain, not only because your wife and McDonald were in the room below when the windows were shut and had a clear view of the only place to which an escaping murderer could descend but also because the windows were bolted on the inside. We arrive at the apparently absurd conclusion that the weapon which killed your aunt vanished away as soon as that lady's heart had stopped beating, that is to say as soon as her blood had ceased to flow."

He took a pinch of snuff.

"In each case the weapon vanished after the blow had been struck. Come back to the murder of the lady. You, Mrs. Gregor, were the last person who saw her alive. She was then stricken with panic. I imagine that her first impulse was to return to bed and hide there. But soon the open windows attracted her notice. What if an attack was made from that direction? Panic does not reason; it acts. She jumped up and shut one of the windows. She was about to shut the other when she heard, far away, the sound of Captain Gregor's motor-boat. That sound, with its promise of safety and triumph, reassured her. She leaned out of the window the better to hear it. As she leaned there was a crash above her and she was wounded. She staggered back, shocked and panic-stricken. One arm was helpless but she managed to close and bolt the window with the other. She staggered across to her bed and sank down…Her heart stopped…"

The doctor leaned forward.

"You all know how much importance Barley attached to that spike in the wall above Miss Gregor's window. He observed, from the pantry on the top floor, that the rust on the spike had been rubbed away at one place and concluded that a rope had been used. There is another explanation.

The weapon which struck Miss Gregor as she leaned out of the window may have struck the spike in the course of its descent. And that, in fact, is what happened."

He rose and resumed his place in front of the fire.

"When Miss Gregor leaned out of her window, Christina, in the pantry above, saw her. The sound of the motor-boat reached Christina's ears also. That faithful, superstitious woman heard in the sound the doom of all those she loved, of you Captain Gregor, of you Mrs. Gregor, of your child. Of Duchlan himself. In a few minutes Miss Gregor's evil influence would be exerted to blast your marriage as it had been exerted to blast your father's marriage, as it was being exerted to destroy your son's health."

Dr. Hailey paused and then added in quiet tones.

"At the moment when she heard the sound of the motor-boat, Christina was engaged in chipping ice from a large block to refill the ice-bag on Hamish's brow."

Chapter XL

The End

The silence in the room was broken by the first clear notes of a blackbird. A moment later the chorus of the birds, that immemorial song of the dawn, broke on their ears. A look of great gentleness appeared on Dr. Hailey's face.

"Christina in that moment," he said, "heard the call of her gods to action. She seized the block of ice and dropped it out of the window. It struck the spike and was shattered into several jagged daggers. One of these struck Miss Gregor and was wedged firmly into the wound it had inflicted. In this hot weather it soon melted; she was dead before that occurred.

"The effect on Christina was exactly what might have been foreseen. Those who feel themselves called by Heaven to take action against the powers of evil, and who are greatly successful, develop immediately a spiritual pride that is nearly, if not quite, insanity. Christina constituted herself the protector of the Gregor family. When she heard that Dundas suspected you, Captain Gregor, she marked him down for destruction. The room above his, as you know, is empty. All she had to do was to wait there till he leaned out of his window and he did that no doubt at very frequent intervals on account of the heat. She knew that McDonald and I were coming upstairs; she heard Dundas wish us good night. He appeared below her. The block of ice was not shattered in this instance, for there is no spike above Dundas's room. It rolled down the bank and went splashing into the burn. The current carried it out into the loch. The procedure was the same in Barley's case except that a bait was necessary to induce him to walk under the window. It was supplied by the dropping of a preliminary block of ice, the resulting thud and splash, heard at the moment when he was about to arrest you, Mrs. Gregor, naturally excited his liveliest interest."

He stopped and bowed his head.

"I planned, to-night," he said in tones of deep regret, "to excite Christina's fears and direct her hostility against myself. That was the object of my visit to the nursery and of the directions I gave. I succeeded too well. I had arranged my hat in such a way that, when I pulled on a thread, it would swing out from the french-window. If Christina was guilty I felt sure she would strike again. Then, as I coughed to give the signal, Duchlan appeared. As you know, I shouted, but it was too late."

He drew a long deep breath.

"The knowledge that she had killed her master was sentence of death to the woman at the window," he added. "Her fall did not kill her; as soon as she knew herself alive she rushed headlong down the bank to the water."

The chorus of the birds filled all the spaces of morning. McDonald rose stiffly, dragging his leg.

"I believe," he said, "that the ice comes from the Ardmore fish-monger. There are herring scales on every square inch of his walls and doors."

To receive a free catalog of Poisoned Pen Press titles, please provide your name, address, and e-mail address in one of the following ways:

Phone: 1-800-421-3976
Facsimile: 1-480-949-1707
Email: info@poisonedpenpress.com
Website: www.poisonedpenpress.com

Poisoned Pen Press
6962 E. First Ave. Ste 103
Scottsdale, AZ 85251